A
QUIET STORM

—

Rachel Howzell Hall

SCRIBNER PAPERBACK FICTION
PUBLISHED BY SIMON & SCHUSTER
New York   London   Toronto   Sydney   Singapore

SCRIBNER PAPERBACK FICTION
Simon & Schuster, Inc.
Rockefeller Center
1230 Avenue of the Americas
New York, NY 10020

SCRIBNER PAPERBACK FICTION and design are trademarks of Macmillan Library Reference USA, Inc., used under license by Simon & Schuster, the publisher of this work.

Manufactured in the United States of America

ISBN 0-7394-2884-5

For Mommy and Daddy

For David

Acknowledgments

I'm blessed to have two women who are brave and patient enough to work with a young writer such as me who required constant reassurance and support. Thanks to my agent, the wonderful and wise Wendy Sherman, and to my talented and brilliant editor, Cherise Grant. I will be forever grateful to you for your faith in me.

Thanks also to my extended family and friends for your encouragement. Lots and lots of thanks, though, to my sibs: Gretchen, Jason, and Terence. You three continue to inspire me to pick up the pen and write. I love you.

For the Lord God will help me: therefore shall I not be confused; therefore have I set my face like a flint, and I know that I shall not be ashamed. —Isaiah 50:7 For the Lord God will help me: therefore shall I not be confused; therefore have I set my face like a flint, and I know that I shall not be ashamed. —Isaiah 50:7 For the Lord God will help me: therefore shall I not be confused; therefore have I set my face like a flint, and I know that I shall not be ashamed. —Isaiah 50:7 For the Lord God will help me: therefore shall I not be confused; therefore have I set my face like a flint, and I know that I shall not be ashamed. —Isaiah 50:7 For the Lord God will help me: therefore shall I not be confused; therefore have I set my face like a flint, and I know that I shall not be ashamed. —Isaiah 50:7 For the Lord God will help me: therefore shall I not be confused;

1

Taste the Rain

My fascination with storms started in elementary school. Third grade, I think. I was standing in line to play tetherball at my school's playground, bundled up in a maroon nylon parka with the white faux-fur collar and the blue-and-green plaid inside lining. My fingers constantly poked through the hole inside the right-hand pocket. Mommy hid my lunch money there. And sometimes, I found a stray Lemonhead or a Skittles, depending on my luck. The other girls on the court were arguing over who was better: Wonder Woman or the Bionic Woman. Was the invisible plane cooler than a bionic ear? Would you rather have Max the bionic dog or those gold bracelets that deflected bullets? I didn't care. I liked Ramona the Brave. Ramona was a rebel. Ramona had spunk. Ramona could kick both of their superhuman behinds. And she didn't need a magic lasso or a bionic audio microsensor, either.

That afternoon, in an instant, the sun disappeared. The sky turned the color of tarnished silver; and the clouds squished down so low it seemed that I could jump and touch them. When I exhaled, miniature white clouds burst from my mouth and added to the miracle happening above. I didn't say a word. I didn't want to share. I couldn't change whatever was inside those clouds. I just prayed that it might snow. Not very likely in L.A. on a February afternoon, but I was a child who believed in snow.

No snow came. Just thunder and lightning and pouring rain. And I, a little terrified and confused, wondered how those same clouds that looked so harmless in their silent journey across the sky, how could anything so peaceful, so delicate, create such clamor and chaos? Why did they make me jump and make my heart pound? And why couldn't I have snow like everyone else in the world?

That night, I lay in bed, still trying to figure it out. But the loudest boom that ever boomed in the history of the world crashed through our house and shook the windows. I grabbed a metallic purple penlight that I got from a school book fair back in October and jumped out of my bed. I scampered into the bedroom closet. My sister, Rikki, who slept in the bed across from me, followed close behind. She hated storms, too.

Sheets of water hit our bedroom window as if they were being chased by the devil and needed to get inside with us. Our closet, stuffed with church dresses, cancan slips, numerous sets of identical shirts and slacks in rainbow-glow colors, and twenty-two pairs of shoes, had always served as a makeshift haven from monsters, parents, and loud, obnoxious relatives. Now it would protect us from tempestuous weather. To pass time, Rikki and I played "Miss Mary Mack" and "Slide" by the glow of the tiny flashlight, which I held between clenched teeth. And when our hands reddened and burned from our games, we prayed, sat still, and waited for silence.

Daddy always liked storms. He'd open his bedroom curtains, then switch on the radio, turning the dial until he found a station playing Christopher Cross or Air Supply. Then he would sprawl out on the bed and watch the sky until he fell asleep. Mommy, on the other hand, tried to ignore bad weather with nonstop vacuuming. She'd carry that Hoover up and down the stairs to every room in the house. Some storms lasted so long that she'd have to vacuum rooms twice.

That night, Daddy came to our room. He saw that we weren't in our beds, so he peeked in the closet. "Rikki, Stacy, get out of there."

Rikki shrank back into the cancan slips. She whispered to me, "No. Don't."

"Now," he said. "Don't make me drag you out." He disappeared into the darkness.

I slipped my penlight onto my pinkie and grabbed Rikki's clammy hand. We crawled out of the closet and tiptoed to the middle of our bedroom. Daddy stood at the window. He had opened our ruffled pink curtains to display pandemonium outside. He beckoned us to come to him. Rikki and I, still holding hands, padded past our glow-in-the-dark unicorn poster and the cabinet of Barbies and stuffed kittens, to where Daddy, a giant silhouette with hands on his hips, waited. I stood on Daddy's right. Rikki stood on his left. He took our hands in his and pulled us closer to him. He ran his large palms over our shiny, pressed hair, then rested them on our thin, pink-flannel-covered shoulders.

Just then, another volley of thunder pounded against our house. We jumped. Rikki cried out and covered her face with her hands. I wanted to run to the closet and make it all go away.

"It's okay," he said, eyes on the sky. The windowpane glistened from the heavy, silver cover of raindrops that slammed against the surface. "Don't worry. It's okay. We're inside."

Daddy saying that it was okay settled it for me. Not Rikki, though. Still unconvinced, she peeked at me through her slender, nutmeg-brown fingers. Her breathing rattled like a small diesel engine. Are you okay? I asked with my eyes. She nodded yes.

"Look there." Daddy pointed outside.

Our eyes followed his index finger to the sky beyond our orange and lemon trees. A brilliant lavender flash cut across the blackness. Our room glowed for a second or two.

"Now count," he said.

I swallowed. "One, two . . ."

Rikki joined in. "Three, four . . ."

Then it happened. An explosion rumbled from the depths of Hell to the soles of my feet, then across my stomach, and finally to the fleshy pockets of my cheeks. The window shook until I thought the glass would shatter. Rikki whimpered but kept her gaze on the sky. Daddy chuckled and squeezed our shoulders.

"A storm's coming," he said. "It's only four miles away. You see, seconds equal miles. Understand?" We both nodded our heads: yes, we understood.

Later, I found out that Daddy's explanation wasn't true; but Rikki never feared storms again. The counting mentally prepared her for the chaos to come. After that lesson, whenever a storm reached our house, she'd laugh and run outside with her mouth open to catch the rain on her tongue. She told me that rain tasted like spoons and sugar.

My mother, like most mothers, feared head colds, bronchitis, and pneumonia. Because she was also a part-time public librarian, she had read that a single bolt of lightning could carry over 100 million volts of direct current and reach temperatures of up to fifty thousand degrees Fahrenheit. "Lightning can roast nerves, damage the brain, form cataracts, rupture eardrums, break bones, and sizzle skin—all in one second flat," Mommy told us. Safety mattered more than rain dances, especially for delicately boned Arika.

When Mommy saw Rikki dancing in the rain from the kitchen window, she would throw up the sash and shout, "Arika! Get in this house right now! Arika, don't make me . . ."

And when Rikki continued to twirl in the rain, I would be sent out to get her. "Rikki, you gotta come in," I said. "Please." Only then did she stop and follow me into the house.

"Do you want to land in the hospital?" Mommy asked Rikki as she toweled her dry and stripped her down. "People must think I'm out of my mind, letting you go wild out there. Are you crazy?"

Daddy thought my sister looked beautiful with her arms outstretched and her face washed over in God's soggy glory. Our mother, however, reminded him that his opinion was just that—his opinion. There would be no dancing in the rain for the Moore girls. And while he called Mommy overprotective, and she called him immature, Rikki slipped into the backyard to burrow her toes in the ground that shimmered with water. It didn't matter to her if the sky poured open like Niagara Falls. She wanted to be outside. And I stood guard at the door, ready to tell her the moment Mommy encroached on the perimeter.

And when she had been called inside yet again and the doors had been locked, we'd sit on our matching pink canopy beds in front of the open curtains and windows, as the wind forced the corners of our unicorn poster to snap against the wall like a snare drum. With the towel wrapped around her snarled, kinking hair, Rikki explained that thunder tap-danced across the sky—kick, ball, chain, kick, ball, chain—just as it tap-danced in her mind. She explained that rain was God's tears: He cried because He gave His only begotten Son to die for us.

Then the lightning came and Rikki and I counted. Thunder, on cue, followed. Car alarms screamed, Mrs. Drake's German shepherds yapped, and God made it clear that, if He wanted, He could do it with water again.

Only after the seconds between the lightning and the thunder passed seventy-five would we eventually fall asleep. By then, the storm had downsized to harmless rain to simple sprinkle to barely-there drizzle.

And the next morning, the sky would be cornflower blue and the sun would pour bright white light into our bedroom. Kids would be riding their Huffys up and down the street. The man next door would be waxing his Pontiac Firebird. Only a few drowned earthworms on the sidewalks and a puddle that could be mistaken for runoff from a sprinkler would remain. It was as if the storm had never happened.

I counted Rikki's storms just like I counted God's. Flashes of light—one, two, three, four—and then a boom. I saw her patches come and braced myself for the havoc. No one else seemed to see her clouds gathering. If they did, they remained silent.

I never danced in the rain like Arika, so I may never know if raindrops truly taste like spoons and sugar.

Someone has to stand at the door to keep watch.

And that was my life.

2

QUEEN OF HEARTS

ARIKA—we called her Rikki—pulled luck from life like a blackjack dealer pulls aces from a deck. In junior high school, she was voted Best Figure and Most Likely to Succeed. She won poetry contests, received scholarships from Bank of America and the Urban League, scored 1,500 on the SATs, graduated salutatorian of her class, and sacked lunches at the Los Angeles Mission.

She taught fourth grade at 59th Street Elementary School, in the heart of South Central Los Angeles–Rolling 60's gang territory. The hearts of the boys in her class fluttered for the first time in their prepubescent lives when they met Miss Moore. The girls styled their hair with their mothers' big-barreled curling irons to simulate their teacher's cascades. Her colleagues stole her lesson plans because Rikki's students outperformed other kids in the school district.

My sister received more Valentine's Day cards, more Christmas mugs, and more PTA accolades than any other teacher at 59th Street School. She earned her students' love with her warmth, her badly delivered jokes, and the Toll House cookies she baked for them every Friday. With her own money, she bought extra books for the classroom if there was a need, and during gang wars that raged outside the safety of the school grounds, she would load into her car her students who had to walk home. She dropped every frightened child at his or her doorstep. She couldn't sleep at night if she knew that she hadn't done all she could to protect them. "Teaching is my ministry," Rikki would say.

Women solicited her presence for teas and receptions, committees of this and boards of that. No debutante could come out, no Snickerdoodle could be sold, and no Christmas song could be caroled unless she sat on the advisory committee or hosted a fund-raising brunch or donated at least one hundred bucks. She never forgot birthdays and anniversaries. She served God and man to make the world a better place. She out-Pollyanna-ed Pollyanna. *At first.*

These same committee members and ladies who lunched expected me to hate her perfection, to belittle her efforts and her stewardship, but I couldn't. Rikki never gloated or bragged. She never acted smug and smarmy . . . how I'd act if I were beautiful, smart, and civic-minded. Who says God doesn't know what He's doing as He hands out gifts?

To add to her abundance, God supplied Rikki with a perfect companion: pediatrician Matthew Dresden. He, too, walked humbly among men even though he was exceptional. Matt spoke six languages, including Mandarin Chinese, and had finished college days after his twentieth birthday. He had joined the Peace Corps in Guatemala for a year. Matt also made the pulses of nurses and fretful mothers at Cedars-Sinai Hospital rise and reach levels not attained with their own boyfriends or husbands. Even when he knew that many of these women's kids weren't sick, he still delighted in making his tiny patients giggle at his magic tricks and funny voices and pretended not to be aware of their mothers' intentions.

Matt met Rikki at a church camp retreat. Some say it was love at first sight. Maybe it was. Maybe it was something else.

It's always been my opinion that a woman should wait at least three dates to sleep with a guy. Rikki, despite her high IQ, fell short by two dates and believed Matt when he said, "I've never met a woman like you, let's spend our lives together, blah, blah, blah" (on their first date, can you believe that?) just as Eve fell for the "You will have eternal life" line from the Serpent. But I'm also a realist. We all make mistakes when a beautiful man has his hands up your skirt.

Despite their premature coupling, Matt called Rikki back for a second date. Their relationship blossomed until they epitomized *the* All-American African-American Couple. Rikki and Matt kissed in line at Disneyland. They called each other "sweet pea" and "love bug." They kept their hands tucked into each other's back pockets. They talked at noon every day just to say, "I love you." I discovered *this* when the cops showed me their phone records.

Six years after they met, Rikki and Matt announced their engagement to a crowd of fifty "close" family and friends over tender Chilean sea bass and steamed asparagus with a divine citrus mayonnaise. I planned this special evening once it became apparent that Rikki was overwhelmed by the font selection for the invitations and deciding whether to use the stamps with the hearts or the stamps with the cupid.

Mommy muttered, "My baby's getting married," the entire evening until tears silenced her. Tears of joy? Tears of sorrow? A mixture of both? To be honest, I don't think she believed that Rikki would *ever* marry. Regardless, Mommy ran out of tissue by the time the waiters served the lemon tarts. Her mascara didn't mix well with the tears and the oil that already soiled her face. I wouldn't say she looked like a raccoon, but . . . well, you decide if you ever see the pictures.

Matt's mother, the widow Zenobia, recited her own mantra that night. "Oh, how wonderful. Oh, how wonderful"—and pretended to dry nonexistent tears with her starched monogrammed hankie. A hankie. In the twentieth century. Can you believe that? Okay, maybe my mother also accessorized with a useless swatch of material that night, but Mommy was *nowhere* near as tacky as Zenobia.

Zenobia Dresden was one of those rich ladies who couldn't find class if it were stapled to her elbow. She decorated with a hatchet and a single color swatch: red. She drove a red convertible Cadillac Eldorado with bloodred leather seats. And her *house.* Eight red velvet chairs surrounded the black-lacquered table that sat in the middle of her dining room. Fake red calla lilies sat in a red vase, which shimmered in the glow of the red-and-white crystal chandelier. Of course, this was set against a photographic mural of a Hawaiian sunset. And yes, there were the animal-print throw rugs, and brass elephant planters here and there, and the black velvet painting of Jesus and His disciples. I have to admit—she had a theme. And she carried it over to fashion—scarlet hankie and all—the night of the engagement dinner.

As Pastor Phillips blessed the food that evening, the widow Zenobia kept her eyes open. I guess she couldn't glare at her future daughter-in-law with closed eyes. Yes, my eyes were also open, but that's different. *I* don't get up in church and call myself a prayer warrior like *some* people. And my eyes were open not because I didn't believe what we prayed for, like *some* people. I don't think I need to name names.

After we all said "Amen," Zenobia sighed, "Oh, how wonderful, just wonderful."

Like a broken phonograph, that woman. Like cheese made from soybeans. Fake, fake, and more fake. She didn't fool me. I knew that Zenobia cursed out Matt the night he introduced her to Arika *Moore* over dinner a year after they started to date. She actually frowned whenever she said our last name. *Moore.* The way some people spit out *Hitler* or *Nixon* or *Cher.*

"You're just like your no-good father, that lousy son of a . . . ," Zenobia said to her son after Rikki left her home. Miss Compton 1995 was her choice of daughter-in-law. Madison Reems (a Madison in Compton, can you believe it?) was a Lena Horne look-alike with an empty Cracker Jack box for a brain. To make matters worse, Matt Senior had, just before dying of congestive heart failure, left the country and Zenobia for Spain and for a dermatologist's assistant who resembled Rikki around the nose and chin. The widow hated Rikki as much as she hated paella and cortisone.

Rikki laughed when Matt reluctantly told her about his mother's feelings, flicked it away with her slender hand. Chalked it up to the widow Zenobia's love of J & B, Crown Royal, Johnnie Walker, Wild Turkey, and schnapps (if someone distilled it, the widow drank it).

Rikki and Matt's relationship endured. But as the time for their wedding drew closer, the gossip mill chugged into overtime. Rikki had never spoken ill of her enemies, had never stolen a boyfriend, wasn't involved in any of that talk show drama. But folks had a bad case of the grapes, you know? Matt hadn't chosen their daughters. What had Rikki done to deserve him?

A friend of a friend of Mommy's told her sister's cousin's niece (who does my hair) that Zenobia said one night after prayer meeting, "I don't trust that Arika *Moore*. And I don't want Matthew marrying her, either. I told him, 'Son, Madison was Miss Compton 1995. She's drop-dead gorgeous, smart as a whip, and more talented than Whitney Houston. Can Whitney play the accordion? Madison can. And she don't need no drugs to keep *her* head straight.' But he says to me, 'Mother, Rikki's just as beautiful, highly intelligent, and taught herself piano, and I love her.' I don't care, though. There's something about that girl that's off, taking all those pills. I can't put my finger on it right now, but it's worrying me. I stay on my knees all the time, pleading with the Lord."

Of course, I told Mommy about this one morning on our way to church.

"Who is *she* to be talking about who's crazy?" Mommy said. "Rikki loves Matthew and that's all that matters. And as far as drugs go, everybody pops something once in a while. Aspirin, St. John's warts, that stuff those ADD kids take. It's all the same." As we neared the church, Mommy tucked a pink lace handkerchief in her bra and pulled on her fuchsia church hat. "Zenobia hates Rikki 'cause she ain't high yellow like Miss Ghetto America, that's all."

True, I guess. But then . . .

Zenobia Dresden *did* rise to the occasion on December 20, 1996, Rikki and Matt's wedding day. It was the last major social event of the year: buppies joining together in holy matrimony before God and society. Everyone came, including our congresswoman, pastors from two of L.A.'s prominent black churches, and a movie star. They probably wanted to see if Miss Compton 1995 would bust into Wilshire Methodist Church with an Uzi and a broken forty-ounce.

Even as she solemnly marched down the aisle on Uncle Gregory's arm, Rikki refused to see pools of envy in the eyes of her guests. She never heard the remarks: "They're not gonna make it" and "I heard that Pastor Phillips said that they shouldn't get married" and, my favorite, "Ain't no decent woman supposed to wear a dress like that."

Instead, Rikki fell for their "You look so beautiful, I'm so happy for you." My poor, turn-the-other-cheek-believing sister. And those hypocrites ate our food—$85.50 a plate. They whispered behind one hand while the other hand, fork in place, stabbed at pieces of cake—$1,800 for three hundred guests. They stole bottles of Martinelli's apple cider as they bitched about the "crazy gold-digger"—$1.99 a bottle. I wish I could send every one of them a bill.

They contributed to the storm, those Judases. They kissed her cheek and wished her well, but then said, "Told you so," when the buzz gradually filtered down to them in their muck and mire. Rikki and Matt fought like the dogs of Hell. Rikki talked to herself and cried for no reason. Rikki threw a $3,000 Waterford crystal bowl at Matt's head. They heard that a scar in the shape of a watermelon wedge remained on the back of his neck.

It never mattered to them if these rumors were true. No

one dared to ask Rikki or Matt or even me. They just ripped through the gossip like foxes in a chicken coop. They rolled around with full bellies, delighted that they had just gobbled up more ugly, hurtful morsels about my sister and her husband.

I disregarded much of it: the lies and the truth, people's whispers, even some of my sister's erratic behavior. I tried to ignore it as I had since Rikki and I sat together on our canopy beds. That night when Daddy taught us about watching storms come. The same night when Rikki told me that she had storms in her head.

3

BEGINNING OF THE END

IT ONLY took two hours for the phones to ring off the hook when Rikki came to church alone one Saturday four years after the wedding. The earth stood still. The sun turned to blood. Frogs flooded the streets and rivers. There was wringing of hands and gnashing of teeth . . .

And just how many pediatricians do *you* know who may have to work on a Saturday? More kids than usual had runny noses and high temperatures. Matt was called in since he *was* a pediatrician. End of story. But no . . .

"I talked to Sister DeHaviland today," Mommy said to me later, refreshed after her Sabbath nap. My mother took pride in her role as the top left branch on the church grapevine. She was frustrated that neither of her daughters expressed interest in carrying on the tradition. "She told me that everybody noticed that Matt missed church today."

"Uh-huh," I said.

"Has she talked to you?"

"Who? Sister DeHaviland?"

"Stacy, don't be silly. You know I'm talking about Rikki. Has Rikki talked to you?"

Irritated, I stuffed the last of a third Krispy Kreme glazed doughnut into my mouth. A wave of nausea forced me to close my eyes. I wished it had forced me to close my mouth. "No, Mother, she hasn't talked to me. Why should she?" And why is it my, your, or *anyone's* business if her husband danced naked at the St. Patrick's Day parade? I wanted to ask; but my mouth was full. A piece of dough lodged in my throat as I croaked, "She seemed fine last time I saw her."

"*Seemed?* Anastasia, you're her sister."

I shrugged and licked the sugar from my fingers. "Yes, I know that, Mother. What do you want me to do?"

"Nothing," Mommy snapped. Then she whined about my flippancy and my coldness and my lack of compassion for her and my big sister. "Don't put yourself out."

"Fine. I won't." I didn't. I knew that I'd become involved no matter my level of apathy. I just wanted some time to myself before the circus came to town. I mean, I had missed church, too, but no one is interested in gossiping about a twenty-eight-year-old, 170-pound woman who does taxes for Catholic charities and freelances as a crossword puzzle writer.

As soon as Mommy hung up, pissed off, and I had placed the receiver back onto the cradle, my phone shrieked again, as if on cue. For a second, I thought about not answering, but as always, I did. As I figured, it was Rikki in hysterics. I couldn't even finish my "Hello" before she wailed, "He wants a divorce! A divorce! Oh, God!"

Stunned, I turned the volume down on *Cops*. "Oh, no, Rikki," I whispered. I knew she and Matt were separated. Matt had been renting a house in the Hollywood Hills, but sheesh, I figured their split was only temporary. A couple who called each other "sweet pea" and made love twenty-three days out of the month didn't *divorce*. If *they* could fall out of love, what chance did we mere mortals who ate peanut butter straight from the tub and shaved our legs once a month have?

"Maybe we should go to Marin," Rikki continued, referring to our family cabin near Muir Woods, twelve miles north of San Francisco. "To talk about it. To try to work it out. Then maybe he'll move back in."

"What if he doesn't want to come back?" I asked, immediately wanting to take back my words.

"Oh, Stacy! You think he hates me that much?"

"No, Rikki, wait."

"He doesn't love me anymore," she cried. "I don't know what I'd do without him!"

"Cheese and bread, Arika. Just calm the hell down. Damn."

Rikki blew her nose, then sniffed. "We just need to get away from all this bullshit. Bastards. They just waited for this to happen." She paused. "Including that woman."

Even after four years, Matt's mother still had her money on Miss Compton 1995.

I grabbed another doughnut from the box on my bedside table. They came in handy in times like this. Hell, in *any* time. "When are you thinking of leaving?" I asked. "Not until it stops raining, I hope." It's a pretty treacherous drive up those wet, winding roads. I found Jesus en route to that cabin last winter. My car spun four times and ran over a possum. For catharsis, I wrote a puzzle entitled "The Odyssey" about it. You know, "to cry in distress, 6 letters across," "a Southern rodent, 6 letters down," "to meet one's Maker, 3 letters down."

"Sooner rather than later," she said, then sighed. "Matt's a fucking jerk. I don't care. Screw him."

"O-kaaayyyy," I said, aware of the acidity in her tone.

"You think he still loves me?"

"I'm sure he wants to work it out." Hell, I didn't know.

My sister and I ended our conversation minutes later. I told her to keep me posted, knowing that I didn't have to say that. Two weeks later, right when *America's Most Wanted* ended, Rikki called again. She and Matthew had just talked. And because of his willingness to try and try, he had agreed to attempt to reconcile with her in the woods. She was thrilled: they would celebrate their wedding anniversary together.

So when the police arrived at the cabin that Christmas, they could not understand why Matt, a dependable and predictable man, had disappeared without explanation.

Months later, Mommy called me again on a Saturday afternoon, and like everyone else she asked, "Why didn't you know?"

I shrugged. I knew *things*. Just things.

4

TO SERVE AND PROTECT

BEFORE I left my mother's womb, God charged me to
protect my sister. At the time, I didn't know what that
involved. But once I learned, I never let Him down.

My mother and father didn't get to wait long between
Rikki's birth and my conception. We're eleven months apart:
I was an IUD baby. People who knew us often forgot that
Rikki was older. Sometimes, my parents forgot, too. You see,
I had to speak up for Rikki, walk her to class whenever I
could, and tuck her in bed after Mommy had already done so.

At nine years old, Rikki demonstrated more sensitivity
than a confused, pimply teenager. Mommy was like this, too.
She cried once because we forgot to write *love* on her birthday
card. But Rikki was worse than our mother. She had the back-
bone of a rag doll. She wept at the sight of a stray cat. She
crumbled if someone looked at her weird. Weak-kneed, she

visibly trembled when threatened and tended to lower her eyes and bow her head to hide her tears. I beat up this girl, stinky Pamela Keller, because of my sister's emotional fragility.

Pamela was a sixth-grader who loomed forty feet above the student population, even the boys. Lettuce and french fries from old lunches sat trapped in her braces. She smelled—even at her age, she needed sticks of deodorant. Every kid stayed out of Stinky Pam's way. She didn't scare me, though.

That morning, Rikki and I stood in line for nutrition. Stinky Pam pushed Rikki, then cut in front of us in line. Frightened, Rikki dropped her thirty-five cents that she had planned to spend on a piece of coffee cake. Pam plunked her cruddy, size-60 Nike tennis shoe on top of the dime and the quarter, then sneered at us.

Rikki broke out in hysterics right there. "Ohmigod," Rikki wailed. "My money! Ohmigod!" Being cut in line, dropping her money, Pam's teeth, it was all too much for Rikki to bear. Tears and gut-wrenching sobs followed. You know, the kind of sobs you make when your parents take your beloved Labrador retriever to the vet, never to be seen again.

I yelled at Pam, "Why'd you cut her?" I grabbed Rikki's head in an attempt to comfort her on my shoulder. It didn't matter that she stood three inches taller than me.

"Because I wanted to," Stinky Pam snapped.

"Punk!" I shouted. "I should kick your butt!"

By this time, the cafeteria's noise level had dropped to near silence. Everyone in the vicinity stared at us. They had been waiting for someone to finally knock Pam from her bully seat. Pam looked around the room. She knew that her

reputation was on the line. If she didn't do something spec-
tacular, no one would ever fear her again. So she pursed her
big lips together, wrinkled her nose, and spat on Rikki's
Buster Browns. *Spit!* Can you believe that?

So I pushed her. Surprised, she fell back. She steadied
herself, then she pushed me back. Then all hell broke loose.
Students whooped and yelled, "Fight! Fight!" Pam punched
me in the stomach. I threw milk in her face, then hurled the
empty carton at her forehead. She pulled my ponytail. I
kicked her in the knee, then landed a mean jab on her nose
like I'd seen on *Starsky and Hutch*.

"Stop it! Stop it now!" Mrs. McGuire, the cafeteria monitor, shouted. Someone pulled me back. Mrs. McGuire
grabbed Pamela. In a matter of seconds, the Great Fight of
1978 was over. We were both sent to the principal's office. In
the end, I broke Pam's nose. She scratched my left cornea.
We both offered lame apologies, even though the principal
saw that I wasn't sorry at all. I was suspended from school for
three days.

Daddy, disgraced, picked me up from the school's front
office. He didn't speak to me during the drive home. Mommy
cried and wondered aloud where she had gone wrong. At din-
nertime, she prayed for guidance and wisdom when it came to
rearing me. I ignored her—she always overreacted.

Later that night, Daddy stood in the doorway of my bedroom. I sat on my bed, my head hung low with shame.

"And what did you accomplish?" he asked. For him, every
action needed a goal, even if you were only a third-grader.

Tears stung my eyes. "Nothing," I mumbled. I wanted to
say, "Well, I kicked stinky Pamela Keller's butt real good." But
I didn't. I didn't offer details, give an excuse, or even utter

Rikki's name. And he never lectured me on why my actions were wrong. He knew that *I* knew those reasons, so why waste words? Besides, he didn't care if my motives were altruistic. I was in a fight. I had been suspended from school. For him, nothing good could come from that.

"Straighten up and fly right," he said. "I don't want to have this conversation again. Ever. You understand?"

"Yes, Daddy."

Then he turned on his heel and went downstairs to watch Walter Cronkite. He didn't say anything else to me that night. His silence was the worst punishment ever.

At the end of my first day of suspension, Rikki came home with a gift. "Here." She handed me cafeteria coffee cake wrapped in a napkin. "I know you like the coffee cake, especially the cinnamon-sugar crumblies."

"Thank you," I said.

"Isn't that sweet, Anastasia?" Mommy said. "She didn't have to do that." She kissed Rikki on the top of her head. "So thoughtful."

And that's how it went, and how it continued to be. I'd take the heat whenever Rikki couldn't handle it. She offered gifts as payment: Hello Kitty junk, posters of puppies hanging on strings, *Mad* magazines, coffee cake, and Shrinky Dinks. She baked those baby chocolate cakes for me in her Easy-Bake oven. When she felt profoundly grateful, I got to play with her Strawberry Shortcake dolls or her remote-control Barbie Corvette. She became more and more grateful as her bouts of anxiety worsened and she found herself, time and time again, in the land of Hopelessness, in need of immediate rescue.

Okay. So I had a distressed sister, a pacifistic father, and a peculiar mother. Other than that, my family wasn't really different from other families in the neighborhood. I mean, we had health and life insurance, we were well-read, and we lived in America. We weren't as well-off as the other families around us: Even though the neighborhood was black, we were the affirmative-action homeowners on the block. The house actually belonged to my mother's parents. When Granddad died and Nana had to be put away, we moved in (after the new coat of paint and the removal of President Kennedy's portrait). White sheets from Kmart stayed over our windows for months until we could get the new curtains off of layaway. Daddy mowed the lawn himself instead of paying a professional gardener to do it. He bought his Volvo in hopes that the noses of 90008 would lower just a little. And to be safe, Mommy's Toyota Corolla stayed hidden in the garage next to Nana's old Buick station wagon.

Nana. Wow. I don't think about her much. I actually don't know much about her. Mommy kept a picture of Nana on the fireplace mantel. She's wearing this pink suit. A gigantic orchid corsage hangs on her collar. She's standing alone, in front of that station wagon. She doesn't smile—pictures offend her, it seems. She stares right at you, looks at you as though she knows something. Something bad.

Our neighbors would "mention" things about Nana from time to time. Like the occasions when Nana would sit in her car all day. How she folded her money into tiny packets of dollar bills and hid them in her bra. That she never discarded old newspaper or aluminum cans. And how she wandered the neighborhood late at night. The day before she was committed, a cop found her walking in the middle of the street in her housecoat and slippers.

Nana wasn't a subject that came up over club sandwiches, dominoes, and soda pop. And if she did come up, the subject would immediately be changed. I made the mistake of pressing the issue once. I think I was seven. My mother and I were sitting in the hair salon, waiting to get our holiday press and curl. An old woman with a purple rinse and a girl my age had just left the shop. They looked so happy together.

"Why doesn't Nana ever come to the shop with us?" I asked. "And why doesn't she live in a house like normal people?" I had so many questions, like why didn't Nana knit us hats and scarves or bake us cookies? Why didn't she send us cards and checks on our birthdays? Why didn't she drive a big old Cadillac or smell like lavender and mothballs? Why didn't I ever sit next to her in church on that fifteenth pew in the center of the sanctuary where we sat every Saturday? I hoped these two safe questions would open the floodgates of my mother's memory.

Instead, Mommy hissed, "Stacy, you ask the rudest questions." Her eyes shot around the salon to determine if any of the other ladies were listening to me as I aired our family's dirty laundry.

"But why doesn't she?"

Mommy leaned toward me until our noses almost touched. Her eyes burned into mine. Her fingernails pinched into my wrist. "Next time, think about what you're going to say before blurting it out for fifty million people to hear," she snapped. "And keep your voice down." Then she pretended to read her magazine, even though her eyes continued to roam the salon, checking and then rechecking to see if anyone was staring at us.

After that, I never asked any other questions. So I learned

to ignore Nana like everyone else in the family until a major holiday like Christmas or Thanksgiving rolled around and we piled into Daddy's Volvo to go visit her.

Nana never spoke to me. She never spoke to anyone, yet we'd visit and pretend to include her in our conversations. She'd sit there with her eyes glazed over, her mouth twisted in a gnarled frown due to over-the-top doses of therapeutic drugs. She'd rub the smooth, horizontal scar on her left wrist.

I thought these visits were the stupidest things, and I must have said so a million times. There was that Christmas we got the Atari 2600. I wanted to spend the morning in front of the television playing Frogger and Asteroids. But we had to go visit Nana first.

"This is so stupid," I said while rifling through my drawers for a pair of tights to wear under my dress.

"Don't be nasty," Rikki said. "Nana only sees us at Christmas and Thanksgiving. She'll feel your negative energy if you don't shape up."

"You sound like Mommy," I mumbled. "And stop being a goody-goody. You hate going, too." Rikki usually cried after our visits.

My parents constantly argued about my grandmother. I remember their scariest fight as though it happened a month ago. It was a Sunday. Rikki and I sat in our room, immersed in the adventures of Nancy Drew and the Hardy Boys. Actually, I had Judy Blume's *Are You There God? It's Me, Margaret* hidden behind Nancy Drew. Daddy had bought it for me even though Mommy considered it trash.

"But she's my *mother*, Clark," Mommy shouted somewhere downstairs. "Not some woman off the street!"

"I don't care," Daddy shouted back. "She's crazy and needs to stay hospitalized! She doesn't need to be here."

"Oh? And *your* mother had all of her crayons in a box?" Mommy shouted. "She *had* to be crazy marrying your father!"

I read my book as Mommy and Daddy fought. I reacted like most kids whose parents constantly bickered: I shut them out. Rikki, though, froze in terror whenever their voices rose with curses that cut the air. And today, she froze. I didn't want to look at my sister down there on the carpet even though her eyes burned into my forehead.

"She's a squirrel, Olivia!" Daddy said. "And you're nothing but a squirrel's daughter who can't admit that her mother's full of nuts!"

Ouch.

"You son of a bitch!" Mommy yelled.

Then flesh slapped flesh. Who hit whom in these fights? Don't know. Don't think it ever mattered. I flinched, the task of shutting them out becoming more difficult. I looked at our closed bedroom door. Rikki continued to stare at me.

I turned to her. "You okay?" I asked, a slight quiver in my voice. I swallowed and hoped the tremor would go away.

Rikki didn't answer. Her breath just rattled in her chest.

I closed my eyes and pictured the Hardy Boys, Nancy Drew, and Margaret lurking in the darkness with one flashlight between them.

"I don't want her around my daughters!" Daddy shouted.

"Well, take your daughters and get the hell out of my house!"

Mommy never, ever, ever let Daddy forget that he didn't buy the house we lived in. So Daddy hated our house. And he hated Nana for going crazy. And he hated Mommy for arguments about what was hers and what didn't belong to him.

My parents went back and forth, trading insults, and talking about each other's momma. Then I heard paper. *R-ii-ppp.* I opened my eyes and gawked at Rikki. "What are you doing?" I whispered. But I already knew. Her fingers slowly tore a page from my Nancy Drew mystery. This wasn't anything new. By now, she destroyed a book every other week. I lied each time this happened, told Daddy that I had accidentally torn it, that I was ever so sorry because I didn't want him to stop buying me books every Sunday afternoon. He would if I (I mean Rikki) kept destroying them. But here Rikki was, breaking my promise. Really, I don't know which television show she watched to get an idea like tearing up people's property, but I really wished she'd destroy her own stuff.

R-ii-ppp. Rikki bowed her head. A teardrop tumbled down her cheek and onto a vandalized page. The paper darkened as it fell to the ground.

My heart lurched. *Are you there God? It's me, Stacy.*

"What are you doing?" I asked. "You're gonna get me in trouble again."

She finally looked at me. Tears stood at the rims of her eyes like coffee in a shot glass. When Mommy called Daddy a bastard, a teardrop fell onto the back of her hand.

"Rikki, don't." My heart pounded as I processed the sound of tearing paper. "Rikki . . ."

And then Rikki screamed. A high, piercing scream that made *me* scream. I stopped after a moment, but Arika kept on. The cords in her neck flexed like piano strings. Mommy and Daddy charged into our room to see their eldest on the carpet with scraps of paper scattered around her, with her mouth wide open and eyes squeezed shut.

"What the hell?" Daddy shouted.

"I made her scream," I blurted. "I told her that she couldn't read my book." The obvious lie didn't matter. My parents seemed satisfied as they always were when I made myself the problem. Without a word, they closed the door and returned to the den to watch the rest of *Gunsmoke.* They grounded me and forbade me to read for a month.

My life as Rikki's sister wasn't always horrible. In junior high school, Rikki's emotional collapses lessened and, for me, having an older sister actually became a benefit. In my opinion, "junior high" was a concept that only a masochist could have thought up: forcing several hundred anxiety-ridden adolescents into an overcrowded school, forcing them to undress in front of strangers for the sake of physical education, then isolating anyone who didn't own at least three pairs of Jordache jeans. And then there was the clique problem— you were a "cool kid," "nerd kid," "welfare kid," "slow kid," or "jock kid." Sheesh. You can understand why kids sometimes have to beat each other up after school. Talk about cruel and unusual punishment.

Not for Rikki, though. Junior high was mecca for my sister, the same person who had gone into conniptions over dropped change at nutrition just a few years back. Rikki had breasts, clear skin, *and* perfect hair. Most of the guys who knew her asked her out. She didn't have to take woodwork or metal. She looked like a jillion dollars on picture day. Everyone said, "Hey, what's up?" to her when she passed. And lucky me, I was her sister. Well, actually, no one knew that offhand.

I still lingered in the training-bra section at Sears. Zits blemished my face and my hair just didn't fall right, no matter how long the beautician left in the relaxer. And I also had to take metal. But Rikki Moore was my sister and rescued me from the pit whenever she could. She wrote my assignments for creative writing when my mind sat blank in my head. When Alex James (the first boy who held my hand, sat next to me on the bus, and kissed me on the cheek just before I got off) started going out with Christina Harmon (she wore braces and had a huge butt), it was Rikki who, finding me in tears on my bed, said, "Why are you letting all of that stress you out? There are fifty million boys at Audubon. There's a top for every pot. An ass for every seat. It ain't that deep, Stacy. You're cute. Relax."

Mommy agreed. "And you're too young for boyfriends. Concentrate on your math."

And when Rikki wore three of the friendship bracelets I had crocheted to school, then started having me do some for all of her friends (also very, very popular girls), my life in junior high changed for the better.

Kendall Finch, considered the prettiest girl in the eighth grade (she had the "advantage": light skin and green eyes), sat next to me in English class. One day, she motioned toward my green-and-white bracelet and whispered, "Hey! What's that on your arm?"

At first, I wasn't aware that she was actually talking to me. I mean, we had sat next to each other for three months and she hadn't uttered a single word to me. She kind of looked past me even though my head blocked her view of the chalkboard. Before that day, I was Stacy the Invisible Girl.

Shocked, I said, "A friendship bracelet."

"Let me see," she demanded.

I held out my decorated wrist.

"I ain't seen one of those in school colors before." She turned my wrist over, then pulled it closer to her eyes.

So I offered her mine. She accepted. I untied the bracelet from my wrist. She plucked it from my fingers. I tied the ornament around her wrist. "Thanks," she said. "What's your name again?"

She hadn't asked for it a first time. "Stacy." And just like that, I was somebody to know.

Like Rikki's friends who loved the bracelets, my new pal Kendall bragged to her friends about them, too. Pretty soon, I was spending ten dollars a week on yarn and different-size needles, which I carried in a little pastel handbag.

"Can you make me some for the election?" Rikki asked me. She had just started her campaign for ninth-grade student body president. "I'll pay you back. Promise." The next day, she stood in the middle of the quad with a grocery bag full of my green-and-white bracelets. She gave one to each passerby and said, "A vote for me is a vote for a friend." She had attached to each bracelet a slip of paper that read VOTE ARIKA MOORE FOR PRESIDENT. She won the election: 375 votes to 63. I like to think that my bracelets had something to do with her victory.

Not only was I friends with Kendall Finch, but now my big sister was the most powerful student on campus. Life got even better. People said hi to me as I walked around the quad. I got a certificate for perfect attendance. I went to Sacramento with my leadership class and lobbied for equal education. Sweet.

Rikki stood between Mommy and me as we started to argue more. She introduced me to guys she knew I liked. She even took up for me when other kids wanted to ostracize me. Once, Kendall and my new friends Star and Helen came over to our house for a slumber party. That night, I pulled on my pajama top as we prepared to climb into our sleeping bags.

"You sleep in your *bra?*" Kendall gasped. She looked as if I had just sacrificed six small children and a kitten.

"Yeah." I tucked my long-sleeved pajama top into my pajama bottoms. I got really cold at night because Rikki kept our bedroom window open. The girls had on these short teddy thingies with their arms and legs out. No one else wore a bra.

Star gawked at my feet. "*And* socks? Why do you wear so many clothes to bed?" Their toenails glistened with bubblegum-pink nail polish. "Are you gonna put on a coat and a hat next?"

My stomach rumbled. I tasted the pizza from earlier. Sweat popped onto my temples. "I don't have that much on. Dang."

"My mother says that you'll get breast cancer if you wear a bra to bed," Kendall said. "It's important that your titties breathe."

Star looked at my chest. "Not like you got any." They busted up, laughing and hooting.

Trapped, I had to make a choice. Take off the bra so that my titties could breathe and grow; or keep on my bra and remain a double-A cup.

"Stacy, you are so *weird*," Kendall said as she squinted her cat eyes. "Who in the world wears a *bra* to bed?"

I guess Rikki had heard our conversation, so she entered the room. She crossed her arms and stood in the doorway. "What's so weird about her wearing a bra to bed? I wear a bra to bed."

The girls hushed in deference to the ninth-grade president and the yearbook's Nicest Figure winner.

"But not tonight." Then Rikki lifted her pajama top. Her breasts—cups in the high B's—hung there as perfect as ripe grapefruit. No female in the room came close to her proportions. "Does it look like *mine* need to breathe?" Silence filled the room. "No?" With a nod, she let her top fall back over her breasts. "Maybe you guys need to wear bras, too."

I placed my hands over my mouth to keep from laughing. The girls got sleepy all of a sudden and someone told me to turn out the lights. Kendall, Star, and Helen found humility that night after my big sister flashed them and shoved her perfection in their faces. And from that moment, they left me and my little chichis alone.

5

So Close, Yet . . .

ALL OF Rikki's teachers considered her gifted. She took
honors everything: math, English, history, and Spanish. She
read on a college-freshman level. She took a few courses at
our local community college, too. Over three years, Mrs.
Beasley, our principal, paid close attention to her star pupil.
When it came to Rikki, she liked what she saw. The October
of my sister's ninth-grade year, Mrs. Beasley invited Rikki to
her office one morning. No one, including the principal,
noticed the bags under my sister's eyes—Rikki only slept one
hour a day.

"Arika, have a seat," Mrs. Beasley said. Then she flipped
through Rikki's file, which was stuffed with commendations,
teachers' letters, and report cards. She whistled between her
teeth as she reviewed my sister's history. Mrs. Beasley was a
powerful old lady. She had been principal for twenty years

and it showed. Even though she barely reached five and a half feet tall, she carried herself like John Henry. Her knuckles and hands were the size of a man's. She walked as though she wore a suit of armor. Even her skirts pleated with purpose.

"Have you thought much about college?" Mrs. Beasley asked.

"No, ma'am," Rikki said as she studied the dusty grizzly-bear figurines planted on the principal's desk.

"Well, it's quite obvious from your test scores, your grade point average, and the breadth of your extracurricular activities that you should seriously consider top universities," the principal said fast. Way too fast.

Mrs. Beasley's dentures slipped from her gums as they did whenever she rambled or let too much air into her mouth. To keep from laughing, Rikki kept her eyes glued to the stained Berber carpet. A giggle escaped, though, and Rikki immediately faked a sneeze.

"Bless you," Mrs. Beasley said. "The high schools in this district can't . . . well . . . they can't meet the standards that you need. I believe you'd be better off in a private school, where your chance to succeed dramatically increases. You should receive more attention. You should be able to choose from a wider selection of courses. Marlborough offers seventeen more AP classes than Crenshaw. So I want to talk to your parents about your education this evening. Is that okay with you?"

"Yes! Oh, God, yes!" Rikki chirped. "That would be the best thing ever!"

Three hours later, Rikki told me that she hated the idea of going to a private school. "And I think Nelson likes me, too," she said. "And he's going to Crenshaw." Nelson Sutherland was also in the ninth grade. He was the cocaptain of the varsity basketball team. He constantly brushed his hair to maintain his rows of S-Curl–assisted waves. He also sat in back of Rikki and me in typing class.

"You remember when Mrs. Ortiz stepped out of the room today? I turned around and Nelson was staring right at me," Rikki said. Then she giggled. "I came this close to asking him if he liked me or not."

"Where was I?" I asked, dumbfounded. How did all this happen without my noticing?

Rikki shrugged. "Then I went up to him after class and he said, 'What's up?' Then I said, 'Nothing, what's up with you?' And he said, 'Inflation!' He's soooo funny! And he's right! Prices *are* sky-high!"

I just sat there with a stupid grin on my face as my sister giggled until she turned purple. I didn't mind these moods so much. Rikki climbed out of her giggly, girly moment, then said, straight-faced, "But if I'm at another school, how will our love survive?"

She sat up three nights in a row, trying to figure out if her education should precede love. Finally she asked, "What do you think?"

I shrugged. "I don't know." *She* was the one who had told me that boys weren't that deep.

In December, Rikki tested, interviewed, and blew Marlborough's Admissions Committee away. Before the end of her ninth-grade year, she won a substantial scholarship to one of the ritziest prep schools in Los Angeles. Girls who attended Marlborough drove their own convertible German imports, wore purple-and-gray uniforms, and were white. And not Valley Girl white, either. I'm talkin' rich, vanilla,

Mayflower white. Not exactly a bastion of diversity, but neither was Crenshaw High School, my alma mater, located in the soul of South Central Los Angeles.

And since no love blossomed between Rikki and Nelson, that was that. Rikki walked through those wrought-iron gates that September. Her scholarship covered tuition and books. Relieved, Daddy had proudly written a check for her uniforms. He had the Volvo waxed. He and Mommy drove Rikki to school on her first day.

Rikki fit in and stood out in her new environment. She was black. She was pretty. She was sassy like Nell Carter or Florida Evans, but not disrespectful like Florence the Maid or Wilona the Neighbor. Smart, but not Harriet Tubman/Oprah Winfrey start-a-race-war smart. She was black, but not too . . . *black*. So they liked her.

I enrolled in high school that next year and eventually found my niche at Crenshaw. I ran track, but not on Saturdays, played violin, but not first chair. I played piano, but my fingers lurched across the keys as if they were made of sausages. I found myself on the honor roll, but nowhere near the top. I was elected to student government, but only as treasurer. I took honors geometry, even though I probably needed to be in regular algebra. Teachers liked me but didn't love me. I had plenty of friends who had come over from junior high, including Kendall and Star. So I wasn't lonely. But I missed my sister.

"Wouldn't it be cool if I went to Marlborough, too?" I said to my parents one night as they watched *Dynasty*.

Mommy smiled and nodded. "That's a great idea, Stacy."

Daddy remained silent.

Rikki actually frowned when I brought up the possibility.

"Can't I do *anything* by myself?" she asked. "I'm tired of having to baby-sit you."

Baby-sit *me?* What world was *she* in?

After Mommy signed a few forms, Crenshaw's registrar forwarded my transcripts to Marlborough's Admissions Office. I received a letter from the school: my interview was scheduled three weeks later.

"You can't go in there half-assed," Daddy said. He still wasn't excited about me going to private school, but he didn't want to see me fail, either. So he put me through a grueling course of mock interviews. I even had to dress up for these sessions, which he conducted in his office downtown. He sat behind his desk, a frown in place, and threw profound, sometimes ridiculous, questions at me:

"What's the one thing that you'd change in the world?"

"Where do you see yourself in three years?"

"What's your favorite ice cream flavor and why?"

Afterward, Daddy provided a written critique of my best and worst answers. Soon, I was ready for the real deal.

I decided to wear a navy blue dress and matching pumps—the same outfit Rikki had worn for her interview. Only I had cramps that day, and a pimple the size of a corn kernel had generated right in the middle of my chin. Rikki suggested that I take a broomstick and some eye of newt with me. I cried in the bathroom.

"Just ignore her, Stacy," Mommy said through the door. "You're way too sensitive." I eventually came out of the bathroom. Mommy thought foundation would hide my blemish. It did not.

My interview was conducted in Marlborough's library, which had to be thirty-five degrees. My uterus contracted as soon as I walked in: it couldn't stand the arctic conditions, either.

Minutes later, a white woman with frosted hair and bright red lipstick entered in a cloud of White Shoulders perfume. "You must be Anastasia," she said, and extended her hand. No cuticles on those nails, not that I could see any—the glare from her behemoth diamond and sapphire ring blinded me. "I'm Dr. Martha Quimby, the principal."

"It's a pleasure to meet you," I said, shivering. I gave a firm handshake and looked her square in her eyes, as instructed by Daddy in our trial runs.

The principal and I sat in two armchairs. I crossed my legs at my ankles and kept my hands folded in my lap. My voice rang as clear as Pastor Phillips's and I reminded myself not to use *ums, uhs,* and *you knows.* One lapse into colloquialism could mean public education for the next seven years of my life.

Principal Quimby and I chatted for an hour about track and violin, Rikki, career choices, the type of tree I'd be, when I led and when I followed, the public figure I most admired, and finally, how I'd spend $2.8 million if I became governor of California. An hour of questioning and no mention of ice cream or my strengths and weaknesses. I wondered if that was a good thing. Principal Quimby asked me if I had any questions. I said no.

She stood. "Thank you for coming in. I enjoyed talking with you." We shook hands and I left the library.

Daddy was waiting in the car. When he saw me, he hopped out to hug me. "How'd you do?"

I smiled as the sun warmed my face. "Piece of cake," I said. The icicles melted from my extremes. My cramps had even subsided. I considered the manicured hedges, the green lawns, and the well-tended mansions across the street. I thought of all the kids back at Crenshaw who would miss me. In my mind, I had even composed the beginnings of the farewell speech I'd give on my last day. I would promise Kendall that we'd remain friends for the rest of our lives. I would look so cool in that purple-and-gray uniform.

Daddy treated me to lunch at Sizzler after the interview. "Get whatever you want," he said. "It's your day." So I ordered the hibachi chicken *and* the salad bar.

"I'm proud of you," he said, then squeezed my hand. "I'm glad you take initiative when it comes to your education. People always point to Arika as the smart one. You are, too, in your own way." He smiled. "You're like me: a jack-of-all-trades, not just a scholar. I'm really, really proud of you, Stacy."

I blushed and buried myself in my ice cream sundae.

I wasn't admitted to Marlborough. I won't tell you, verbatim, what my rejection letter said, but it wished me luck with my academic career. It was signed with a stamp of Principal Quimby's signature. It was addressed to "Anesthesia More." I crumpled the letter into a little ball after I read it and tossed it in the kitchen garbage can. Then I fished it out again.

I wasn't exceptional enough. Maybe I grossed out Principal Quimby with my zit. Maybe I grossed out Principal Quimby with my interview answers: future writer who wanted to be a mahogany tree, who led most of the time and followed whenever I knew the leader knew what she was doing, probably just what Alice Walker did, which is why I admired her the most, and in the best of worlds, Alice and I would spend all that budget money on literacy programs for poor black kids in the inner city.

Rikki didn't seem too upset about my rejection: "Oh, well," she said. "They don't let in *everyone* who has a relative going there."

I didn't resent her for that. Wait. That's not true. I just didn't let *others* know that I resented her.

Daddy sighed when he read the letter. "Crenshaw's not an *awful* school," he said. Yeah, and it ain't a great one, either. He took me to get a scoop of black walnut ice cream. "Let's go to the golf course. It'll do us both good." He never mentioned my rejection from that exclusive private school for girls again. Bless him.

Life went on. Rikki thrived at Marlborough and I kept keeping on at Crenshaw. Since we went to separate high schools, Rikki and I didn't hang out Monday through Friday. Saturday didn't count since church and family monopolized our time. Sunday was it for us. And on Sunday afternoons, Rikki and I rode the city bus to Fox Hills Mall in Culver City, another Los Angeles suburb. For most of the black kids in L.A., Fox Hills was *the* place to hang out and flirt. And it had a Judy's, a Contempo Casuals, and a Sam Goody. All of your needs were met.

Can you see us, in those tight, heavily starched Levi's with creases in the leg as sharp as an iron could make them, swinging our hips down the cool, gaudily lit corridors that smelled of pretzels and chocolate chip cookies, strolling from store to store, our hair long, dark, and lovely, flipped and curled past our shoulders? We were fly girls.

And we enjoyed the lustful stares of the boys who watched us pass. "What's your name?" guys with flattop haircuts or bald heads asked. And if they were cute, Rikki and I would look at each other and smile.

"Rikki," she'd say.

"Stacy," I'd say.

And if they were cute, and if their K-Swiss tennis shoes sparkled, and if they smelled of Polo cologne, we'd give them our phone number written with pink ink (of course) on a piece of Hello Kitty stationery. We'd smile and slink away, never caring if they called or not. And to be honest, we hoped that they *never* called—Mommy would beat us blue. Yeah, Rikki and I were better than best friends back then.

Don't get me wrong. Naturally, there was plenty of drama with two teenaged girls under the same roof. For instance, Rikki wanted to wear bows and crucifixes like Madonna, and the torn, off-the-shoulder sweatshirts and leg warmers like Jennifer Beals in *Flashdance;* but since she wore that uniform (the one I thought was so damn awesome), she had to change into her outfits as soon as she got home. That meant she only had three hours to be fly.

Hell, in public school, I got to wear almost anything I wanted: tight, stonewashed jeans with zippered legs, slouch socks and Converse high-tops, neon this and pastel that, miniskirts, Esprit and Reebok whenever my parents could afford it. I could wear as many Swatch watches on my arm as I wanted, even though I only had one. I had a good time, and Rikki hated me. "You think you're the bomb," she said. "You're not. Far from it."

"Whatever," I said, then pulled on my bubble-gum-pink Converse.

It got worse, though. There was the Jacques Hilbert Incident that October. Jacques had green eyes and that blond hair mixed black kids had. He also had several pairs of K-Swiss and drove his daddy's old Beemer. Every girl at school wanted Jacques. I ran track with him, so I didn't trip óut as much. I introduced him to Rikki when she came to one of my meets. She fell in love. They went out a few times shortly after.

One night, Rikki invited Jacques to our house. I invited Tommy Green, who didn't know that I had a mad crush on him. Mommy ordered pizza and provided the Dr Peppers for Rikki and New Cokes for me—hey, if Max Headroom drank it, so did I. Jacques arrived first.

"Hey," he said to me. He hugged me—a hug that lasted a little too long. I pulled away. Rikki glared at me. "What's up?" he asked.

"Nothing," I said. "Congratulations on the race." He had come in first at a big meet against some school in the Valley. "You blew them away."

"Hey, Rik," Jacques finally said. He hugged her and kissed her cheek. She took him to the den to meet Mommy and Daddy.

Tommy called to cancel, so Jacques, Rikki, and I retreated to the living room to play Trivial Pursuit, the game that compelled me to memorize useless pieces of crap in order to beat my sister at *something*. An hour of game play passed. Rikki and I were squares and Jacques knew it. We had both of our parents, lived in a two-story house, drank Dr Pepper *and* New Coke, and played Trivial Pursuit. He sat quietly as Rikki and I answered questions from those damned little cards. I think he got one right.

Around nine-thirty, he yawned and stretched. He had figured out that he and Rikki wouldn't have the chance to make out with me there and with Mommy and Daddy watching *Dallas* twenty yards away.

"Hey, I gotta go." He stood and brushed potato chip crumbs from his Levi's. "It's getting late."

"So soon?" Rikki cried. "What's wrong?"

"It's getting late, Rikki," I repeated. Jacques smiled at me and I smiled back.

Rikki looked at me, then at Jacques, then at me again. "What the hell's going on here?"

I walked past her. "Let's walk him to the door."

She grabbed my *Flashdance*-styled sweatshirt. "You're trying to steal my boyfriend!" she shouted. "Ho!"

As I pulled away, my sweatshirt ripped. "Will you chill out?" I shouted.

"Rikki," Jacques said, "I didn't say that we were—"

"Shut up," she yelled. "Right in front of my face!" Tears flooded her eyes. She yanked me again and tore more of my sweatshirt.

And I had worked so hard to rip it the right way. "Let me go!" I shouted.

"I hate you!" Then she slugged me in the nose.

Oh, the pain. Throbs of white heat spilled over my face. Sticky wetness dripped between my fingers. Is this how stinky Pamela Keller felt when I clocked her back in elementary? Man. Karma's a bitch.

Jacques ran from the living room to get my parents in the den. He shouted, "Rikki's beating up Stacy!"

Rikki, cowed by the sound of violence, had stumbled behind the couch. She muttered, "I'm sorry, Stacy, I'm sorry."

Jacques returned to the room and held me in his arms. My nose bled over my lips and onto his polo shirt.

"I'm sorry, Stacy," Rikki said again.

Mommy and Daddy swept over my sister. "Are you okay?" they asked her. They checked her face and body for cuts and blood.

Jacques's jaw dropped as he watched. "Stacy's the one bleeding," he finally blurted.

Daddy looked at me. "Oh." He came over. I stepped away from Jacques. I wanted a hug and to hear words of comfort. I wanted Rikki to be grounded for life.

Daddy shook his head, then said, "She got you pretty good." Then he chuckled and guided me to the bathroom as Mommy saw Jacques to the front door. Rikki hovered outside the bathroom as Daddy cleaned me up until Mommy called her downstairs.

I skipped school until the swelling on my face subsided. Mommy hid my black eye with her Fashion Fair foundation. Jacques never called Rikki again and I didn't speak to her for a week. Remorseful, she left pints of black walnut ice cream and glazed doughnuts at my door. I ate them, but didn't care to thank her.

The January of Rikki's senior year, God flipped Rikki's switch. She wrote essays, but her words rambled on into infinity. She immersed herself in books and stories, but couldn't remember what she had read. She sat in class lost and confused. Frightened, she ran from the classroom and cried in the bathroom on several occasions. Mommy and Daddy met with Rikki's counselor. The counselor had no answers to Rikki's sudden behavioral change. Everyone agreed that she was stressed out because of college applications, essays, and SAT scores. Universities would start sending out admission letters in the next month or two, and what high school senior didn't fret about that?

Rikki started to lock her bedroom door more. She ignored us at dinner. She'd listen to one album for weeks. Prince got played for two months straight. Now, I like Prince. I always chose him whenever my friends had that major debate on who was better, Prince or Michael Jackson. But back then, I didn't listen to his music every single day of my life. Rikki did. She played that *Purple Rain* album until the tape spilled from the cassette. I'm glad it broke because the songs made her cry.

Sometimes, my parents noticed her melancholia. "What's wrong with her now?" Daddy asked every week.

"Don't take that tone, Clark," Mommy said. "Did you say something to her, Stacy?"

"No," I said every single time we had this conversation.

"Why don't you guys do something fun?" Daddy suggested. "Here." He had bought two pairs of brand-new roller skates.

"Clark, they already have skates," Mommy said.

Daddy wouldn't have known that because Mommy never let us skate around our neighborhood. According to her, a car could hit us or we could be kidnapped by some pervert. Gangbangers and drug dealers hung out at the roller rinks, the beach was too far, and the park was too dark.

For the first time in her life, Rikki was failing. I didn't want her to get kicked out of school, so I attempted to do my part. "Want me to study with you?" I asked her. Maybe she needed someone to talk to. Maybe she needed me.

"I'm not a baby," she spat. "What makes you think that I want to be around you, anyway? What makes you think I care?"

I shrugged. "Whatever. Have it your way." I rose to leave, but she grabbed my wrist.

"Where are you going?" she whimpered. "Stay."

I sat. She covered her face with her hands. "I'm not a virgin anymore," she whispered.

"Huh?" My heart pounded. What did she mean, not a virgin? I assumed that neither of us was interested in *intercourse;* especially since Mommy had told us that we could get herpes or VD from too much kissing. But here was Rikki, actually letting some guy put his . . . *thing* in her. "Who?"

"Garry McAlpine."

"*Scary* Hairy Garry? From church?" I asked, shocked. He had tufts of hair on his back. It poked through his clothes. His ears were larger than a silver dollar. His hairline started right above his eyebrows, like Frankenstein. He made bombs and read *Soldier of Fortune.* He put cats in the microwave and watched them explode. I shivered. "Ugh."

Rikki placed her face in her hands again and sobbed. I patted her back. "So are you two going together?" Ick. When did she have time for sex? And was he to blame for her problems? Sheesh. I'd cry, too.

"He hasn't called me back," she wailed. "And I already bought him a Valentine's Day card, but it seemed so fake and stuff, so I wrote him these." She thrust wrinkled pieces of paper in my hand. "They're poems. Read them."

"'Garry, I see the sun in your eyes. Your love has touched the bottom of my heart. Forever, forever, you and me.'" O-kaaaay. "You wrote *this?*" Rikki had published poems in magazines and newspapers. Really good stuff. But what I had in my hand right then was . . . well, it was crap.

Rikki nodded.

I read the next one: " 'Garry, my love, you are like a dove sent from heaven above. Awaken the fire within. Use its light to guide your way to my soul. If you let it dim, I shall die.' " I grunted. "At least that one kinda rhymed," I mumbled. *Cheese and bread.*

She fell into my arms and cried until Mommy banged on the door. It was time for dinner. "Rikki, we should go eat," I said.

"I don't deserve to eat," she muttered. She hid her face in the pillow. "I'll never be a virgin again!"

She was right, so I couldn't argue. I arrived at the dinner table alone. Rikki's poems were in my pocket. I planned to bury them in the backyard or, better yet, burn them.

"Where's your sister?" Daddy asked.

"Sleeping," I lied. "She's pretty tired."

From that night on, Rikki took her meals in her bedroom—that is, if she ate. Simple things in our life transformed into major battles with her, like washing dishes or putting up groceries. She barked at people when she spoke. And now we both argued constantly with Mommy.

One Saturday morning, I chose to wear my new apple-green dress to church. As I combed my hair in the bathroom, Mommy came in. She looked me up and down, then said, "You're not wearing that."

"Huh? Why?"

"Because it's riding up your behind," Mommy snapped. "You look cheap. Like a streetwalker." And as far as streetwalkers went, Mommy looked like my madam in her too short purple skirt and silk camisole.

"You're the one who bought me this dress." I had tried it on and modeled it for her at the department store. "I want to wear it! We're already late!"

"Fine. We won't go to church, then."

I sighed and threw up my hands. "Fine. I'll change." I took off the outfit and found a pink dress—the same style as the green dress—and pulled it on.

"Now, that's better," Mommy said as she changed purses.

"Why are you so concerned about what she's wearing?" Rikki said. She had emerged from her room in this somber, black frock. She wore no makeup and had pulled her hair back into a tight bun. Her eyes sat deep in their sockets. Her mouth was set in a frown.

Mommy stuck her hand in the dish of peppermints and grabbed thousands of candies. "Excuse me for not wanting people to think that I've raised some streetwalking Jezebel."

The three of us walked down to Mommy's Corolla. Mommy scooted behind the steering wheel. I sat in the front passenger seat. Rikki sat behind me. "Who cares what people think?" I said. "That's not why you go to church, anyway."

"Don't get your tongue pulled out," Mommy warned.

"And don't mess with God," I said. *Honestly.*

"Who the hell are you talking to like that?" Mommy shouted.

"Will the both of you just shut up?" Rikki yelled. "Just shut up! All you two do is bicker back and forth and I'm fucking sick of it!"

Mommy and I froze in our seats. I saw my sister's reflection in the vanity mirror. She clutched her purse tight to her chest. Her eyes were squeezed shut.

"Look at the clock!" Rikki shouted. It was eleven forty-five. "By the time we get to church, it'll be twelve-fifteen. And in case either of you *heathens* has forgotten, service ends at twelve-thirty!" She kicked the back of my seat, then jumped out of the car. "You made me miss my blessing!" She glared at Mommy and me as she stormed into the house.

She didn't come out of her room that afternoon. During the week, she went straight to her room when she got home from school. I often heard her crying in the bathroom. She wouldn't let me in or tell me to go away. She avoided my parents and me as much as possible. It was as if a ghost lived in our house.

On the Sunday morning of my spring debutante ball, I was eating Frosted Flakes and reading *Hollywood Wives*. I, along with twelve other sixteen- and seventeen-year-olds, would be formally presented to society by Alpha Kappa Alpha, Incorporated, at the Carson Ramada Inn that Sunday evening. My knees throbbed from rehearsed curtsies and waltz classes, and from the cheap white pumps I had tried to break in. My fingers ached from extra music lessons. My piano teacher, Mrs. Matthews, ate evil for breakfast and little girls for lunch. She also rapped my knuckles with a ruler if my fingering wasn't correct: child abuse. She scowled and never said, "Great job," even when I flawlessly played a piece. I hated Beethoven because of her. I was convinced that I would throw up as I played "Für Elise" because I hated *her* so much.

That morning, Mommy sat next to me at the breakfast table with a needle and thread. She had to take up an inch and a half on the white confection of a dress I'd wear that night. Daddy sat across from us with his face hidden by the Metro section of the *Los Angeles Times*. He tossed the paper on the table after a while. "I'm sick of this. Where's your sister?"

I wanted to say crying a river 'cause she gave it up to Scary

Hairy Garry McAlpine, who had dumped her three days before Valentine's Day. Instead I said, "I don't know." And I could care less. I continued to read the book I had brought to breakfast.

Mommy glared at me. "This house ain't that big. Tell her to come down for breakfast. We need to be at the mall when it opens."

Before I could stand, Rikki emerged from the hallway. Her hair, a frizzed-out corona, hovered around her head. Her fuchsia bathrobe sagged around her like old skin. Her face looked ashen and hard.

"Good morning, Arika," Mommy said. "Glad you could join us."

Rikki grunted, then plopped in the chair across from me. I stared at her. She stared back at me.

"What's wrong with you today?" Daddy asked as his eyes grazed the top of the paper.

"She's fine," Mommy said. She turned to me. "Stacy, what have I told you about bringing books to my table?"

I put Jackie Collins away and watched my mother pour Frosted Flakes and milk into my sister's bowl. "Now eat," she told Rikki. "We have things to do."

Rikki sneered at me and grabbed her spoon. Her teeth looked sharp, as if she had grown fangs overnight. Mommy continued on with her stitching. Daddy turned the page to the obituaries. I was first to notice Rikki's robe sleeves darken into maroon. And I was first to notice a dark drop of liquid hit the milk in her cereal bowl, then swirl into an amoeba-shaped pattern between the flakes. I looked at Rikki, who now smiled at me. "You're bleeding," I croaked. Another drop hit the milk. "Mommy, Rikki's bleeding!"

"Shut the fuck up," Rikki said, and kicked me beneath the table.

"What did you say?" Daddy asked. He had missed the "You're bleeding" part, but had heard the curse right away. Typical.

Mommy finally noticed Rikki's cuffs and her cereal bowl. She backed away from the table as if a live wire had jolted her. Rikki held out her wrists like a young girl proud of her stamp collection.

Daddy shouted, "No!" and jumped across the table. "Call nine one one!"

My ears and neck burned. I tasted acid and sour milk. I wanted to scream, but I couldn't. I just sat there. I couldn't look away. Daddy touched Rikki, who screamed, then blacked out. He tied my white dress around her wrists. "Stacy," he shouted, "move your ass! Call nine one one!"

Mommy also fainted and hit her head on the stove. I ran to the hallway and called 911. I returned to the kitchen and held Rikki as Daddy tended to his wife. When my mother regained consciousness, she was a different woman. Her face was murky, queer, and pained. She looked fatigued, like a soldier in a ceaseless war. Her frown took no true shape—as if her lips wouldn't commit. Her body slumped, just like her mouth.

The ambulance arrived ten minutes later. Our neighbors gathered on our lawn. Mommy, in her own oxygen mask, rode in the ambulance with Arika.

"I don't want to go to the hospital," I told Daddy as we stood in the driveway. You could still hear the faint cry of the ambulance siren. Our neighbors now stared at us from their own lawns.

Daddy frantically searched for the key that would unlock his car. "Your sister needs you. Stop being selfish."

"Well, can I change?" I still wore bloody pajamas.

"Get in the car," he said. *"Now."*

I climbed into the Volvo. Daddy slammed the door behind me. We drove in silence. I spent the morning of my debutante ball in the Cedars-Sinai emergency waiting room. It didn't take long for the doctor to stitch up my sister's wrists. She screamed and cursed the entire time. "I want to die! You can't make me live!" she shouted. She told Mommy and Daddy that she hated them for bringing her back and forcing her to stay alive when she didn't want to. Eventually, the orderlies restrained her. The attending physician sedated her with Valium, then pumped Thorazine into her IV.

I stood at the admitting desk, listening as my parents told the nurse Rikki's age, the date of her last physical, whether she was allergic to penicillin, the first day of her last period. Eventually, a candy striper led me to the waiting room, where I sat, alone, while my parents were escorted to my sister's bed.

An hour had passed when a woman screamed behind the double doors. I jumped. It sounded as though the doctors were tearing out her heart. Was that my sister? I walked toward the doors and peeked through the mesh glass windows. Nurses and huge orderlies scrambled into a room. A second later, the woman was rolled out on a gurney. She was strapped down, like an animal. It wasn't Rikki. Still, my heart ached for her. Where was *her* family?

Rikki's doctor, a guy named Lowenstein, sat with my parents and me in his office. Certificates covered the wall, as well as pictures of happy children with dogs, cats, and stuffed animals. He looked like Woody Allen if he lived in California. "Is this her first attempt?" he asked.

"She broke up with her boyfriend," I blurted.

"She broke up with her boyfriend," Mommy parroted.

"Yes, it's her first," Daddy said, annoyed with both of us.

"She has a broken heart, Clark," Mommy said. "Doctor, you know how teenagers get. And I know that listening to that rap music doesn't help. I'll throw it out as soon as we get home. Really. It's no problem."

"Are you gonna put her in a straitjacket?" I asked.

Mommy glared at me. "Shut up," she said through clenched teeth.

I went back to counting the blood splatters on my pajamas.

"How are Arika's sleeping habits?" the doctor asked.

"She doesn't sleep," I blurted.

"Stacy," Mommy growled.

I shrugged. "Well, she doesn't. She stays up all night studying and writing poems and stuff."

"My daughter's exaggerating," Mommy said, clearly embarrassed.

The doctor, though, stared at me for a moment. "Have you noticed anything else, Stacy?"

I didn't look at my mother, even though I felt the heaviness of her glare.

"Well?" Daddy said.

"Um . . ." I drew a deep breath. "Sometimes, she's, like, really excited about something, so she'll talk really fast, but she'll switch subjects, and she won't make sense. Then she'll start crying and stuff." I wanted to mention that she was also having sex, but I wasn't *that* stupid.

"Has she taken any drugs?" Dr. Lowenstein asked.

I shook my head no. "Sometimes, she acts like it, though. I mean, she acts strange sometimes."

"Strange?" the doctor repeated.

Mommy sighed: here I was again, airing the family's dirty laundry, but with a white man this time.

I was sure that I wouldn't live to see my next birthday.

"Doctor, can you help us find counseling?" Daddy asked.

"Counseling?" Mommy screeched. "Over my dead body!"

Daddy and I glanced at each other, as though *that* were a viable option.

"Arika may be suffering from manic depression," Dr. Lowenstein said. "And you're right, Mr. Moore. Your daughter really should see someone. She keeps talking about dying. She threatened to stab herself in the throat with a fork. Sounds horrible, but then we want her to vent her feelings and not bottle them up, so she could explode again."

Mommy flicked his comment away like a piece of lint on her sleeve. "My daughter is not crazy. She just has an overactive imagination. She wants to be a writer when she grows up. She talks to me all the time. And to her sister. She was in love. She just needs rest."

"Olivia," Daddy said. "Come *on*. She just tried to kill herself."

"A friend of mine is a psychiatrist," the doctor said. "He's a great therapist." He slid a business card toward Mommy, who only stared at it. "Especially with teenagers." Daddy took the card and shoved it in his jacket pocket. "And, um . . ." The doctor scribbled on a small pad. "He'll probably start Arika on . . . um . . . lithium." He tore the slip of paper from the pad and handed it to Daddy. "Just to give you a heads-up."

"Eskalith?" Daddy read.

Dr. Lowenstein straightened his tortoiseshell glasses, then folded his hands on the desk. "It's lithium. Don't worry. It's a pretty common medication nowadays. Like Tylenol."

The Swedes, creators of the Swiss Army knife and IKEA, had discovered lithium, atomic number 3 on the periodic table. And like most drugs in the world, it became the cure for everything, so much so that a man created a drink a long time ago. He called it Bib-Label Lithiated Lemon-Lime Soda. Drinking it would give you more energy, shiny hair, a clear complexion, lots of enthusiasm, and shiny eyes. The key ingredient? Lithium. The beverage? 7UP, the uncola. For whatever reason, the drug was eventually taken out of the drink.

Too much lithium can make you nauseated, make you fat, or slur your speech, among other things. Way too much lithium can, well, kill you. "But she'll be fine," Dr. Lowenstein said. "She just has to take it regularly. He can even prescribe it in a syrup form. Just dilute it in fruit juice. But make sure she eats something first. She has to take it every day for it to work, okay? And have her cut back on her cola, too. Dr. Jordan will go over this with you again, so don't worry."

He smiled and leaned forward. "Millions of people around the world are on this. It may take at least a week before she starts to feel better, but it'll balance her out, help her cope better."

Daddy handed the slip of paper to my mother, who didn't even look at it.

6

WALK IN THE LIGHT

MY PARENTS drove me home that evening. They planned to return to the hospital after they had dropped me off. Before they left the house, Mommy told me that my friends couldn't come over to visit. Of course, there would be no curtsying or waltzing at the Ramada. Both my parents and Rikki's doctor decided that I shouldn't visit Rikki in the hospital. They planned to keep her for a week. "Well, can I go to choir rehearsal on Wednesday night? We're singing for the eleven o'clock service on Saturday," I said. "I'm sure Mrs. Curtis will pick me up. I'm gonna be bored being here all by myself."

"You're asking me to let you ride in the car with *that* alcoholic?" Mommy screeched. "I don't need to worry about you getting in some accident with a big rig when I already have to deal with your sister!"

"Mommy, Mrs. Curtis doesn't even drink Mountain Dew," I said. She had Jesus bumper stickers all over her minivan. "You worry too much."

"Well, what do you want me to do?" Mommy shouted. "My nerves are shot!" She rushed downstairs, where Daddy waited to take her back to Rikki's bedside. "Your sister isn't feeling well. I will not leave her in the hospital *alone* just so that I can take *you* to some choir rehearsal."

"Aren't you supposed to be bringing me up in the way I should go?" I asked. "We're talking about *God,* Mother. Worship."

"And where in the Bible does it say that you need to be in a choir to worship God?" she asked. "I worship God and I can't carry a tune."

Hopeless. No singing for me that week.

So I cleaned the house. I scrubbed the blood out of the white carpet upstairs and downstairs. Only a pink tint remained. Kool-Aid? Melted lipstick? No one would ever think blood. The dining room table sparkled after countless swipes with a dust cloth and Pledge: nothing more than milk or gravy had wet its surface. I stuffed my bloodstained ball gown into a brown paper bag, then shoved the bag deep into the trash can. I soaked the bloody towels in the laundry room sink, then tossed them into the washing machine.

Until then, I hadn't noticed how big our house was. My first night alone, I jumped each time it creaked. I whimpered with each rumble from the water heater. Whenever the neighbors' German shepherds barked, I wondered if an intruder lurked outside the windows.

I wandered the hallways and stood in each room for minutes. Don't know why. Have no idea what I wanted to see. I remained in the bathroom the longest. The razor blade that Rikki had used to slice her wrists stuck to the side of the sink. Its pale gray sheen was still speckled with liver-colored liquid. I wrapped tissue around my fingers and pried the weapon from the porcelain. Then I wrapped it in more tissue, then a washcloth, rendering it more harmless, and placed it in the wastebasket. I would empty it later.

I stared at my reflection in the mirror. I had forgotten that spots of dark red still stained my pajamas. My eyelids looked swollen; my eyes were just raisins in my head. I stripped and stepped into the shower. I stayed under the water, destroying my new relaxer, for over thirty minutes. I got out and pulled on sweats and socks.

It was almost eight-thirty when I stepped into the kitchen. My stomach growled. Even though I was almost seventeen, I (Rikki, too) was forbidden to use the stove when my parents weren't home. Mommy hadn't gone to the grocery store in days; we didn't have bread or meat for sandwiches. Everything in the cupboard, except the Tabasco sauce and pumpkin mix, required fire. I sat at the table and waited.

Daddy walked into the house first, around eight-forty-five. He trudged upstairs without a "Hello" or a "Hungry?" Moments later, water pounded against the shower walls. Mommy eventually came in from the garage and found me seated at the breakfast table. Her flip haircut was rumpled and tangled. Her skin had darkened as though the blood had died in her veins. Her lips were chapped. She clutched her purse to her chest along with a plastic bag that contained Rikki's soiled bathrobe.

She offered me a limp smile, kissed me on the forehead,

and said, "You must be hungry." She was right—I hadn't eaten since breakfast, ten hours earlier.

She rummaged through the cabinet and pulled out a box of instant macaroni and cheese. She found hamburger patties in the freezer. I remained at the table and watched her move, zombielike, between the stove and the refrigerator. Twenty minutes later, she scooped macaroni onto a plate next to the hamburger, which sat in grease. She kissed me again and walked upstairs.

I mumbled a blessing over my food and stuck my fork in the mound of pasta. The noodles resisted my bite—undercooked. The cheese tasted chalky—not enough milk. Blood seeped from the center of the hamburger patty. And I ate it even though I gagged, even though my stomach threatened to vomit with each bite I took.

After I forced down my meal, I pushed the plate away. The air still reeked of fried meat. The house was more silent with three people in it than when it had been just me. My throat clenched and tears burned at the back of my eyes. I wanted to throw my plate at the wall. I wanted to smash my glass of fruit punch on the ground. I wanted to destroy that kitchen, to burn down the house. I didn't. I willed my hysteria away.

On Monday, Mommy permitted me to miss school until further notice. That evening, again Daddy entered the house silently; Mommy found me in the kitchen and kissed me on the forehead. She prepared my mac and cheese and burger, then called Mrs. Kaye, the debutante ball's organizer. "Stacy got bit by a black widow," Mommy said. "Honey, she was so swollen up, Clark and I thought she was gonna die. . . . Yeah. . . . Yeah. . . . The doctor told us that she needed rest. . . . Girl, please . . . Yeah. . . . Me, too. . . . Okay. . . . Bye. . . . Yeah. . . . You're a fool. . . . Yeah. . . . Bye."

Over those following days, I watched soap operas and cartoons. I found peanut butter and stale saltines in the far reaches of the kitchen cabinet. That was lunch. I rummaged through the attic and found Rikki's warped Michael Jackson *Off the Wall* cassette, two *Hustler* magazines (Daddy's, I presume), and an old box of Mike and Ike candy from Halloween, which I immediately devoured. I found the rest of Daddy's razor blades in the trash. Now a pack of disposable Gillettes sat in the medicine cabinet.

We didn't interact as a family then. Just moved around each other like barges in the bay. Since I took my dinners alone, I hadn't talked much to my father. He snapped anyway when he addressed Mommy. They'd argue in their bedroom. About what, I don't know. Then they would leave for the hospital. No one said "Good-bye, Stacy" or "See you later, Stacy." They just stalked from the house to the garage. In a way, I was glad to have the house to myself. I could live without holding my breath.

On Friday afternoon Cedars-Sinai discharged Rikki. I rushed to the door to welcome my sister back home. This time, Mommy didn't kiss me on the forehead when she entered. Rikki's beauty had been downgraded to pinched and grim. Her face was haggard and chalky. Her eyes held no expression. She wore bandages around her wrists.

Mommy guided Rikki to the chaise lounge in the den. "Now, you just rest, okay?" she told my sister.

Rikki sat there, dazed, her wrists immobilized by the clumsy, white bandages. I sat in the bay window across from her. I wanted to say something to her. What could I say, though? How are you feeling? What did you do in there? Did you like the food?

"Hungry?" Mommy asked.

"Yes," I said.

"I'm talking to your *sister*, Stacy. You're old enough to fix yourself something to eat." Mommy kissed Rikki on the forehead and left the room. Cabinets opened and closed. Silverware clanked and jangled. Minutes later, Mommy brought out tomato soup and orange juice on a tray, the meal she considered a cure for every illness, mental or physical, real or imagined.

My stomach growled. Since when was I old enough to fix tomato soup *on the stove?*

Daddy came downstairs after his shower. He peeked in on us, then retreated to the guest bathroom. We heard him cry and regain his composure. He retreated upstairs. Mommy didn't go up to comfort him. She remained in the kitchen.

Rikki and I waited to see what would happen next. I whispered to her, "Did it hurt?"

She nodded yes, then shook her head no. "I was in this black . . . space." Her voice was raspy and quivering. "I started running through this long, dark tunnel. It didn't feel like I was in *this* body. Lighter. I felt lighter. And I kept running and I saw this brilliant light. It was a warm light. Quiet and peaceful light." She smiled and closed her eyes. "It was God. I *know* it was God." She scowled at me. "But those wicked *bastards* made me come back. They didn't care that I was being born again." She turned away from me once Mommy popped in to check on her progress.

As a result of my sister's suicide attempt, Daddy made it a point to come home before midnight at least twice a week. Mommy included representatives from all the food groups on our dinner plates. We now said a blessing before we ate. We even played Yahtzee on Saturday nights. "Quality time,"

Mommy said as she flipped through a women's magazine for some how-to-make-a-happy-home advice.

Okay. I'll admit it. I *liked* the balanced meals and Daddy being around. I liked the board games and the point to love each other more. Unfortunately, Daddy and Mommy still argued, and then he wouldn't come home before midnight. He offered weak excuses for not being with us:

"I have to work late."

"The guys are getting together for drinks."

"Golf..."

"Meeting..."

"Why is it any of your concern? I'm a grown man and *I'll* come home when I wanna come home."

Mommy continued to put his dinner on a plate, then into the oven. She waited up for him. Or maybe she went to bed once Rikki and I fell asleep. She never complained to us about his absences. We didn't ask her where he was, either: all in the name of becoming Regular Family of Normal, USA.

After a few times, Yahtzee and meat loaf got a little stale. "Can we have a pizza night?" I asked. "We need to get out of the house."

"That's a great idea, Stacy!" Mommy said. Surprise, surprise. "What do you think, Arika?"

Rikki, close to catatonia, shrugged.

Done deal. Pizza night it was. I chose Thursdays. Daddy had to work late on Thursdays, Mommy said.

"We'll never go if we're waiting on him," I said, pissed off.

Mommy agreed, another surprise. We went to Shakey's Pizzeria without him. Over a medium cheese and ground-beef pizza and Mojo potatoes, Mommy and I chatted about school, television, and clothes. Rikki silently poked at her pizza slice. It was too difficult to ignore her, so I asked Mommy for quarters. She gave me two dollars. Shakey's had a brand-new video arcade, complete with Pac-Man, Ms. Pac-Man, and Baby Pac-Man. I grabbed Rikki and pulled her to the arcade, bustling with other teenagers. I placed two quarters on the game console and waited to play Frogger.

"This is so fucking fake," Rikki muttered. "Who does she think she's fooling? We're not like everybody else. We'll never be."

"At least she's trying," I said. "Daddy's not even here."

"He's an asshole, too," she sniped. "Like pizza and Yahtzee's gonna keep me from killing myself."

"What will? Nobody knows what to do for you 'cause you don't talk to anybody. How are we supposed to know? If you want my opinion—"

"I don't want your opinion," she snapped. "You're just a kid. But you can tell your mother that I'm not interested in being saved. Tell your father that, too. They can both kiss my ass." She turned and left the arcade.

Later I told Mommy about my conversation with Rikki. "You know she didn't mean that," she said. But she knew. She had paled as I spoke. Her trembling hands covered her mouth. She shook her head and stared at the carpet. "You should go to bed now," she told me with that limp smile. I heard her cry later that night and thought of getting out of bed and going down to the den to comfort her. I pitied her. I pitied us. But I didn't know her enough to share the pain. Probably because she had never made an attempt to get to know me.

My parents never called the therapist, Dr. Lowenstein's friend. I'm sure Mommy found that business card, burned it, and dumped the ashes over the Pacific Ocean.

For we are saved by hope: but hope that is seen is not hope: for what a man seeth, why doth he yet hope for? But if we hope for what we see not, then do we with patience wait for it. — Romans 8:24–25 For we are saved by hope: but hope that is seen is not hope: for what a man seeth, why doth he yet hope for? But if we hope for what we see not, then do we with patience wait for it. — Romans 8:24–25 For we are saved by hope: but hope that is seen is not hope: for what a man seeth, why doth he yet hope for? But if we hope for what we see not, then do we with patience wait for it. — Romans 8:24–25 For we are saved by hope: but hope that is seen is not hope: for what a man seeth, why doth he yet hope

7

A Matter of Life and Death

PIZZA NIGHT didn't work. Mommy tried it twice, but Rikki didn't bite. Mommy and I tired of talking to each other, and pretty soon there wasn't much to say. Rikki just sat there anyway, staring at her pizza. Soon, she began to mumble. I only caught a few words: *stupid, bullshit,* and *baboons.* She sighed countless times, then placed her head on the table. Of course, this behavior alarmed Mommy. On our last pizza night, my mother touched Rikki, who snatched away and snarled, "Leave me alone."

Exasperated, Mommy phoned Pastor Phillips when we got home. Rikki and I stood nearby to eavesdrop. "We're home, Pastor," Mommy whispered into the phone. "Yes. . . . Yes. . . . Okay. . . . See you soon." She returned the phone to the cradle. Rikki and I returned to our seats in the den.

"Why is the pastor coming over?" I asked.

Mommy didn't respond. "Now, you just rest, okay?" she told my sister, then went upstairs to find Daddy. Rikki followed her, then returned a minute later.

She whispered to me, "Their door's closed, but I heard her and Daddy talking. I think they want to exorcise me."

"Exorcise?" I said, breathless. "Like in the movies?"

She nodded yes.

We didn't talk much about exorcism in church. At least not formally. There was mention of the incident where Jesus sent a group of demons into a herd of swine, but that *word* was never used.

"But you sound normal to me," I said, drawing on my Hollywood canon of possessed heroines.

"Well, *they* think I'm evil. But they're the ones with the problem. And what they're about to do to me? It's not right. A *real* man of God would know that and leave me alone." She closed her eyes and lay back.

I wondered if we would have to cleanse the house with oils and incantations. Anxious, I sat back in the window and watched my sister for any sign of strange behavior.

Pastor Phillips pulled into our driveway around ten-fifteen that night. His Cadillac Seville clunked until the engine cut off. I heard his car door slam and his feet drag against the pavement like a mummy's. My mother rushed to open the door. I shivered. I was always afraid of Pastor Phillips. He was a pip-squeak really, only about an inch or two taller than me, but I guess it was how he wore those inches. Despite my nervousness, I was still too damn curious to run up to my room, lock the door, and hide.

It didn't take long for the pastor to enter our living room. He nodded in my direction, then turned his gaze to my sister. He didn't smile, but then again, he never smiled—at weddings, baby blessings, life . . . His eyes were even worse. Any flickers of emotion hid behind those clouded pupils. Mommy helped him out of his black fedora and moth-eaten overcoat. Comfortable now in his suit, he mumbled a thank-you to my mother and turned his attention back to Rikki. After much consideration, he jerked toward my sister. Rikki sat up, like a cobra on alert.

He stood over her and clucked his tongue against his dentures. "Arika, Arika, Arika," he said in that baritone that preached sermons of fire and brimstone every Saturday. "Collusion with the devil. You know what that means, gal?"

Rikki's eyes, red and teary, focused on the carpet. Pastor Phillips moved his hands toward her face. She flinched. The pastor grabbed her pointy chin and forced her to look at him. "What's gotten into you, gal? Know ye not that ye are the temple of God, and that the spirit of God dwelleth in you? If any man defiles the temple of God, him shall God destroy; for the temple ye are."

Rikki sighed and looked away.

"Gal, I'm talking to you."

The room fell silent under all its flounces, ruffles, and lace doilies. Mommy and Daddy stood motionless in the doorway, with Daddy clutching Mommy's shoulders. A draft lifted the curtain's hem the way the wind lifts a lady's dress: innocent, but voyeuristic.

"Maybe she's got laryngitis," I said, even though I had just finished a conversation with her.

Mommy shushed me. Daddy sighed. "Maybe you should go upstairs, Stacy."

"Leave her alone," Rikki snapped.

My parents jumped, startled that my sister had finally spoken.

"Have you accepted Jesus Christ as your personal savior?" Pastor Phillips blurted.

"Of course I have. You were *there*, Bertram." Rikki chuckled and looked at me as if to say, What's *with* this guy?

Pastor Phillips touched Rikki's shoulder. She flinched again. He reached for her and made contact. Rikki still resisted. They wrestled for about ten seconds until she tired. The pastor held her shoulders down with his hands. "Let us pray," he commanded.

My parents closed their eyes while I kept mine open. If there *was* evil in the room, I sure as heck wanted to see it coming. Mommy and Daddy held each other as Pastor Phillips prayed. Both peeked from time to time to see Rikki's shoulders shake as the old man shouted his requests to God.

"Oh, Heavenly Father," Pastor Phillips prayed, "we need you right now. Right now, sweet Jesus." He paused, then said, "I exorcise you, unclean spirit, in the name of Jesus Christ. Come out from this servant of God, Arika Diane Moore. Accursed and damned spirit, heed the word of the Lord. Depart from this servant of God, the same God who created man. The same God who created this world. The same God who sent His Son to die for His children." He told whatever or whomever to flee from my sister and return to the fiery depths of Hell. He implored the Holy Spirit to fill the space that the devil occupied and to prepare my sister for a place in the kingdom, in Christ's name. Seven minutes more of admonitions, and then Pastor Phillips said, "Amen."

We (but not Rikki) mumbled, "Amen." Mommy wiped

away her tears. Daddy disappeared into the kitchen. My heart pounded. I wanted to see Rikki's head spin, or to hear Latin curses in a demonic voice. *Something.* But none of this happened, of course.

Rikki didn't cry. She didn't even whimper. I don't think she believed any of it: that she still lived despite her efforts not to, that Satan or his imp lurked in her innards, that God was interested in her or this exorcism.

Pastor Phillips reached into his battered satchel. I hoped that he was about to pull out a vial of holy water. Instead, he handed Arika six pamphlets that she had already read for baptism class several years before. Still polite, my sister took the materials. Her gaze returned to the carpet.

"You must repent and be rebaptized," Pastor Phillips told her.

"Why?" I asked.

"Stacy, shut up," Mommy said.

"But she didn't do anything wrong," I said.

"She has, in fact, done something *very* wrong," Pastor Phillips said. "It is an abomination to the Lord to commit suicide."

"But she didn't *commit* suicide. She *tried* to commit suicide. It didn't take." I didn't want God angry at Rikki for something she didn't mean. I looked to Mommy for assurance and support.

"Anastasia," Mommy said, "go to your room. Now."

"This really has nothing to do with you, sweetie," Daddy said. He had returned to the doorway.

I didn't understand. How did Rikki's state of mind *not* involve me? Hadn't my parents told me over and over again that I was *supposed* to watch over her?

The adults in the room stared at me. Rikki then lifted her eyes to mine. Nothing there begged my presence.

So, feeling like crap, I left my perch on the window. My clothes stuck to my skin. A river of sweat ran between my shoulder blades. I wanted to grab Arika and get the hell out of there. I wanted to take her to a place that gave her peace, like the peace she had found in that tunnel. Instead, I shuffled toward the staircase. I turned a final time to look at my sister. She smiled. And in that smile, I saw that something still ran amuck in my sister's head. But at least God still owned her soul. I didn't. The devil didn't. I went upstairs and prayed.

To everyone's surprise, except mine, the exorcism failed. Put simply, Rikki was not possessed. She wasn't paranormal or violent toward others. She didn't spit or flip out whenever Jesus' name was uttered. She believed in Him more than any of us. The entire ceremony seemed like a waste of time.

But something else happened in our house after Pastor Phillips's exorcism. Rikki read the baptism pamphlets that he left. She found her chain-referenced King James–version Bible, the one with her name inscribed in gold on its cover, in her desk drawer. She flipped from page to page for texts that related to the pamphlets. She studied hard, but rarely spoke to me or to Mommy and Daddy.

As a result of her self-imposed religious retreat, Rikki's chores became my chores; and her homework became my homework. Daddy drove to Marlborough every day to drop off what I did, then picked up the next day's assignment. I heard him tell Mommy that he feared that Rikki would lose her scholarship because of her chronic absences, and my dangling participles and ridiculously wrong calculus equations. And if she got kicked out, where would she go? Back to Crenshaw with me? Mommy told him that she was alarmed, too, and said that she would get me a tutor as soon as possible.

I was also scared. Daddy would be disappointed in me if Rikki failed. And Rikki's teachers would eventually wonder why their star colored girl had dumbed down so much and so quickly. I was amazed that no one saw behind our charade. I mean, I was a grade behind Rikki. And there's a big difference between someone who studied regularly and someone who dipped into a textbook once a week.

I constantly lied to Rikki's friends at church and school about her whereabouts, her silence, and my brush with that black widow. I hated every day of my life and wondered if I would go to hell for bearing false witness as I honored my parents' instructions to just "make something up if anybody asks."

My friend Shawna came by one afternoon in April to show me her formal portrait from the debutante ball. "And Mommy's gonna send my picture to *Jet*," she said. "Ain't that *da bomb?*" She was my only friend who owned a pair of fuchsia Guess? jeans *and* the matching jacket. That ranked pretty high with me at the time, especially since I had that one purple Sassoon T-shirt that I wore to death. What Shawna thought of me meant more than what *I* thought of me. And now her picture would be in *Jet*?

Rikki, seated on the floor, didn't look up from her Bible pamphlets as Shawna droned on about pledging and Spelman and her brand-new tennis bracelet. I had hoped that Rikki would tire of my friend's monologue and retire to her own room down the hall.

An hour later, I walked Shawna to the front door. "Why is

Rikki reading that stuff?" she asked. "I mean, what's the Apocalypse and the four angels' message? What's wrong with her? Is she some religious freak now?"

I shrugged. Shrugs can be safe. At least, safer than lying.

Shawna zoomed away in her teal green Volkswagen Jetta, and I returned to my room and my sister. I picked up a Jackie Collins novel and read.

An hour in silence passed until Rikki broke it. "Does it scare you?"

"Does what scare me? The book?" Actually, all those writhing, naked bodies and the senseless Mob violence aroused me.

"No, you scrub."

I sat up. "Who are you calling a scrub?" Not only had she ignored me since her suicide attempt, now, as she spoke, she insulted me.

"The Book of Revelation," Rikki continued. "Doesn't all that stuff about hell, dragons, and whores scare you? I've read this fifty times and it still freaks me out."

"I don't know. I haven't read Revelation." I picked up my book and resumed reading about Lucky Santegelo's sex-capades with Lennie Golden.

Rikki sat on my bed and took the novel from my hands. Her muddy brown eyes hid behind her bangs. "Sometimes, I have nightmares about this stuff," she whispered.

I brushed her hair aside and said, "What kind of night-mares?"

She placed one of her wrinkled pamphlets in my hand: "Your Soul and Hell." "Nightmares about this. And some-times, I wake up and I can't move. I try to scream, but nothing comes out. In one dream, I was frozen in a block of ice." She clutched her shirt. "You and Mommy and Daddy were standing around me. I called your name, but you didn't hear me."

I squeezed her hand. "I'm sorry." I meant it.

"What's the point of all this?" The pamphlet slipped from her fingers to the floor. "We're all gonna die anyway, no matter what we do. It's in the plan."

My heart jumped. I wanted to run to Mommy. To tell her that Rikki had death on the brain again. But I sat there as my sister stared at my Prince and Tom Cruise posters.

"But not everybody's gonna die," I reasoned. "Some people will go to heaven without dying."

Rikki frowned at me. "How do *you* know? You haven't read Revelation, remember?" She moved away from me. "Heaven's way in the future, Stacy. What about today, with the old people, and the kids with cancer, and the fucking trees? Did you know we're killing the earth's atmosphere with hairspray? Whenever a cow poops, we're just one step closer to the end of all things!"

Amazed, I said, "No."

"Mommy and Daddy, they're gonna die, too. And you're gonna die and I'm gonna die. So what's the point? It's in the plan."

A shiver danced up my spine. My fingers tingled. "Maybe you should stop reading those pamphlets. They're hella depressing."

She stared at me. After a long pause, she smiled, then nodded her head. Her eyes turned chestnut brown again. Outside, bluebirds chirped in the citrus trees. "You're right. You're absolutely right. Screw the plan, right? Forget that I'm going to die, right?"

"Maybe you should find some happy stuff in the Bible. Some stuff that will cheer you up."

Her smile grew wider. "You're right again, Einstein." She ran to her room. She returned seconds later with a fabric-covered journal that Mommy had given her for Christmas. She found a pink highlighter in my desk and turned to "In the beginning God created the heaven and the earth." She dragged the marker across that verse. "That definitely makes me happy," she said. She read to the end of the first chapter, highlighting occasionally, and continued on. Once she reached Job, she threw out the pastor's pamphlets.

She turned page after page, passing "Lord, how are they increased that trouble me! Many are they that rise up against me" in Psalms, past "I will greatly rejoice in the Lord, my soul shall be joyful in my God" in Isaiah. And she read on and highlighted every text that comforted her. And as she found these passages, she wrote them over and over, page after page, in her journal.

I also kept a journal. I wrote things like "Damien looked at me! Maybe he'll ask me to the dance." Or "Mommy gets on my nerves. I can't wait to go to college." Nothing holy or profound found its way into *those* pages.

I sat with my sister and her Bible like this four times that month. Believe me, I didn't want to stay, but she begged. And those tears in her eyes didn't help, either. She'd pore over pages that she hadn't highlighted. "In case I overlooked some inspiring word from God," she explained.

Somehow, Pastor Phillips discovered that Rikki had chucked his literature. I think Mommy found the tracts in Rikki's wastebasket on cleaning day. Needless to say, he wasn't happy. Mommy assured him, though, that Rikki voraciously read the Bible. That made the pastor angrier: Rikki had questioned his authority and now she had found God without him.

"She needs to repent," the pastor told Mommy. He held out more pamphlets to replace the old ones. "To take the bad with the good." You see, Christians like him believed that spiritual growth required healthy doses of angst, shame, and fear.

But Rikki ignored the pastor's admonitions and his literature. Charged with energy, she immersed herself in church life. She volunteered for Sabbath school programs, served as a junior deaconess, and fed the hungry lines that wrapped around our church on Tuesday evenings. Her grades at school stabilized and improved until her name topped the honor roll that semester, as it had before her "accident." Rikki then landed a lead role in *To Kill a Mockingbird.* Not only did she get into U.C. Berkeley, she got in on full scholarship.

The Saturday before Arika's graduation from high school, Pastor Phillips, after his sermon, called for members in the congregation to rededicate themselves to God. The organist started in with "Just As I Am," and those who knew the words sang. Others just closed their eyes and gently rocked their bodies back and forth. Rikki, in tears, stood from her seat and plodded to the altar with the other sinners, fornicators, and their friends, to ask for mercy. Mommy saw her go, then squeezed her eyes shut. I'm sure she prayed that everyone wouldn't see her daughter at the front of the sanctuary.

At the end of every service that month, Rikki returned to the altar for rededication. But then Rikki didn't attend church the next week, or the next. Every Saturday, she gave Mommy some excuse for staying home: cramps, headaches, carpal tunnel syndrome. I didn't know what Rikki did at home alone. I didn't want to know. Clearly my mother didn't mind that Rikki stayed away from church. Rikki cried in public and dedicated her life to God again and again and again and in front of so many people.

Daddy also didn't care that Rikki ditched. He had stopped going to church when I turned fourteen. "They're all hypocrites," he said to me as he threw his golf bag over his shoulder. "And Rikki's smarter than that. I thought you were, too."

During the third church service we attended without Rikki, I noticed that Mommy's smile had returned. In her sharp soprano, she sang hymns with more life. She kissed more cheeks, shook more hands, and loitered several minutes after the service in the parking lot. Sometimes after then, she went to a friend's house for a potluck. The sun shone because trouble stayed at home suffering from carpal tunnel syndrome or improving his handicap on the links in Pasadena. For her, our little family had found peace again.

When we came home from service one Saturday, I finally asked Rikki why she no longer attended church.

"I wanna tell you something," she said. "But you can't say anything to Mommy, okay?"

"Okay." I leaned forward.

"I'm having weird dreams again," she whispered. "There are these bodies of people and animals in my bedroom. They're decaying and maggots are crawling all over the place. It stinks." She paused, then said, "I want to throw up, but I start laughing."

Okay.

"When I look down at my hands, they're all bloody. I have clumps of meat underneath my fingernails. Stacy, I think I killed those people and those poor, poor animals."

I chuckled and kicked off my pumps. "Arika, you didn't kill them for real."

"*Obviously,*" she snorted. "But I did in my *subconscience.* And what's that verse about killing in your heart?"

Hell, I didn't know. "You go to the altar because you're a murderer in your subconscience?"

"In my *heart,*" she corrected. "Stacy, I can't keep playing with God. Sinning, then repenting; sinning, then repenting. I have to face it: I'm not worthy of God's grace. And I'll get mine. Watch. I'll get mine."

In the end, it was Daddy who got his. He died from a massive heart attack two weeks before Rikki left for college. That afternoon, I had been sitting with him in his bedroom. We were admiring his new set of golf clubs. He was particularly proud of his titanium driver, even promised to let me use it whenever I wanted. A golf tournament blared on the television, but we weren't watching it.

I noticed, after a while, that sweat glistened on his forehead and temples, even though the room was air-conditioned. He kept squeezing his left arm as he talked. Then he froze and looked at me, dismayed. His face blanched and he whispered, "I think I'm having a heart attack." He eased back on the bed. "Go get your mother."

Confused and near tears, I darted from the room down to the den, where Mommy clipped coupons from the newspaper. I shouted, "Something's wrong! Daddy's sick!" She immediately ran upstairs. I called the paramedics.

Rikki came out of her room as I ran back to my parents' bedroom. "What's going on?" she whispered.

"Daddy's having a heart attack," I shouted. I pulled her arm. "Come on!"

She pulled back and stepped away. I left her there and returned to my father's side. Mommy sat on the bed next to him. She held a wet towel on his forehead. I took his hand and prayed that he suffered from a hernia, gas, *anything*. Not a heart attack.

As we waited for the paramedics to arrive, his breathing became more strained with each passing moment. "Watch over your sister," he told me. He took a deep breath and died.

"Mommy," I said, and stepped away from the bed.

Mommy gently shook Daddy and said his name. Rikki slipped into the room and stood over us. She clutched his hand, then knelt on the ground.

"Clark?" Mommy said again. She bent over to listen to his chest. Then she gasped and screamed, "Oh, God!" She screamed again, then ran out of the room to find Mrs. Drake from next door. Rikki followed her.

I remained at my father's side. The paramedics arrived thirty-five minutes later. By then, Daddy's skin had turned waxy, his lips and nails paler. I touched his skin, now purpled and bruised.

I never looked at the paramedics who attended Daddy. One of them smelled of Drakkar Noir cologne. I can't smell that cologne today without remembering the afternoon my father died.

Mommy cried somewhere in the house. Rikki wandered from room to room, but avoided Mommy and Daddy's room. Mrs. Drake stood with her arms around me, but didn't speak.

One of the paramedics pulled his stethoscope from his bag. He lifted Daddy's arm, placed the silver disk on his wrist, and listened for a pulse. After a moment he said to me,

"Sorry, sweetheart, but your dad's gone. Probably a heart attack."

Daddy was forty-seven.

I sank to the ground. Mrs. Drake knelt next to me. I sobbed in her arms. Daddy had died before the paramedic told me, but hearing someone say it made it official. The morticians came for Daddy within the hour. Mommy signed some papers and immediately left her bedroom. The morticians slipped a yellow tag around Daddy's toe, then wrapped him in a white sheet.

We followed the men as they navigated the gurney down the stairs out of our house. We stood hugging in the front yard as they loaded my father into the back of the minivan. As the automobile hauled Daddy away from us, Mommy collapsed to the ground. Rikki and I continued to cry. Even though I knew better and had seen them wrap that sheet around him, I wanted that van to come back. I wanted someone to admit that they had made an awful mistake and that Daddy was alive—he had just stopped breathing for a spell. Of course, that didn't happen.

Five days later, Mommy, Rikki, and I sat in the front pew of our church. Daddy's bronze casket sat ten feet away. I sat between my mother and my sister, who cried throughout the entire service. I cried on and off. When the time came, people got up to talk about how great Clark Moore was, how he had affected their lives. Then we sang or listened to songs— sad, old hymns that, I guess, are required at funerals: "Pass Me Not, O Gentle Savior" and "His Eye Is on the Sparrow." I didn't understand how these songs helped soothe the hurt—folks just seemed to cry harder.

Pastor Phillips gave the eulogy. Daddy would've had three

fits if he knew. It wasn't an exceptional speech, nor was it inspirational. The pastor included the usual topics: the Second Coming, Lazarus, that Great Gettin' Up Mornin'.

The time came when the attendants opened the casket for the final viewing. The body in the casket, the one wearing the Brooks Brothers suit, didn't resemble the man I called Daddy. No. That wasn't him lying there. There was no half-smirk on his lips or crinkles around his eyes. Sorry. This wasn't my father. I expected Rikki to throw herself on the coffin. She did not. Instead, some other woman did. She screamed and wailed Daddy's name. She wore a dark suit and a black hat with a veil. Both Rikki and I looked at Mommy, as if to say, Who's *that?* Mommy glared at the woman through her tears as the deacons pulled the lady away. Then Mommy's shoulders shook violently and she fell back into her own pit of anguish.

For the rest of the day, folks kept telling us that Daddy was in a better place, that he was in heaven looking down on us. Daddy would've had another fit if he knew that. Even though he had stopped going to church, he was still an Adventist who believed that when you die, you're dead. No going to heaven until that Great Gettin' Up Mornin', and that's only if you're good. But of course I didn't argue the point. These well-wishers just wanted us to take comfort in *something.* But no matter where my father was—in heaven or on earth in that casket—he wasn't with me and there was no comfort in that.

We made our way to the cemetery where my father would lie. American flags and pinwheels poked from surrounding plots. A couple placed a bouquet of sunflowers on a child's grave. Incense, sweet and smoky, wafted in the breeze. Late-afternoon fog had set a chill in the air. I wore my favorite dress—the blue one with bright brass buttons down the middle. My feet ached from my new patent leather pumps. Mommy and Rikki clutched my arms until there wasn't any feeling left. People around me wailed and cried into tissues. The woman who had thrown herself on the casket stopped in front of my mother and leaned in for a hug. Mommy glared at her and mumbled, "You bitch." The other woman, alarmed, moved away from my mother as quickly as she could.

Hours after the funeral, guests left our house with aluminum-foil-wrapped plates of fried chicken, red beans and rice, and cabbage. I didn't know most of them, even though Daddy had spent thirty-five years of his life with them at his office. Jocelyn McNamara, Daddy's secretary, was the last to leave our house that day. On her way out, she and Mommy whispered back and forth for a bit. Mommy frowned a lot and cried into her handkerchief. Jocelyn just patted her back.

Eventually, she and Jocelyn walked to Jocelyn's car. I followed them to the door. Jocelyn reached into the front seat. She pulled out an expandable folder and handed it to my mother. Mommy clutched the file to her chest and nodded. Jocelyn kissed her on the cheek and offered a last hug. Mommy returned to the house and placed the folder in her bedroom.

That night, Rikki and I were watching television when we heard our mother crying in her bedroom. Then Mommy ran past our room down the stairs. Her Corolla's engine roared to life and raced down the street.

While she was gone, Rikki and I tiptoed, hand in hand, into her bedroom. The folder was on the bed, its contents spread across the comforter. Rikki and I sat and began to rifle through the mess. There was Daddy's day planner. Doctors' appointments had been penciled in, then crossed out, twice a month over three months. There were papers on cardiovascular diseases and treatment options. There were also letters from a woman named Tracy. Letters that encouraged him to commit to her once and for all, to get his health together, and to leave his wife. There were a few pictures—the woman in the pictures was the hysterical woman at the funeral.

Rikki ran from the room in tears. I scattered the materials that we had touched across the bed, then trudged downstairs to the refrigerator. Someone had cleaned the kitchen for us, so the countertops and fixtures sparkled and smelled of bleach. I stood there, numb from grief and exhaustion, with the dishes of turkey breast, red beans, and sweet potato pie around me. I didn't know what to do. If I cried, what would I cry about first? Death? Life? Lies? What's first? What's worse?

Daddy cheated on Mommy. And Rikki. And me. He gave his heart to some woman outside of our little circle. He was sick, but didn't tell us. I always thought he was a noble, honest man. A liar? Not my dad. But he was. And if *he* was, then any man could be.

I didn't cry. Instead, I filled a plate with funeral food and buried my pain beneath gluttony.

Mommy returned to the house. She didn't see me in the kitchen. She ran upstairs to her bedroom. Soon, her weeping mixed with Rikki's. Rikki and Mommy had always cried the same way: a long wail punctuated with two controlled sobs. Wail. Sob, sob. Wail. Sob, sob. I couldn't tell one from the other.

I climbed the stairs close to midnight, deep in my own mix of grief, anger, and delusion. I entered Rikki's room. She lay there, somewhere in the dark, whimpering. I switched on the lamp and saw that she was in the bed. I sat next to her. My hand brushed back her damp hair. Before I knew it, my eyes filled with tears. I slid to the floor and cried. Rikki sat up, shocked at my display of emotion. She wiped my face with a tissue. "Let's promise that we'll never do that," she said.

"Do what?" I asked between hiccups.

"What Daddy did."

"Not say anything about his heart? Or about—"

"Stacy," she said, her eyes flickering with tiny specks of red.

"Rikki," I said, recognizing the fire in her tone.

"If my husband ever cheated on me, I'd die of a broken heart," she whispered. She pulled the comforter to her chin. "But not before I killed him."

"Well, Mommy can't do that because Daddy's already dead."

"Serves him right. When you make a promise to be faithful, you're supposed to keep it."

"I feel so sorry for Mommy." It was the first time I ever said those words and meant them. She didn't deserve that kind of humiliation. How many people at our house that afternoon knew about Tracy?

"I'll never cheat on my husband," Rikki said. "Promise me that you won't either."

"Promise." I didn't even have a boyfriend at the time. *Husband* was just a word.

She grabbed my wrist. *"Promise."*

"Yeah, I promise." I shook free from her grasp. What did she want? Blood?

A month later, I drove to my father's grave. Someone had placed a basket of lilies on the grass. I sat next to his plot, just as people did in the movies (my only point of reference for death then). The sprinklers had just cut off. The wet grass seemed sloshed with silver. The Forum rose past the marble mausoleums in front of me. A lawn mower roared somewhere behind me. Although I feared that the gardener would mow right over me, I remained seated. I wondered if I should do something else. A speech seemed unnecessary and stupid. No graveside confessions were in order. And tears—couldn't dredge up any from my soul.

His bronze nameplate had arrived. It now marked where he lay.

Clark Richard Moore

May 3, 1941–August 16, 1988

Beloved Husband and Father

8

ACTING OUT

ALTHOUGH SHE was about to leave Los Angeles, Rikki returned to our pew the Saturday following the funeral. Mommy was shocked, but in too much pain to question or protest. My sister and I held hands during the service. She didn't cry or walk to the altar. She kissed and hugged people after service. She thanked them for their prayers and dishes of food. Too bad Mommy stayed home that day.

"Daddy died because I rejected God and stopped going to church," Rikki told me as we drove home. "I don't want Him to take away you or Mommy for something *I* do."

"Rikki," I said, "I don't think God—"

"And I'm gonna tell you something, but you *cannot* tell Mommy. Deal?"

"Deal."

She took one of my hands from the steering wheel and

held it to her chest. "I'm gonna see a doctor when I get to Berkeley," she whispered. "I'm gonna get better. Even if that means I have to take pills."

Rikki eventually left for school. Mommy helped her pack and told her to take the Volvo. Daddy, of course, wouldn't need it. Mommy and I drove with her up to Berkeley and planned to fly back. We met her roommate, Shoshanna, a birdlike white girl, whose face was pitted from bouts of severe acne. She had already decorated her side of the dorm room with a crucifix and candles. She reeked of cigarettes and patchouli oil. She didn't smile the entire time Mommy and I stood there.

Rikki didn't cry when she dropped us off at the airport. She had a new life to begin. Her smile brightened as Mommy and I disappeared into the crowded terminal.

Rikki and I talked every week. She told me that she missed me dearly. I told her that I had applied to Cal. She said that she hoped that I got accepted because she couldn't wait to hang out with me again. Once, before we hung up, Rikki admitted that even though her medicine made her wobbly and a bit nauseated at times, she hadn't felt more balanced in her entire life.

Christmas came and Mommy wanted us to drive to Fresno, California, to visit a second cousin whom Rikki and I didn't know. I was not pleased. Rikki and I had already planned to shop with some of her scholarship money. "I don't want to spend my Christmas break in cow country with a bunch of chain-smoking, alcoholic Baptists! And didn't you say this cousin of yours beats his wife?"

"That's none of your business," Mommy said. "We're spending the holidays with family, so deal with it."

My bickering with Mommy didn't upset Rikki the way it had in the past. The air of distraction and desperation about her had evaporated. When she smiled, her eyes sparkled. That December, she was alive and seemed to be happy because of it.

"You look good," I told her.

"Thanks." She took out a tiny gold box from her purse and shook it. Something rattled inside. "I call them the Regulators." She stuffed the box deep into her purse. "And my therapist is incredible. She has manic depression, too, and she's so accomplished." Rikki turned to me. "You haven't said anything to Mommy, have you?"

I smiled. "Not a word."

"So you don't think she suspects anything?" Rikki asked, concerned. "You don't think I'm acting too normal, do you?"

"Mommy's not that observant." I had pierced my ears on the sly weeks back and covered them with tiny, clear bandages. And what would our mother say? She couldn't speak without acknowledging Rikki's condition before the pills. This meant she couldn't admit that Rikki was better *because* of them. So, if she *did* notice, she kept quiet. It was safer for her and safer for us.

9

FACE-TO-FACE WITH GOD'S GREAT CREATION

TO MY delight (and surprise), I got into Cal. Mommy was happier than me—Rikki wouldn't be alone way up there in Berkeley. I told her that Rikki had a life of her own and just because we would be sharing a dorm room didn't mean that we'd hang out all the time. Kendall didn't get into Berkeley, so she planned to attend Cal State Northridge in the fall. We promised to write and call.

College: what a beautiful idea. You could party as much as you wanted as long as you passed all of your courses. I hadn't been away from my mother's house for a month when I pierced a second set of holes in my ears and dyed my hair auburn. Academics was important back then; but as a freshman who no longer lived at home and didn't have a curfew, sex was more important. I drew to fornication like Texans to a barbecue. My first college boyfriend was Michael York, a sophomore who had a tattoo. I lost my virginity to him after we had dated for a few weeks. That was pretty uneventful, but then nothing compares to the love scenes in a Jackie Collins novel. Still, I went from boy to boy, looking to play out those vignettes.

I learned that music swapping was the best way to meet guys, so I collected and maintained the most extensive hip-hop collection of any female there. Want to dub the new Boogie Down Productions tape? See me, and if I liked you, well, you got a bonus. Scary stuff when I think about it now.

As I got used to living with Rikki again, I noticed that days would sometimes pass when she didn't take her medication as instructed, or she'd miss a therapy session. I forced myself to mention my concerns.

"Oh, I'm fine," she said. "Can't you tell that I've gotten better?"

I nodded, but still . . . There were signs that I didn't know whether to ignore or to freak out about. She went to church every Saturday and to prayer meetings on Wednesdays. You could say that I was overreacting, but church on *every* Saturday? In college? C'mon.

She invited me to join her. Ha! I wasn't having no part of religion at that time of my life. Not with all the sex and free alcohol everywhere.

That fall semester, I flunked linguistics, French, and marine biology; but I sang a mean alto in the gospel choir. At the start of winter quarter, I decided to major in comparative literature. I liked to read, so why not? Not surprising, my course of study paled in comparison to Rikki's. She majored in education and sociology and minored in journalism.

"There are kids in the tenth grade that read on a third-grade level," she said. In some schools, students had to share textbooks. Some classrooms had rats and falling ceiling tiles. "What about the children? Who will teach the children?" she asked.

She wanted to make a difference in the classroom, and not as an administrator like Daddy. "I'm a doer, not a dreamer," she said, near tears.

For Rikki, her second major in sociology and the minor in journalism were all related. You couldn't teach effectively in the inner city if you didn't understand the larger social problems, challenges, and history of that community. And how would people know about the problems if you didn't write about them? "I'll write the truth," she vowed. "Not a bunch of manufactured crap that lulls you to inaction and pats you on the back even though you haven't done squat."

"And only you can do that?" I asked.

"Don't make fun. You're a product of those schools. Look at how limited *your* education is. You should be thanking me."

I don't know how she did it. Triple loads of course work and she still passed, though sometimes barely. She read without sleep and attended every lecture. She wrote papers in half the time it took the typical student, then rushed off to complete mandatory hours for her internship. In between the class work, she joined every black club on campus, pledged AKA, and wrote a weekly column for the campus newspaper.

"This is what college is for," she said. "Where else in the world will someone listen to your opinion, then have you write ten more pages about it?"

"It just seems that you're in way over your head," I said.

"I want to take a class in anything that's ever interested

me. I only have three years left. And I have to bust my butt if I want to graduate summa cum laude."

Honors in college didn't matter to me. Would summa cum laude help me push one pile of paper from one end of the desk to the other? No. I think not.

I had my first pregnancy scare that winter. One night, with one winner I can't even remember, the condom broke. I know, it sounds pretty lame: the condom broke. But it did. Weeks later, I missed my period. I panicked. Nearly lost my mind. No matter how hard I squeezed, nothing happened. I tried to will menstrual cramps, but I only got headaches. My breasts were tender and my complexion was flawless.

"That's what you get for not using condoms," Rikki said. "You don't have an excuse."

"We did use a condom. It broke. This can't be happening." I needed a second chance. I'd do anything for a second chance. Not a day passed by without a plea bargain to God.

Rikki, tired of hearing me whine, went to the drugstore and purchased a pregnancy test. "Here." She threw the blue box at me. "Shut up and pee."

I tiptoed to the bathroom with the box hidden under my sweatshirt. Three minutes dragged on into eternity. My hand trembled as I waited for the sign. "Please, God. Please." At 3:18 P.M., a minus sign appeared in the test window. It was the prettiest pink symbol ever created by man.

I ran to our room and waved the stick in the air. Rikki hugged me. We went for pizza to celebrate. I have *never* been so scared to pee since then. Death didn't terrify me as much as the thought of being pregnant. Relieved, I cried. I even attended service that Saturday. I promised God that I would never have premarital sex again. I was celibate for three months. But the star point guard on the basketball team tempted me. We had just won a game against Michigan. We all went out to celebrate. Things happened. My, my, my . . . he was a beautiful man.

My sister got to play my confessor and heroine that time. And after this lapse in the way things should be, we fell back into how things were.

It started with an earthquake one Tuesday, a little after four o'clock in the afternoon. I was sitting on the windowsill with my reader while Rikki lay in bed watching the news. We both shrieked as our room jolted beneath us and threw us both to the ground. The shaking lasted forever and registered 6.9 on the Richter scale. The RA evacuated the dorm. We didn't return to our rooms until the school engineers issued a clearance six hours later.

Even though we had grown up with earthquakes back at home, Rikki and I still cried with each aftershock. Neither of us slept because we could hear the earth rumble, then feel it move seconds later. To deal with stress and fear, some students drank or talked to shrinks. Rikki didn't talk to anyone, not to me, not even to her therapist. She went to the store every day and purchased canned food, water, and a first-aid kit. She stored all of this under her bed.

I didn't mind her constant anxiety about earthquake preparedness until the day she came home with a pallet of sweet corn, three more gallons of water, and seven extra first-aid kits. "I think we're covered, Arika. Where are you going to put all of that?"

She didn't answer me as she walked to my closet, pushed aside my clothes, and piled the supplies on the floor.

"That's *my* space," I shrieked. She had already placed a box of toilet paper there.

Rikki came home the next day with more food, candles, flares, and flashlights.

I warned her. "If you don't get rid of some of this crap, I'm moving out." It was an empty threat. On an overcrowded campus, there *were* no places to go.

"Don't you want to be prepared?" she finally asked. "I'm just trying to protect us, Anastasia. You haven't done jack." And she kept buying supplies until neither of us could move around the room. Then one afternoon, I came home after class. Everything was gone. I could sit on the floor. I could see my poster of Bo Jackson. Friends could come over and didn't have to pretend that whatever was going on in our room was normal.

In April, I received a flyer that announced the annual retreat at the church campgrounds in the mountains. My sister saw the mailer and sent in her registration. Mommy sat on the camp committee and saw Rikki's completed form and check. She called me. "You need to go, too," she said.

I didn't want to go. Salvation was something you found once you stopped caring about strawberry wine coolers, tickets to see Al B. Sure!, and Victoria's Secret catalogs. You know, once you passed thirty. "Why can't she go by herself?" I asked. "She's nineteen years old."

"She may give away all of our money or do something just as extreme," Mommy said. Was this the same religion that I practiced? We weren't the Hare Krishna or the Moonies. No one ever gave away her possessions or shaved her head in the name of God in *our* faith. "And she shouldn't drive up to the mountains by herself," Mommy added.

"But I have class on Friday nights. And isn't it too late to register anyway?"

"Anastasia, you actually think it's safe for her to go alone? Are you nuts? Have you been doing drugs up there, too? Don't worry about paying. I'll take care of it. You're going and that's that."

I packed a bag and promised myself extra helpings of debauchery when I returned to Cal on Sunday night. Rikki and I left early Friday morning. We reached San Bernadino ten hours later. As Rikki drove her Volvo up those winding roads, dense patches of platinum fog hugged the space around us. Some snow still covered rocks and grass. It was five hundred degrees below zero, but my sister insisted on rolling down all the car's windows.

"Can't I roll up *my* window?" I asked. It was so cold, puffs of white left my mouth, froze, and hung in the air like icicles.

"Stop whining. All of this crisp mountain air cleanses the soul," she said. "And you need as much cleansing as you can get."

I added that comment to the other bones of contention that I had collected over the years. There were so many, I almost had a skeleton. We rode in one bone: Daddy's car. I had also asked for a car, *any* car, after I graduated from high school. Mommy told me no.

"Both of you don't need a car," she said.

I got a watch for graduation instead. The doggone thing broke three months later.

Rikki turned up the volume on the stereo. Her favorite gospel group, the Winans, shouted from the speakers. "This is going to be an incredible weekend," Rikki said.

"Yeah." I pulled my jacket closer to my body and prayed

that we reached the campsite before I froze to death. "The higher we go, the closer we get to God."

She slammed on the brakes. The tires skidded. The back of the car fishtailed. I yelled. "Blaspheme again and I'll put you out of my car," she growled. Her eyes, hard and dark as coal, challenged me to rebuke her.

"Okay. Sorry."

She drove on. She hummed along to the music.

"Will there be guys up there?" I asked. "Or is this one of those ladies-only retreats?"

"Is that all you think about?"

I paused, then said, "Yes. Yes, it is."

"Well, if you're looking to have sex, these men aren't the type. They're Christians."

I'm sure I've slept with a few Baptists, Methodists, and Adventists who weren't my husband, but whatever.

We saw Matt as Rikki pulled into the campground's parking lot. If appearance equaled piety, Matt was the pope. He stood next to his Mercedes-Benz with a group of—hell, I didn't know if they were men, women, or Romulans. Matt made me sweat. He warmed my chest. God's goodness shone as Matthew hovered over that group of humans like a seraphim. He laughed at a comment someone in that group made, and I wanted to laugh, too. In an instant, I knew that no one else in the world was like him, certainly not men at Cal. Not even the professors. Not even the mighty chancellor of the university himself.

I temporarily climbed out of my cloud of infatuation for cabin registration. The lobby bustled with the chatter of good Christian girls who, according to my sister, held no interest in sex.

"Well, *I* heard that he doesn't have a girlfriend," one female with a bad weave said.

Her friends, a motley crew of females, gave each other high fives. Ha! As though one of *them* actually had a chance.

"He just finished medical school," Attila the Hun whispered.

"And Jeannine said that he has a big . . . you know," Bad Hair Weave said. Then they burst into fits of laughter.

I wondered, Who was this Jeannine and how did *she* know about his you know?

Rikki shook her head and left to find our home for the weekend. Matthew intrigued me. He was twenty-five years old and drove a luxury sedan. He intrigued Rikki, too, but she had come to the mountaintop to find more of God. This meant that I could snag Matt since it was obvious that I was the second-prettiest girl there.

My evil plan sputtered into action as I stood next to him during the evening mixer. I held out my hand. We shook. "Hi, I'm Anastasia." I used my full name now. It was more sophisticated and adult. "Have we ever met?" I asked. I batted my big brown eyes. Guys had a thing for my eyes.

"Matt," he said. "No. I'm sure I'd remember you." And he smiled.

Later, I sat next to him for vespers. He couldn't remember my name. "So, do you go to Bethany now?" I asked. "I've been a member all my life and—"

"We should probably listen to the speaker," he whispered. He turned away from me.

So I broke out the classic move: I brushed my leg against his leg during the program. And he didn't budge! I knew then that *he* knew that I wanted to peg him, plain and simple.

At the end of the program, he stood. "Good night, Annie."

Annie?

"Oh," I said, miffed but persistent. "I wanted to show you the bear." The campground staff kept a brown bear in a caged den. The trail leading to the bear was wooded and somewhat secluded.

Matt yawned and stretched. "I'm pretty tired. It's been a long day, so I think I'll head back to my cabin."

"Come on, Matt. You're supposed to be here to fellowship. We can't fellowship in a cabin." Then I went in for the kill. "Actually, we can but we just met."

He just stared at me for what seemed to be forever. Then he laughed. The laugh that had made me want to join in earlier now made me feel young, stupid, and slutty.

"Good night, Annie." Then he waggled my head as if I were some kid who had just offered him a bottle of Coke after a game. Matt didn't see me as a siren or temptress. He saw an infatuated eighteen-year-old named Annie with stale pickup lines.

"He's gay," I told Rikki that night before we fell asleep.

"He's gay because he turned you down?" She flipped over in bed and looked at me as if I'd grown wings and a beard. "Don't be ridiculous."

"He has to be. No straight guy is *that* polite. Plus, he didn't even flirt with me. And once you throw in the bear thing, you gotta ask yourself, How many straight guys do you know would turn *me* down?"

"And I'm the crazy one."

"Explain it, then."

She smiled and shrugged. "He wasn't attracted to you."

"Bullshit."

Rikki frowned and threw her pillow at me. "Shh! This is holy ground."

I tossed back her pillow and stared at the beamed ceiling. "There's only one explanation. He doesn't like women."

Boy, was *I* wrong.

Rikki had left for breakfast when I rolled out of bed the next morning. I made it to the cafeteria in time to see her and Matt chatting over bowls of Cream of Wheat. They looked as if they had known each other in a former life.

I would have been embarrassed if he knew we were sisters, so I skipped breakfast and lunch that day. I also stayed away from every service that afternoon. I wandered around the campgrounds, alone. Everywhere I looked, I saw perfect beauty: the dark green-blue of trees, the amber patches of random, bare ground, the colorless pulse of sun against the bright blue sky. Tiny cabins dotted the spaces between the imposing cedar trees. Bluish pearl mist hung over the mountains across from the mountain where I stood. I wondered if someone was standing over there, taking in the same view but from the opposite side.

It was so quiet here that I heard the roar of the river that slivered its way from the mountaintop to the mysterious place below. And if I couldn't hear the rushing river, I heard weekend campers singing "Side by Side We Stand" or "Precious Memories."

Rikki didn't notice my absence because she and Matt never left the other's side. I didn't get it. Rikki and I looked so much alike that guys in malls thought we were twins. Damn it, I was perfect now—flawless, milk-chocolate skin, 36B-cup breasts, a tiny waist, and of course, the eyes. I wasn't stupid anymore, either. I could talk at length on Kafka, Dickens, and W. E. B. DuBois. I spoke a semester's worth of French. It was only right that I win this contest.

What frustrated me most was that Rikki didn't even try to snag Matt. She never wore lots of makeup. She never giggled like some silly girl. That weekend, she even hid her cleavage beneath sweatshirts. And she had strikes against her. She cursed and cried when she hit her low. She popped pills, but not as much nowadays. She had even slit her wrists. And despite this, *Matt chose her.* How unfair was that? They exchanged numbers that Sunday before we left. He even told me good-bye and acted as if nothing had happened between us. I guess nothing had. He watched us drive toward the main road. He called her twelve hours later.

10

COMING BACK
TO THE MIDDLE

FOR MONTHS, I envied my sister. She had this incredible man who made me see stars, planets, and galaxies beyond. When it came to Matt, I was a drooling, stumbling fool in love. But I eventually outgrew my jealousy once Rikki and Matt began to exclusively date during her third year in school. I even rejoiced a bit at her good fortune. God and I weren't always in touch back then, but I knew He meant for Matt to find my sister. God knew that he would love her almost as much as I did.

Meanwhile, as I dated one tattooed frat boy after another, Rikki waited for Matt to call every night at ten o'clock from UCLA Medical Center, where he worked as a pediatric resident. Sometimes, she drove to Los Angeles on minor holidays or on odd breaks in his schedule. Her world depended on Matt's calls and their visits. Hysteria threatened our lives when neither of these happened.

After one of their weekends together, I found two condoms (not mine) on the floor near our closets. I asked Rikki about them. She told me to mind my own business, then snatched the rubbers from my fingers. After all that time "being good," Rikki had fallen off the wagon.

At times she'd cry and run to her car and threaten to drive away for good. She told me that Matt was a dog and that he was out creeping with some other girl. She said that she'd never forgive him; but Matt would call. He would apologize for his neglect, which was, of course, unintentional or nonexistent. He assured her that no other women were in his life, and definitely not in his bed.

To be honest, I never thought that Rikki and Matt's relationship was abnormal or unhealthy. Their relationship, in my mind, was just intense. But then, I didn't know anything about healthy relationships. My parents always fought loud and often. And Mommy cried at least twice a month. So when Rikki cried, I just comforted her in my arms. Real love made you cry, right?

Rikki started to skip classes. She withdrew from our group of friends and hid out in our dorm room with the curtains closed. She wore the same Body Glove T-shirt and black sweatpants day after day. She rarely showered. She left long messages on Matt's voice mail at least three times a day. Then she became a vegetarian. Now, *that* offended me. "Living things shouldn't eat other living things," she said.

"Don't vegetables live before they're ripped from the ground, steamed, and served with a wedge of lemon?" I didn't believe what I had just said, but I couldn't resist the argument. College does that, you know.

She thought about my response. "You're right." Then she threw herself on the bed and cried. Once she calmed down, she resolved to live off water and Slim-Fast bars. This lasted for two days. She gave up after she realized that the chocolate coating on her diet bars came from living cocoa beans that hung from some living tree in Central America. I was honored to treat her to a Fat Burger double cheeseburger later that night.

Rikki recorded love songs from the radio. Initially I thought, No big deal. Everyone dubs a collection of their favorite love songs, then names the tapes "Slow Jams." My sister, though, recorded stacks upon stacks of tapes of songs by Shirley Murdock, Whitney Houston, the Force MD's, Janet Jackson, Luther Vandross, Anita Baker, and anyone else on an urban radio's playlist. Some tapes duplicated others in songs and in artists, but I kept my mouth shut.

Then I started to notice a pattern. When Rikki got stuck on recording Public Enemy, she then spouted about the lack of students of color on campus. Affirmative action had failed us. It was time to take matters into our own black hands, by any means necessary. She thought of joining the Nation of Islam.

Sade equaled depression. Love sucked. Love hurt. No one loved her. Matt hated her. Mommy hated her. Alone. She was alone.

Billie Holiday expressed extreme depression. What was the point of living? Maybe she'd just go to sleep and never wake. I took her Billie Holiday tape and smashed it.

"Always and Forever": she recorded that over and over again on both sides of a cassette.

"So I don't have to keep rewinding," she explained.

And then, without any warning, she would stop listening to the tapes. She'd also forbid me to play them as well. One hundred and seventy-four cassettes sat in the middle of the room and caught dust and my toes in the middle of the night.

Two and a half weeks later, as she browsed through her collection, she decided to categorize and alphabetize each tape, by date of creation, then by most favorite to least favorite. This took her two full days, days in which she ignored class and sleep. After the tapes were sorted, then sub-sorted, then sorted after that, she searched for and found three milk crates in the grocery-store loading area. The tapes went from the floor to the containers, and for that I was grateful, even though the arrangement now sat in the middle of our room.

Then it got *really* weird. Matt told Rikki in passing that he hated to work late because he missed *Cheers,* his favorite television show. From that night on, Rikki taped every *Cheers* rerun that aired. If she wasn't home, she'd set the VCR to record the show or assigned me to tape it. Sometimes, she would record love songs as she recorded *Cheers.* She cried on nights like this. I had to leave the room.

She ran out of money—being a recording studio was an expensive habit. And she couldn't write checks because she bounced checks regularly. The bank had called and threatened to close her account if she continued. She had to reimburse them $1,297 immediately. "I don't have the money," she cried into the phone. "I don't remember what I bought. It's a mistake. Maybe somebody stole my checkbook."

I took the receiver from her once her sobs made her incomprehensible. I told the bank's customer service agent that I was her sister and that I would make a deposit at the bank that afternoon. I'd just have to drain my savings account, that's all, then work another two hundred hours plus overtime to replace the funds that were supposed to pay for the next semester's tuition. Yep. No problem.

I hung up and Rikki thanked me. "I'll pay you back. Promise."

Her checkbook wasn't stolen—it was in her purse. The check register, though, was blank, so I examined her canceled checks: drugstores, grocery stores, military supply stores, and a membership to the NRA. Each check had her loopy, left-slanted signature. Rikki shuffled through the checks, too. "I don't remember," she said. "I don't remember."

Part of me thought that Rikki wouldn't learn her lesson if I paid her debt. The other part of me knew, though, that my sister could never learn some lessons. And *that* made me sad.

It wasn't long before she came to me and asked, "Can you loan me twenty dollars?"

"For?"

"Tapes." On these occasions, she'd shower and change her clothes and maybe take lithium. She didn't want me to think that she was, well, sick.

"I don't want you spending my money on that crap," I said. Hell, I now worked thirty hours a week at the Gap, folding sweaters the Gap Way, folding blue jeans on that wall rack the Gap Way, smiling at customers until my face froze the Gap Way. Rikki still didn't have to work. She was a Regent's Scholar: full ride over four years.

"I won't spend all of it. See, look." She held out one hundred or so coupons for video- and audiocassettes. "But I can't use the coupons if I don't have the cash."

True, but it still freaked me out.

She sent Matt his tenth *Cheers* tape. He told her that it wasn't necessary to record every episode. She burst into tears on the phone.

I looked up from *The Tempest*. "What's wrong?"

Matt, I'm sure, attempted to console her because she told him, "No, I understand" and "I know you didn't mean it." She cried while he rambled on about his love for her and her wonderful heart, and so on and so forth. In the end, Matt continued to receive taped *Cheers* episodes once a week.

"I can watch them whenever I want," he told Rikki. "No one I know cares for me like my sweet pea."

But in Rikki's senior year, the *Cheers* tapes pushed him to call me from Los Angeles. Rikki was interning at the elementary school that afternoon. Matt and I chatted about classes, Mommy, and politics. Finally he said, "Stacy, can I ask you something? Just between us?"

"What's up?"

"It's about Rikki." He sighed. "Don't take this the wrong way, but . . . but I think . . . does she have a history of . . . well . . ."

"Do you want to know if she has a mental problem?" I blurted.

"Well, yeah. I'm just noticing . . . things. I have for a while now."

"Uh-huh."

"Well?"

"Well, what?" I asked.

"Is she taking something for . . . it?"

I laughed. "What do *you* think? Does she act like she's on medication?"

"Is it me or are you being a smart-ass about this?" he spat. "How can you be so friggin' cavalier when your sister has problems?"

"Matthew, if I plucked a hair every time Rikki tripped out, I'd be bald. I've lived with her my entire life. You've known her for two years. Don't tell me how to react!"

Matt immediately backpedaled. "I'm just saying that I love Rikki. I'm concerned about her, that's all. I didn't mean to sound . . . I'm sorry."

I told Matt that my father had wanted to get Rikki into counseling back in high school, but Mommy wasn't having it. That Rikki sneaked to get treatment once she came to Berkeley, and that Mommy still didn't know.

"Have you talked to her about her recent mood swings?" he asked.

I admitted that I hadn't. He asked if I minded if he gave it a shot. "No," I said. "Maybe she'll listen to you."

I really hoped she would. Rikki had entered an environmental-awareness phase. You see, the ozone was dying. So she combated the lack of oxygen by placing forty plants around the apartment and playing Yanni for them. I didn't care much since we lived in an off-campus apartment: I had my own room again.

Rikki and Matt talked later that afternoon. I pretended that I was studying hard for midterms. She caught me looking at her and took the phone into the bathroom. She left the apartment after her conversation and returned an hour later. I sat at the computer, writing on socioeconomic issues found throughout Kafka's works. "Don't you have some guy to screw?" she asked me.

"Don't you have some hymn to write?" I said.

She leaned against the desk, then tossed a paper bag in my lap. I opened it. A vial of pills was inside.

"So you're on them again?"

"Yep. And Matt and I decided . . . well, we're not gonna sleep together for a while. I think that's best."

I nodded. "Whatever helps you feel better." I'd cut my throat first, but that's me.

Medication and abstinence worked. That spring, my sister marched across the stage to receive her bachelor's degree with a clear head and a light heart. She didn't graduate summa cum laude, not even cum laude. Her counselor had suggested that she drop her minor in journalism. Too much time had passed and the course work that she had missed couldn't be made up. Rikki didn't give the commencement speech or receive special commendations, either. For the first time in her life, she was average, ordinary, getting by, and unimpressive.

But she shrugged it off. "I have my degree and that's what counts." She was Arika Diane Moore, Version 3.0.

Mommy and I held hands during the ceremony. We both cried because Rikki smiled; because Rikki was *there*. She didn't have plants or tapes or military surplus supplies in her life. Just Mommy, Matthew, and me. I thanked him afterward: "If you hadn't talked to her, I don't know if she'd be here today."

"I love her," Matt said. He did.

After a small dinner party thrown by friends and sorors, Rikki and I took a walk outside our apartment. It was warm out. The streets were deserted. The horizon was lost in the fog from the Bay. Hills rose behind us in blue and purple hues. Cal sat to our north: a brick and stucco assembly rambling in all directions.

"Who would've thought way back in elementary school, when you beat up Pamela Keller, that we'd be here," Rikki mused.

Stinky Pamela Keller. "That was a million years ago," I said. "I wonder what she's doing now."

"Still beating up third-graders, I bet." We laughed. Rikki hugged me. "It wasn't Matt, you know, who got me here. It was you. And God, of course. I'm smiling because of you. You're the best sister in the world."

I blushed and broke from her grasp.

"Why are anesthesiologists like beans?" she asked.

I shrugged. She knew I hated mushy moments. "Why?"

"They both give people gas."

I laughed. Arm in arm, we returned to our apartment. She was prepared to save the children. The storm was over.

But medication fools you. You think that you're back to normal because you aren't crying or shouting at the top of your lungs. Your mind keeps track of conversations for a change, and thoughts of death are crushed under your heel. You think you're doing it on your own, so you skip a pill here. And you skip another one. So the moods return. You cut off your hair. You isolate yourself from friends and family. And once again, you're totally off track.

11

THE HAPPIEST DAY OF HER LIFE

RIKKI DECIDED to live with Mommy after she graduated from Cal. Matt had asked her to move in with him, but she didn't believe in "shacking up." The next year, I returned to Los Angeles to work as a junior accountant for a publishing house that put out crossword puzzle books each month.

"Wouldn't it be great if you two shared an apartment?" Mommy asked. I guess she had forgotten how exhausting a life it was with her oldest daughter.

"Yeah, Stacy," Rikki said. "It would be just like old times."

Mommy promised to help us find a place. Neither she nor Rikki had asked me if I was interested in returning to old times. They probably knew my answer.

We found an apartment on the Westside. Mommy ate dinner with us every night. Rikki even had a key made for her. Both she and Rikki talked constantly, and Matt was in and out. Rikki worried about home-invasion robberies, grout in the shower, and the size of our mailbox. Most times, I hated coming home from work.

The vegetarian controversy came up again, but fiercer, after I cooked dinner one night: Salisbury steak, Stove Top stuffing, and sugar snap peas. Mommy blessed our meal and complimented me on the menu. Satisfied with myself, I began to eat my steak. Gravy and those yummy mushroom buttons covered my fork. I looked up to see Rikki glaring at Mommy and me. Her eyes shifted back and forth.

"What the heck's wrong with you?" I asked.

Mommy looked up from her plate. She wiped her mouth with a napkin. "Sweetie," she said to Rikki. "Is everything okay? The food's really good. Eat up."

Rikki sneered, "I'm just disgusted." She shook her head. "It looks like you're eating shit."

I studied my plate, then chuckled. My goodness, it *did.* "Yeah. Where's the beef?"

Rikki didn't laugh. Mommy didn't, either. Mommy touched Rikki's hand. "Sweetie, please don't talk like that at the table."

"Mother," I said, "she just said that my food resembled crap. Who cares that she cursed?"

"How in God's name can you eat animal flesh? And then hide it in gravy. You call yourselves Christians?" Rikki pushed away from the table.

Mommy didn't say a word. She just stared at the pitcher of juice in the middle of the table. I sawed off another piece of steak, poked a mushroom on it, and stuffed it in my mouth. I kept my eyes locked onto my sister's.

"Your bodies are temples of God," Rikki said.

"And God said that we can eat cows," I said. "It has hoofs and eats grass. I'm not a heathen, Arika. I know Leviticus."

"Stacy, please," Mommy said. "Don't make this worse—"

"And who made you in charge of what I eat?" I asked. "You can't cook to save your life. You need to grow up and shut up because I'm tired of your shit."

Mommy and Rikki gasped. Mommy said, "Stacy, please. Why don't you finish your dinner in your bedroom, okay?"

"What? This is *my* apartment. I pay half the rent here. I'm not going anywhere!"

Mommy gave me The Look. I got up and took my plate to my room.

The next night, I returned to the dinner table. Rikki sat across from me. I had hoped that she would be out with Matt. No such luck. Mommy set out mashed potatoes and a green salad in the middle of the table. She bought out rolls and a platter of this . . . stuff. "What the hell is this?" I asked.

It was meat loaf that didn't have any meat in it. "Just try it," Mommy said. "Please." Desperation glimmered in her eyes.

I took a bite. My mouth started to itch. I spat the chunk into a napkin. "I can't believe this," I mumbled, and watched Mommy and Rikki stuff themselves. I didn't touch this veggie loaf even though it appeared on the table for a week; and even though Rikki had tossed out every meat product in the house.

"Does this mean that we can't eat cheese, butter, milk, or ice cream?" I asked. "If I'm correct, that pint of double-fudge rocky road in the freezer is made from cow by-product."

Rikki sighed and left the table. She ran to her room and slammed the door behind her. I let her and Mommy carry on with the veggie crusade for one more week. Then I stopped at the grocery store. I picked up ground sirloin, cube steak, chicken breasts, and Hebrew National beef franks. As usual, Mommy let herself into the apartment. She saw me cooking in the kitchen. Good ol' American cattle sizzled in a cast-iron skillet. She almost gave up the ghost. "What in heaven's name are you doing?" she asked, wide-eyed.

"Cooking." I pressed on the patties for emphasis.

She stood there a moment and watched me. Her nostrils flared. "Smells good."

Nothing like the aroma of fried beef and onions to break a former carnivore's back. "Thanks," I said. "Is Rikki with Matt?" It was close to eight o'clock and she hadn't gotten home. It was also raining, so she'd never get home in time to stop me.

Mommy nodded, then stepped closer to the meat and me. Lettuce, tomato, mustard, Miracle Whip, and a big bag of Lay's potato chips sat on the countertop. I moved the skillet to the back burner and turned off the gas.

"You made three patties. You can't eat all of that by yourself, can you?"

I shrugged and placed my fixings onto the first bun. "I'll probably throw one away."

"Rikki will see it."

"Yeah. Guess you're right."

"I'll eat it." Mommy quickly plucked the hot hamburger from the pool of grease and dropped it onto the second bun. Then we sat at the table with our burgers and chips. It was close to nine-thirty when we finished. I didn't get a chance to wipe the grease from the stovetop or air out the house before my sister got home. Rikki had a cow, but I was a meat-eater once again.

The next year, life improved tremendously. I met Dr. Eric Warren. You could say that we had a "cute meet." I stood in back of him in line at Cedars-Sinai Hospital's cafeteria. I had just gotten a check for my first published crossword: a whopping $75. I was a conqueror—most people who try their hand at puzzle-making give up in piles of crumpled paper and eraser debris.

Rikki was upstairs in Matt's office. She needed me to drive her to the mall since she had cut up her driver's license into eensie, weensie pieces (too many cars on the road killed the ozone, and no ozone meant death). Anyway, Eric stood in front of me. He wore those sexy blue surgery-room scrubs that make almost every man look good. He was tall—six foot two—and muscular from basketball, not weight lifting. I couldn't tell if he was cute since I stood behind him; but his hairline was very neat. No razor bumps, no nicks, just smooth skin the color of new pennies. I stared at his neck for an eternity. I even closed my eyes and fantasized about running my tongue across that smooth swatch of skin.

As I continued to lust, I didn't notice that he was moving away from the counter. His elbow rammed into my nose. His cup of coffee slipped from his hand, but not before it spilled onto my tank top and the bare skin above it.

"Damn it," he shouted. "I'm so sorry!"

I doubled over in pain, but managed to sneak a peek at his face: chiseled and beautiful. Then a curtain of tears draped across my eyes. Oh, the pain. It felt as if thousands of cotton balls were burning on my chest. Then all of a sudden, the pain disappeared. Every nerve had died a quick death.

No one else moved to help me, to ask if I was okay. No napkins were thrust in my direction. I guess they knew that a doctor was in the house. And he didn't need no stinkin' napkin.

"Damn. I'm an idiot," Eric whispered. He reached toward me and placed his slender fingers on my shoulder. He gently guided me away from the line and to a table.

"Cheese and bread, will you stop pushing me?" I snapped. I closed my eyes. Oh, the pain. I knew my skin had to be peeling away from my skeleton like a fruit roll from its wrapper.

"Just breathe deeply," he advised. He knelt in front of me and waited.

After a minute, I whispered, "You couldn't drink milk, could you?" My voice sounded wet. I smelled boiled me.

"You should get that checked out," he said, honey-voiced. "Want me to take you up to emergency?" He had dimples even though he didn't smile. Flecks of gold danced in his brown eyes.

"I'm fine. Shouldn't I, like, put ice on it or something like that? Butter?"

He smiled. "Yeah. Something like that." And I was his.

Thanks to Eric, I suffered from second-degree burns. He rubbed burn ointment on my inflamed chest that night: our very first date. I, too, broke my three-date rule. Over and over again. I moved into his beachfront condo in Santa Monica five weeks after we met. Rikki was pissed off: I had chosen to be with Eric instead of her. But she still faked happiness and excitement when I announced my engagement months later. She was angry with me, but still agreed to be my maid of honor.

Eric and I married six months later on the rooftop of the Bel Age Hotel in Beverly Hills. Twinkle lights in the ficus trees, a string quartet, and these adorable baby lamb chops . . . what a night. Of course, Rikki wore that strapless black bridesmaid gown like Naomi Campbell. And, yeah, her hair glistened as though it had soaked in a vat of mink oil, but it was *my* day and I made a stunning bride. I had the Princess Diana meets Dorothy Dandridge meets Chaka Khan look. You know. Demure, but va-va-voom. Mommy had insisted that Pastor Phillips perform the ceremony. That was the only detail she thought about. "I didn't raise you like this, Anastasia," she said. I agreed: anything to shut her up.

Eric and I honeymooned in Greece, courtesy of his parents, Wesley and Lillian. We had lots of drunken sex on those islands. Took walks on the beach. Stuffed ourselves silly. We returned two weeks later to a condo full of toasters, rice cookers, and Egyptian-cotton towels. Those days, Eric rubbed my feet with eucalyptus oil. He even brought me hot-water bottles when I had cramps. We hosted parties and lunches, took road trips, and played video games.

Eric knew Matt, of course, so we'd all hang out together. Rikki got over my so-called desertion and focused on her relationship with Matt. She constantly dropped hints whenever they passed a jeweler. She would threaten to leave him if he didn't seal his commitment to her. She always cried, "And Stacy and Eric just met," whenever we came over. "And look how quick he was ready to commit to *her.*"

So, after six years of dating, 130 taped episodes of *Cheers,* and countless recordings of love songs, Matt proposed to Rikki on December 24, 1995. They sat in his living room, in front of the Douglas-fir Christmas tree they had purchased together. They decorated it with ornaments that signified their years as a couple: a music note (the tapes), a heart (their love), and a Hollywood sign *(Cheers)*. Matt presented her with a diamond engagement ring in a platinum Tiffany setting.

She told me of their engagement the next morning.

"Did you say yes?"

"Of course I did. Now I'll never have to worry about pre-marital sex and hell again." So she worried about other things: the cake, the garter belt, and her dress.

"I can't wear a white wedding gown," she said as we pored over glossy bridal magazines. "It would be lying."

"Fine," I said. "Here's a nice red dress. You'll look just like your future mother-in-law." I didn't argue. I waited for her to feel better, for the sun to shine again. Three months later, she picked her gown. It was white. It cost a small fortune.

She cried on December 20, her wedding day. I know, brides cry. It's custom. They don't *weep,* though. Rikki wept. Wept as if she had been told that she'd die after the wedding. The other bridesmaids knew by now that crying was what Rikki did. They pulled on their dresses as if the bride weren't standing in the middle of the room, bawling like a kinder-gartner.

"Oh, Rikki," I said, and attempted to hug her through my yards of peach taffeta. "If you keep on, you're gonna get makeup on your dress."

She cried harder.

Mommy shooed me away. "This is normal. All brides cry. I cried on my wedding day and . . ." Then Mommy began to cry.

Uncle Gregory, Mommy's older brother, came in the room. He swaggered over to Rikki and said, "You look gor-geous, sugar." He pinched Rikki's arm and kissed her on the eye. He stood in for Daddy that day. Uncle Gregory lived in

Atlanta, gave us bicentennial quarters every time he visited (including that day), and smoked the smelliest cigars never made in Cuba. He partied with strippers every night, had whirlpools in each room in his house including the closets, and had been arrested more than twice for soliciting hookers. But he was the only older male left in our family. I would've cried, too, if he marched me *anywhere.*

"Out, Greg!" Mommy pushed her brother out to the foyer. He had started hitting on any woman who wasn't related to him. It was time for the wedding to start anyway. The three bridesmaids left the room. Mommy followed them. Rikki and I remained. Her deluge of tears had slowed to a hiccup and a sigh. "I already miss you," she said.

"Arika, you're not leaving Los Angeles."

"I know, but you're always there, waking me up from my nightmares, eating dinner with me, protecting me from Mommy."

Our eyes met in the mirror. I considered her reflection. She *was* beautiful.

"Well, our mother thinks you're the prettiest, smartest woman in the world," I said. "Living in your shadow was pretty safe. I just existed. Like moss on a sequoia."

Tears welled in her eyes. A sob escaped from her throat. "How could I betray you like this?" she wailed. She tore off her veil and grabbed my hand. "I'm just an ungrateful bitch who's deserting my sister, the only person in the world who truly loves me, for some *man* I've only known for, what, six years? What kind of person does something like that?" Then she threw herself to the floor like a Tennessee Williams character.

I stood there, shocked, speechless. "Want some water?" was all I could say as she lay there.

She said, "See? That's the problem. You always give, give, give. I always take, take, take. And I took Matt away from you at camp! I knew you liked him, but I did it anyway."

My cheeks burned at this mention of ancient history. She forgot that Matt wasn't attracted to me, that he thought of me as a kid sister, that I had had my chance, nothing happened, and that was that. He chose her and I had to get over it. And I was *so* over it. Eric loved me. Life was swell.

Rikki couldn't see Matt's absolute devotion because of the guilt she had from being in love. She wanted a life with him and that scared and depressed her. "He's going to cheat on me. Like Daddy cheated on Mommy."

"That's not true," I said.

"He'll leave me for his nurse, and the next thing I'll get from him will be divorce papers from his lawyer. I'll be so fat and so ugly that nobody will want me except for some loser who surfs the Web and plays Dungeons and Dragons all day." She pulled herself from the floor into a chair.

"Cheese and bread, Rikki," I sighed. I retrieved her veil from the floor. "It's your big day. You're getting married in six minutes and you're talking about divorce and affairs and the Internet."

She tossed her bouquet into the wastebasket. "What am I doing?" she screamed. "I don't know what's happening!"

I expected Uncle Gregory to hear her and bust down the door. He'd slap her and she would come back to her senses. Then we'd go and get her married. But Uncle Gregory never came. He was probably hitting on Mrs. Orenstein, the pigeon-toed wedding coordinator, inviting her back to his hotel room for a forty-ounce Schlitz malt liquor, some barbecued corn nuts, and a porn movie.

As usual, I was left to do the comforting. As I knelt next to her, my heel caught in my petticoat. I fell back on my butt and my dress fell over my face. I thought slapstick was supposed to make everyone laugh. Here I was, the female Soupy Sales, but Rikki just cried harder and louder.

I sighed and disentangled myself from my gown. "Look, Arika, what do you want? I mean, Matt's in love with you. You'll have lots of babies, a cat, a dog, and a Volvo. You'll collect art and eat gourmet meals from china every night. *Essence* will do a story on you and you'll live happily ever after, the end. You know it. *I* know it. Everybody except his mother knows it!"

"Why does she hate me so much?"

Oops, I did it again.

Rikki pulled her bouquet from the trash. "I remember watching those sitcoms with the evil mother-in-law character. I always thought that stuff was funny, and I'd laugh and laugh. But it's not funny. It's not funny at all."

In the background, the organist played "Sheep May Safely Graze," the song that accompanied the bridesmaids' procession down the aisle. There was a light rap on the door.

"Yes?" I shouted.

Mrs. Orenstein entered the room. She clapped her pink, freckled hands and peered at me with watery, blue eyes. She smelled of Porcelana and spearmint.

"Enough bonding, ladies," she chirped. "We have work to do. Someone's getting maaareeeeed."

"You're getting maaareeeeed," I told Rikki. "Buck up."

Rikki smiled. She wiped away her tears with an antique ivory handkerchief that Mommy had given her. It was Nana's—something old. I replaced the veil on her head.

"Don't you look beautiful? Tears and all," Mrs. Orenstein said.

"Thank you," Rikki mumbled.

"Oh, I just love weddings," Mrs. Orenstein said. "Let's get going, ladies!"

I helped Rikki stand. I brought the gauze from her veil over her face. She looked so far away behind that netting. "You okay?" I asked as the wedding coordinator pulled me toward the door.

"Does it matter?" Rikki swiped at her veil as though she were trapped in a web. I blew her a kiss and wondered, as I marched down the aisle, if she would show up at the altar. She did, thanks to Uncle Gregory.

Arika cried throughout the service: during the Lord's Prayer, the marriage homily, and the exchange of vows. I'm sure that Mommy thought she sensed her daughter's over-whelming joy and cried, too. I'm sure that everyone thought Rikki cried because Daddy wasn't there: he didn't get to march his little girl, now decked out in a splendid $3,000 gown, down the aisle.

But as I considered Matt, I knew he wasn't fooled. Like me, he knew that Rikki's tears came from a deeper, darker place. A place that drilled past our father's death, past her fear of a new life. Like me, he knew that he had to find that place and roll a huge stone over it before that something got out. But where could he find a rock that big?

12

Near the Mouth
of Madness

As soon as Rikki and Matt exchanged vows, our world found peace. Rikki was right—she didn't worry about premarital sex now that she was married. And I didn't have to worry about her now that she had a husband. Finally, Eric had me all to himself.

With my husband's encouragement, I switched priorities. I did accounting only part-time and concentrated on my freelance crossword-puzzle writing. Rikki bought me a reference library, complete with an unabridged dictionary and thesaurus. The set even came with books on etymology and linguistics. And when I sold a puzzle to a major women's magazine eight months later, Rikki copied it, framed it, and hung it in her classroom behind her desk. "My sister's a published writer," she'd tell anyone who asked about the puzzle.

She kept copies of it in her drawers and handed them out, Bible-study style.

Rikki and Matt immediately settled into their new life. They went to dinners and lunches with friends and colleagues. Matt visited Rikki's classroom to give special talks to the parents and students. Rikki decorated Matt's office with construction-paper apples and colorful charts. They gave away thousands to charity and scholarship funds. They vacationed at least once a year. They were even profiled in *Ebony* magazine.

Matt told Rikki that she didn't have to work; but Rikki told him that she loved teaching. She also liked maintaining their house, a fabulous property. Kind of. The house itself was beautiful—you really can't go wrong in Brentwood. It was a Mediterranean, two-story structure painted ancient mustard. Magnolia trees protected most of the rectangular windows from prying eyes. The house was set back and above the street. Low brick walls ran in two levels to contain the rambling yard, which was structured like a rice field. You had to climb twenty-three brick stairs to reach the front door. It was an Italian hacienda, L.A. style.

Once you entered my sister's home, you could tell that she had decorated each room according to her mood. For instance, one room was a library. In there were books about everything: illnesses, children, the environment, or car repair. The floors and the walls hid under or behind books that Rikki read four or five times, then tossed, never to be opened again. Sometimes, she cataloged the books by author; or she'd sort them by topic. It reminded me of the tapes back in college.

No paint in the house was a true white or a true blue. One wall was burgundy because the first two coats were brown, then red. Or it was coral because Rikki had slapped on yellow first, then changed her mind and wanted pink. Other rooms were half-painted and half-wallpapered. It didn't matter. The house had rooms, heat, and water. Matt wasn't home enough to care about its appearance. He rarely saw the house in daylight.

Of course, this bliss couldn't last forever. After being married for almost three years, Rikki began to call me every day. She constantly complained that she was always alone, that Matt stayed at the hospital night and day.

Eric also worked wacky hours, and whenever he came home, Rikki decided to call then.

"Can't you *not* pick up?" Eric asked me. "Just once? You don't even talk to her when she calls."

"She's my sister, sweetie. You know I wouldn't if I didn't have to." Then he'd leave the room until I had finished my one-sided conversation with my sister.

But then, Rikki would recruit me to run errands with her on Wednesdays and Sundays—the days Eric would typically get off. I wasn't happy about this invasion and often tried to get out of these field trips. But Mommy would call: "What are you doing that's so important?"

"Well, I would like to spend some time with my husband," I explained. We were about to celebrate our fourth wedding anniversary.

"So you're gonna let *sex* interfere with you and Rikki's relationship?" Mommy screeched. "Do you want her doing something to herself?"

"She has a husband."

"But she only has one sister. Go to the grocery store with her this last time. Please?"

So I would; but it was never a "last time."

Now Eric and I rarely spoke. When we did, it always led to an argument. One night, I had forgotten to meet him for dinner with a colleague and his wife. Rikki and I had gone to the movies. I apologized to Eric when he got home, but he ignored me. The next night, he didn't come home. He didn't call, either. So I paged him every hour. No response. I didn't sleep that night, and when he trudged into the house early the next morning, I nearly bit him in half.

"If you're fucking around, you need to stay with that bitch!" I shouted, among other things.

"That's what you're thinking?" he shouted back. "You paranoid—"

"You call me a bitch and you're outta here."

He smirked. "This is my house. My name's on the title."

"What's yours is mine," I spat. "I'll burn it down. Leave you and your girlfriend homeless."

"Why are you so suspicious of what I'm doing?" he said softly. "Aren't you usually worried about your other husband? Oh, I mean your sister. And as far as I'm concerned, you and me—we aren't married." And he turned and went into our bedroom. I slumped to the couch, speechless. Eric left the house with two suitcases and a rice cooker.

Later that night, I picked up the phone when it rang, hoping it was my husband. It was Rikki. I told her about the argument. To my horror, she didn't express any sorrow: "He's always been jealous of us. He needs to get over it. Fuck him."

Matt was devastated. He called—I guess Rikki told him the news. "He'll come back," he said. "Eric knows that this isn't your fault. It's mine and I'll tell him. I'll promise him, and I promise you, that Rikki and I will stick to her treatment. No ifs, ands, or buts. And I'll keep her from bothering you all the time."

Matt talked to Eric over pizza and pool that following week.

"And what did he say?" I asked Matt over lunch.

Matt looked away. "He didn't say anything. He just kept shooting."

Eventually Eric called me. I apologized and promised to do better. He told me that he needed space—from me, from Rikki. He told me that he still loved me. That he wouldn't throw away four years of marriage because of this. He gave me his new address and phone number. I hung up and ate two pints of black-walnut ice cream, popcorn, and a bag of cookies. It was my first wedding anniversary alone. That month, I gained fifteen pounds.

Matt kept his promise about getting Rikki back on track. He stood over her as she took her daily medication. He even had the phone company temporarily block my phone number so she couldn't call. He sent Mommy and a few of her friends on a monthlong vacation—now there was no one to make me feel guilty.

Rikki and I only saw each other a few times over the weeks. She gawked at my weight gain, but never commented. Eric and I had dinner occasionally. He, too, never remarked on my appearance. He didn't say when he would come back, either. We spent my birthday together. I weighed close to 170 pounds. We made love that night. Afterward, I decided to join Weight Watchers.

But Matt's schedule at the hospital worsened and Rikki gravitated back to me. "I want to have a baby," she told me. Matt, though, wasn't ready. He and Eric had planned to open a health clinic for the poor. Matt wouldn't be around as much as he wanted. To him, a baby right then wouldn't make sense.

"I can understand that," I said as Rikki and I drove home from church. I was disappointed after hearing Matt's decision. The route my life had taken, I'd probably never have children. Rikki was my only hope of having little ones crawling all over me.

"But I have a feeling that if I got pregnant, he'd be happy," she said. "What does he expect? I'm almost twenty-eight. I can't wait forever."

Uh-oh. "So . . . what are you thinking?"

"Oh, I don't know," she said with a smile. "Accidents *do* happen."

"Won't you have to get off lithium if you're pregnant? Won't Matt notice . . . stuff?"

Rikki shrugged. "He's not around long enough to notice *stuff.*"

Six months passed and Matthew and Eric finished the planning stages of the clinic. All they needed was the chief of medicine's approval. They hoped to get that at a dinner party the chief was giving at the end of the month. Eric had asked me to go with him. Thrilled, I said yes. Finally, Rikki had missed her period and woke up feeling nauseated.

"I went to the doctor today," Rikki said. "For another pregnancy test." She went every month now.

We were sitting next to each other at the hair salon.

"Ooh! Exciting," I squealed. "What did the doctor say?"

She shrugged and looked away. "That I'm not pregnant. Total false alarm. That the nausea's from the lithium that I've been taking. One of the six thousand side effects of being on this *shit,* even though I'm not on it anymore."

"What? Is the doctor sure?"

She leaned forward and placed her chin in her hand. "She said that I might be infertile. That something could be wrong with my fallopian tubes or that I could have hostile cervical mucus or that Matt could have a low sperm count." Tears filled her eyes. "She asked me if we were having emotional difficulty. That's the term she used: *emotional difficulty.*"

"Hell, who doesn't have emotional difficulty?" I touched her hand. "I'm so sorry, Rikki." I smiled and tugged her fingers. "I know this isn't the end of you trying to have kids. You guys are rich. You can do all the artificial fertilization stuff." I just prayed that she didn't ask me to become a surrogate mother.

Rikki shrugged again. "Yeah. The doctor did say that there are surgical procedures we can try. And fertility drugs. And counseling. You know, for the emotional difficulty. But we both have to go in and be tested before we can go any further."

"And Matt still doesn't know?"

She shook her head. "You're the only person I've told. Matt would flip out if he knew I was trying to get pregnant. I'm not ready to bring this up yet. Especially with this party. Mind if we put this one on the back burner, at least until I've figured out what to do?"

I nodded. Her secret, of course, was safe with me.

"Maybe it's good that I can't have babies," she said with a sigh.

"How in the world can *that* be good?"

"I could pass my brain to the baby. She could wind up just like me."

"Oh, Rikki. You can't inherit something like that. Don't think that way. Positive thoughts."

We left the salon three hours later—it takes forever to get your hair relaxed, washed, and curled. Since it was late, we stopped for take-out Thai food before Rikki dropped me home. We returned to our car to see a stray mutt sniffing through the restaurant's Dumpsters. Rikki stopped in her step.

"I don't think he's gonna bite you," I said.

"That's so sad. Isn't he just adorable? He just needs some love and a bath."

"Yeah . . . ," I said, uneasy. "We should get back in the car before—"

She snatched my brown-bagged take-out order. She tiptoed over to the dog.

"What the hell are you doing?" I shouted.

"Shh! You're gonna scare him away!"

Rikki eased closer to the poor creature. She reached into the bag and pulled out my container of garlic pepper beef. "Here you go, sweetheart," she cooed. "Hungry? Here you go."

The dog stopped his forage through the trash and considered the pretty black lady with the nice hair and aromatic bag. He had a rounded muzzle, a thick neck, and a gray, woolly coat. A white spot sat at the base of his throat.

I hated to admit it, but he was a lovable little guy. He hopped in his step. He smiled, even though, technically, only dogs like Snoopy, Marmaduke, and Scooby-Doo could smile. Five minutes later, the dog rode in the backseat of the Volvo en route to his new home. "I'll call him Mr. Thai," Rikki said. "Because he likes Thai food." Indeed. The mutt didn't even leave a splash of gravy. "And I'm gonna take him to the doggy salon tomorrow. Get his hair and nails done."

Mr. Thai lived in the pantry. Rikki walked him every day. She even dressed him in pom-pom caps and sweaters. She loved that dog. She took him everywhere she went unless Matt forced her to leave him behind. He ate $50-a-bag gourmet dog chow and received monthly pedicures (or would that be manicures?), weekly vitamin-enriched shampoos, and regular trips to the dentist. He slept with Rikki and Matt, to Matt's chagrin. Sometimes, he ate directly from Rikki's fork.

Rikki had always loved animals. As a child, she had begged our parents for a dog, but for once, they told her no. They gave her every animal except a dog. Goldie the Goldfish arrived at our house in a plastic bag. Daddy won him for Rikki at our PTA carnival one year. Rikki forgot to change his water, but that never bothered Goldie. He swam around his filthy bowl in that murky, ginger-colored water for months. Rikki decided to change his water one night because a transparent film prevented the fish food from dribbling to the bottom. The next morning, Goldie was floating on his side. He was not asleep.

Rikki insisted that we hold a funeral service for Goldie. In tears, we buried the goldfish that starry night beneath the peach tree in our backyard. Daddy said a few words of remembrance. Then we sang "Jesus Loves Me." Mommy stayed inside—she thought the entire episode was ridiculous. Rikki and I continued to cry and Daddy ushered us back inside the house. We sat in the kitchen and stuffed our mouths with s'mores and hot chocolate. Mommy had even brought out extra marshmallows.

After an appropriate grieving period, Daddy brought home two gerbils—Peaches and Herb. Gerbils were pretty exciting—they were mammals! Rikki and I watched them work out in their gerbil gymnasium and waddle around the cage. We'd take them out sometimes and kiss their soft, furry faces. Someone (I still say it wasn't me, even though it was) failed to lock Peaches and Herb's cage and the couple escaped. Rikki and I didn't find them for days. We both cried and left out pellets in case they were hungry. We found Herb the next week, drowned in the toilet. And Peaches? Poor Peaches: squished to death. Rikki accidentally sat on her in the bed. Rikki refused to sleep in her bed for weeks.

My parents and I thought Rikki buried Peaches next to Goldie in the backyard. But days passed and our bedroom began to stink. No matter how often Mommy dusted and sprayed, the stench worsened. I looked under Rikki's bed one day, in search of my tennis shoe. I found a smelly shoebox and opened it to discover Peaches's corpse covered in maggots, her tiny mouth stuffed with a cotton ball. I screamed and dropped the box. Mommy rushed in. Minutes later, Peaches found her final resting place in the garbage can.

And finally, there was Birdie the Parakeet. No one in our house liked birds, but here we were, the proud owners of a squawking, petulant creature. Birdie was pretty smart. She flew from her cage, out of the window, and to freedom the first time Rikki changed her cage liner. We never saw Birdie again.

After this, Rikki settled for Chia Pets. She had three: a dog, a sheep, and a cat. She watered them every day. Watered them too much. They lived for a month.

I eventually found the courage to ask my parents for a rabbit. They looked at me with a mixture of fear and disgust. "Rikki had a rabbit," Daddy said. He also died at the hands of my sister. Poor, poor Hopper.

Matt didn't like gerbils, parakeets, or dogs, but he realized that Mr. Thai made Rikki happy for the moment. And that this was a good thing until Mr. Thai bit Matt on his right hand. He needed four stitches—Matt, not the dog. "This is frickin' out of control," Matt shouted after Rikki refused to get rid of their canine boarder.

"I love him!" Rikki said. "He's my baby, Matthew! He needs me!"

"This is unhealthy, Arika," Matt said. "You're treating that dog like . . . Are you hiding something from me? What's going on?" She still hadn't told him about her visits to the doctor.

"Nothing's going on." She threw herself on the couch and sobbed. "What difference does it make, anyway? You only care about those snotty-nosed kids at the hospital!"

Matt went over to her and patted her shoulder. "Sweet pea, I think you need to talk to someone. It looks like your mood swings have come—"

"I don't need a shrink!" Rikki yelled. She pushed him off the couch. "And I don't need *you* telling *me* that I'm crazy!"

"I didn't say that." Matt attempted to smile. "We could all use therapy at one time or another."

"Fine, lovebug. *You* lie on some fucking couch, then." She ran outside to play catch with her dog.

I stayed away from Mr. Thai as much as possible: allergies.

"What's up with your sister running a pound out of the house?" Eric asked me over dinner.

"Huh?"

"She's got ten dogs off in there."

I grunted.

"I didn't think you'd be shocked," he said, pushing his broccoli around on the plate.

"Nothing she does really shocks me anymore."

Rikki had decided that Mr. Thai needed siblings, so she brought home Lester the German shepherd. Lester had been wandering on the side of the freeway when Rikki saw him. She got out of her car and rescued him. Then she saw Bruno the Chow, Oleander the Terrier, and six other mutts that had roamed the streets of Los Angeles.

By now, Matt was beyond shock: "It stinks in here. Dog hair's all over the place!"

"I'll get a maid," Rikki said. "Just for them."

"A maid for dogs? That's ridiculous!" Matt shouted. "I'm calling the shelter to pick these things up."

"I'm not getting rid of them," Rikki shouted. "And they're *dogs,* Matthew, not things. They eat and breathe and think, and if you kick them out, I'll go live in the streets!"

"Rikki, these *dogs* carry disease!"

"Not anymore. I took them to the vet to get all of their shots. And I had them spayed and neutered. See?" She showed him the veterinarian's bill.

"Five thousand dollars for a vet?" he asked, amazed. "How in the hell did you pay this?"

Rikki flicked his sentence away like a dog slaps off a flea. "Credit card."

Matt stopped going home. He didn't know how to banish the animals without Rikki going over the deep end. He took extra shifts to give him an excuse. Not that Rikki paid any attention to him. She only thought of her dogs.

"You gotta know what brought this on," Matt said to me over lunch. "She's acting like these animals are her children."

I looked away and fiddled with the zipper on my jacket.

"Do you know something that I should know, Stacy? You two are always keeping secrets from the rest of the world."

"Matt," I said with my eyes still averted, "just give her time. She'll work it out of her system."

He narrowed his eyes and clenched my wrist. "If I told you that I was three minutes away from leaving her, that I'm *that* fed up with her . . ."

I sighed. "Fine, but you can't tell her what I told you." I hated myself—her secrets had always been safe with me. Until now.

"For the sake of your marriage, I'll tell you." And I told him that Rikki had stopped taking lithium again because she was trying to get pregnant. That possibly she was infertile. That she was scared to tell him since she knew that he didn't want a child anyway. I shared my opinion that Rikki needed to be a mother to *any* living creature since she couldn't be one to her own species.

"Damn it," Matt said. "I don't believe this. Damn it!" After he kicked the chair a few times, he promised me that he would let the dogs stay until they solved their conception issues. "And I'll do better by her," he said, more to himself than to me. "Promise."

My sister's behavior worsened when K-9 Clips rejected her credit cards after she had brought the dogs in for baths and haircuts. Rikki's personal credit had been mangled in every credit agency's computer in America since college. She still shopped hard when she wasn't feeling well. She bought Cuisinarts, pillow shams, pocket watches, leather pants, and juicers. She bought Matt a top-of-the-line Tag Heuer watch for their anniversary. She didn't wear or use the stuff she bought; rarely did she remember that she had them. Creditors, though, had long, long memories. And in case they forget, or someone in their office died, they compiled something accurate and true. It's called a credit report.

The K-9 Clips cashier called the bank for my sister.

"It's got to be some type of administrative error," Rikki told the customer service representative. "I pay my bills! This is absolutely ridiculous! Somebody's out to ruin me!" But she didn't pay her bills. There was no vendetta. In her lifetime, Rikki had been required by at least four credit card companies to cut up their plastic into tiny, tiny pieces.

After the K-9 incident, Matt's accountant pulled out her fifteen-page credit history and circled all of her late payments (or no payments) with a red felt pen. Afterward, Rikki retreated to the bathroom. Matt called me twice that night. "What if she slits her wrists again?" he asked, terrified. Days like that day, I regretted that Rikki had told Matt about her suicide attempt before she accepted his wedding proposal.

As I talked to Matt, Eric was folding his surgical scrubs. "She's still locked in the bathroom?" he asked.

I nodded yes.

"Can you come over?" Matt asked. "I'll treat you to lunch at Shutters or something. Wherever you want to go."

"Lunch at Shutters? Yum."

Eric got up from the floor, grabbed a medical journal from his bag, and waved good-bye from the couch. He knew the drill. He didn't look up when I left the house.

I arrived at Rikki's twenty minutes later. "Arika, sweetie," I said to the door. "Come on out. You'll be okay. Matt's not upset. Right, Matt?"

"Right. I love you, sweet pea. I just want you to come out, all right? Who cares? It's just money."

We eventually coaxed Rikki back to the other side of the bathroom door. She hadn't done anything too drastic—just cut off chunks of her hair. Matt consoled and hugged her. I swept up the mess she had made. The next week, Rikki had five platinum cards from the major players in her name and a snappy, new hairdo. So did the dogs.

Two days before the chief of medicine's dinner party, Rikki found the shortest, skimpiest dress Fred Segal had on his racks: a strapless black number that hit the thighs way up there and dipped in the torso way down there. Her breasts spilled out from the seams like a pork roast from its strings.

"That's a little . . . a little too little, don't you think?" I asked.

She waved me away. "I got it, so I'm flaunting it." She bought the dress for a cool $1,540.

We flitted from that store to Nordstrom's M.A.C. makeup counter. Rikki chose Russian Red, Jet, and Film Noir lipsticks, Diva and Raisin eye shadow, some sparkly, platinum lip gloss, and apple-red and shocking-pink nail polish. She went away, then came back to purchase twelve more shades—from goldenrod to aquamarine to eggplant—of nail, lip, and eye wear for a total of $400. Then she darted to the shoe section and purchased three pairs of patent leather stilettos—the kind of stilettos only disco queens and drag queens wear—for another $700 plus tax.

"Then I'm gonna keep them on *after* the party," she said, winking at me. "Matt likes me naked, drunk, and nasty. You'd never know that, huh? He's such a damn Republican sometimes."

Exhausted and poor (my puzzles hadn't sold well that month), I sat on a bench in the middle of the mall. Thousands of shopping bags, none of them mine, sat at my feet. My arms ached from schlepping them for Rikki, who immediately forgot about each purchase after it was made. I no longer reminded her after she left her sixth bag. From my seat, I watched her spend more money at the Hickory Farms kiosk. "I feel like summer sausage and a jalapeño cheese roll," she had told me. She hated summer sausage and was allergic to jalapeño. There was no danger, though. She'd never eat any of it.

Afterward, she pulled me into Frederick's of Hollywood. Panties, camisoles, and garters of every shape and size glowed in phosphorescent light. Women, as diverse as the underwear, held up articles of clothing to their bodies. Others came out and modeled their selections for too-kind friends.

"Oh, yeah," Rikki shouted. "Now we're getting to the good stuff!"

Embarrassed, I kept my eyes on the floor and my hands far away from the merchandise. Rikki picked up a pair of red, white, and blue crotchless panties. "Listen to this, Stacy!" She rubbed the seat of the underwear. "Stars and Stripes Forever" played. I almost ran out of the store in tears.

She shouted out the instructions for body butter, then asked me from across the store whether black or red fishnet panty hose would complement her new stilettos. "Buy something for yourself," she suggested. "Eric will like it. He's gotta be a freak if he married you."

"No thank you. And Frederick's is for amateur sluts and ladies who lunch." I purchased my whips, chains, and naughty underwear in the privacy of a shop near my apartment, *and* without a committee.

"Fine. Then I'll get you something," she said, wandering toward the panty bin. Back in college, Rikki had bought me my first sexy bra, black satin with underwire. I wore it religiously until the straps grew thin. It's still in my lingerie drawer. I hope to wear it again once I become less . . . voluptuous.

"I don't want anything. And lower your voice."

"Coward," she said. "These look like you. Here." She tossed a pair of leopard-skin panties in my face. "You have to surprise Eric when he corners you in the bathroom. Don't you want something sexy covering the good stuff?"

Women clawing through panties were starting to stare at us. "Rikki, the house will be full of doctors and their wives. And if you don't shut up, I'm leaving you here."

She exaggerated a yawn. "You bore me when you act so damn responsible and adult." She tossed more panties in my direction. She held up a sheer pair. "Think Matt's gonna freak when he sees me?" she asked with glee. "*All* of me?"

"Yeah, because we're going to be the only black people at the party, and you'll look like a whore on a night when his career's on the line. Which brings me to your dress, Arika. Don't you think you should wear something a little less Hollywood Boulevard?"

She laughed. "You're just jealous." She purchased a tube of purple body glitter, a sheer merry widow, my leopard-skin undies, three pairs of fishnets, and those patriotic musical panties. Rikki's credit cards worked like Mississippi slaves that day. She spent over $3,200 between all of her purchases. But nothing awful happened as she bought. No cashier said,

"Mrs. Dresden, your card has been denied." That's because she used Matt's cards and he was rich.

The night of the party arrived. I walked into the chief of medicine's Bel Air mansion on Eric's arm. This house was the largest frickin' private building that I've ever visited. It stood three stories high. Enough grass was on the lawn to donate to each family in my old neighborhood. Grecian columns stood on both sides of the front entrance. As we stepped inside, a spiral staircase swirled to the heavens. Cupolas and loggias and porticos were everywhere—if it ended with a vowel, the chief had it built in. The backyard was big enough for a cabana, six palm trees, a swimming pool, and a volleyball court. It was a villa for modern city living.

Eric and I left our coats with the butler, then entered the palatial living room. I immediately spotted Rikki. She stood near the back, toward the patio. She looked like a prom queen from 1984: short hair made into big hair, break-your-back heels, and heavy makeup. She drank from two glasses of champagne. She leaned on Dr. Irving Lerner, the chief of medicine and master of the house. He was a large man with a shock of thick, white hair that had been that way since he'd turned thirty. His skin had been bronzed to perfection by a Saint-Tropez sun. His teeth were capped and straight. He reminded me of Tom Wolfe, but without all the white.

"What's up with your sister?" Eric whispered. "And what did she do to her hair?"

I shrugged, but my stomach pulled and twisted. My entire body dreaded what it saw.

Then Rikki laughed. My heart pounded against my chest. I recognized that laugh. Oh father, I *knew* that laugh: it was a Witchie-Poo meets Scarlett O'Hara cackle. I almost fainted when Rikki handed the used glasses to a passing waiter, then placed her hands around the waist of the glassy-eyed doctor.

Eric whispered, "Oh my—"

"Do you see Matt?" I released Eric's hand. Matt wasn't in the room. Maybe he had left the house to walk off his rage.

"I'll go look for him," Eric said.

"And I'll go get her." I muscled my way through the masses and tugged Rikki by her elbow. She whipped around and batted her gooey eyelashes at me. Purple, pink, and gray eye shadow hovered above and below her blood-shot eyes. Her skin sparkled as if she had crashed into Tinker Bell.

"Stacy, baby," she slurred. "I'm so glad you made it. I was starting to worry. You know the doc, don't you?"

I nodded to the chief, then said, "Let's go outside for a minute." I wanted to pull her away, to wipe her face, and to have us both melt down into nothing.

"I'm surprised you actually got here. You and Eric are constantly banging each other. I didn't think you could tear yourself away!" She cackled. "What's with you nymphos? What's your secret? Spanish fly?"

The chief laughed. Large red splotches covered his face. His eyes glistened with thirty-year-old Scotch. His chubby hand inched closer to Rikki's twenty-eight-year-old breasts.

This was not good.

I backed away from the two as they babbled on in language only drunks understood. I searched for Eric and found him and Matthew in the kitchen. Matt paced as waiters with silver trays of wine and stuffed mushrooms weaved around him. "I found him," Eric said.

"Did you see your sister?" Matt shouted. The little vein in

the middle of his forehead stood out like a cobra in a basket. "Did you?"

"Yeah, I saw her. You can't help but to see her."

Then I tugged at the leopard-skin panties I was wearing.

"I shouldn't have trusted her to come by herself," Matt said. "But I couldn't get away."

"This is awful," I said. "What are you going to do?"

"Me?" Matt asked. "You mean *you.*"

"No, I don't. She's your wife. In sickness and in health."

"And she's your sister. Blood is thicker than water."

"She needs help," I said. "Not just medicine. Psychiatric help."

"Ain't that the truth," Eric said.

Matt ignored that crack. "What do you suggest that I do *now,* Stacy? *Tonight?* She's out there, looking like some hooker, draped around my boss!"

"I suggest you take her home and lock her up in her bedroom," I said. "It doesn't matter now, does it? Didn't you see her when she got dressed?"

"No, I didn't," Matt snapped. "I told you that we met here. She was fuckin' toasted by the time I came."

At that moment, the chief walked into the kitchen. Concern and Jack Daniel's stained his face. Matt stopped pacing and smiled. "It's a great party, Dr. Lerner. We're just getting some fresh air. You've met my sister-in-law, Anastasia? Dr. Warren's wife."

Dr. Lerner nodded toward me. "I'm glad you're enjoying the party, Dr. Dresden, but you should come out to the living room. Your wife . . . well, you should come out to the living room."

We dashed from the kitchen. Someone had turned up the

stereo, and now Johann Sebastian Bach blasted from the speakers. A small group of Dr. Lerner's guests watched something going on in the middle of their circle. Some giggled nervously; others clutched their throats in horror. Matt and Eric edged toward the center. They pulled Rikki from the crowd and rushed her outside.

"What happened?" I asked Eric when he returned.

"She was grinding up a visiting pediatric surgeon. Matt's screwed."

Matt returned to the party minutes later. He was alone.

"What did you do with her?" I asked.

"She's in the car."

The chief came over. "Is everything okay?"

"She's a bit tired," Matt said. "I apologize for her behavior."

The chief left. I touched Matt's arm and summoned my most empathetic smile. "Should I go out and talk to her?"

He stared at me for a moment. There wasn't any fear in his eyes or anger. Nothing. "No need. She's asleep." He turned, retrieved his coat from the butler, and left the mansion.

13

WHEN THE BOUGH BREAKS

As WE grew older, Rikki and I still resembled each other, but not as much as we did when we were teenagers. My brow naturally wrinkled now. My eyes, set deep in my face, suggested disapproval with everything that passed before me. I frowned easier than I smiled. My gait was that of a Sherpa who traversed Mount Everest twice a day.

Rikki's skin had the waxy pallor that soon-to-be-drug-addicts had. There was a vacancy and dullness to her eyes, dark circles below them because of sleepless nights and crying fits. She was thin one day and bulged the next. Medication wasn't the Holy Grail for life's little monsters because Rikki didn't take her medication regularly: it made her *feel* like crap. Her blood pressure skyrocketed. She frequently got diarrhea. Her face twitched. Her weight fluctuated. Complicate it with the mental problem she already had, then ask, Why would she take it?

But she wore a forced grin that said, "It's okay. *I'm* okay."

I noticed our physical departure from each other the morning after the party. I drove to her house to check on her. The dogs' maid let me in and directed me upstairs to Rikki and Matt's bedroom. The door was open. As I stepped in, the acrid odor of sickness overwhelmed me. Someone had used pine-scented cleaner to cover it up.

Matt sat next to my sister on the bed. Rikki's eyes were puffed and swollen. He turned to me. He still wore his clothes, now wrinkled and soiled, from the party. "She doesn't remember any of it." He spoke as though she weren't in the room with us. He spoke as if he didn't believe that she could actually forget.

But she didn't remember: not her dress or the makeup, the fishnet stockings or stilettos. Not the shopping trip with me. Or the summer sausage and cheese. She didn't remember fondling Dr. Lerner or dirty-dancing with the surgeon. It was as if the day, the week, had never happened.

"I don't know what to say," Rikki said in a hoarse whisper. "I'm sorry."

"Please, sweet pea," Matt said. "We have to do something about your blackouts."

"I'm okay. I just had a little too much to drink."

"Rikki," I said, "Matt's right. You were out of control. And it wasn't just the alcohol."

"I'll be fine." Tears broke her voice. "I just lost it a bit, but I'll do better. I promise. I swear. You don't think I'm trying? I tried taking the pills, but I get nauseous and throw up. I start trembling, like I'm nervous or something, but I'm not. And I get all bruised up 'cause I'm walking into walls. Is that the kind of life you want for me?"

"No," Matt said. "We just want the best for you. Maybe we should try counseling."

I left Rikki's house close to midnight with no immediate solution to our problems. My head ached. I tried to call Eric, but he wasn't at his apartment. Mommy called, though. I summarized the past forty-eight hours for her and mentioned that Matt was now considering counseling for Rikki.

"Counseling?" Mommy shrieked. The idea of Rikki in therapy was still preposterous to her. "I won't allow it."

"It isn't your decision anymore; it's Matt's. What are you scared of, Mother? That we'll have you committed, too? Or do you think we'll forget Rikki like we forgot about Nana until she died?"

"My mother has nothing to do with this. Rikki's not insane!"

"She's schizophrenic or manic-depressed or whatever the doctor said she was a long time ago, but you wouldn't believe him, so we didn't do anything about it! Now look."

"You know what? I don't need *you* telling me what I believe or what's wrong with my daughter. All that Oprah–Dr. Phil crap is hogwash and you fall for it!"

"Oprah has nothing to do with my sister having bats in her belfry and a kennel in her yard!" I shouted. "I'm sick of being the only one in the world who sees this! I'm sick of pretending that we're so normal and perfect, that I'm fat because I eat too much and not because every day of my life sucks! And it sucks right now because *you* get the privilege of ignoring the shit that hit the fan over twenty years ago! I'm sick of it!"

Mommy gasped. "Don't be disrespectful. Who the hell are you talking to like that?"

"Do you want her to disappear or get kidnapped because she finally disconnected? Do you even care about Rikki? About me? Hell, do you even *know* either of us? Why don't you just give her a gun? It'll be quicker that way."

Where was Eric? Why wasn't he here?

"You're overreacting, as always," Mommy said. "We solved all of these problems when you two were teenagers. She wouldn't hurt herself. She wouldn't hurt a fly."

My mind grew weary with this conversation. I hated listening to my mother revel in the destruction of her foes' and their children's lives when she didn't see that my life and Arika's slowly wasted away. Pastor Phillips had told Daddy years before he died that we lived under a curse and that God was chastising us for our sins. Maybe the pastor was right.

My doctor had warned me that I was gaining too much weight, that my health was in danger. "You're too young to weigh one hundred and seventy-two," he said. "Your blood pressure is high enough that I may have to put you on medication to regulate—"

"I don't want to take any pills. What if I change my diet?"

"And decreased your stress levels?"

"And exercised more." *More?* Hell, I never exercised.

He nodded. "I'll give you a month to make a change. If you don't improve . . ."

I thought about it and realized that if I didn't take care of myself, how could I care for Rikki? And to take care of Rikki, I had to break away from her first. My doctor referred me to a nutritionist, who put me on a strict diet. I threw away all the food in my cabinets and refrigerator in order to make a fresh start. I came home from the grocery store with five bags of healthy, low-fat vittles. I took my first two-mile walk around my neighborhood. The fear of chemical dependency and a heart attack motivated me.

Eric told me some of the rumors about Rikki that had generated from that night in Bel Air:

". . . oral sex on Dr. Lerner."

". . . dancing on the piano with a wine bottle in her hand."

". . . dragged out kicking and screaming. She even knocked over Mrs. Lerner's collection of Hummels."

"You're kidding about the Hummels, right?" I asked.

"Nope," he said. "I'm amazed that Matt still has a job. People can't believe that you two are sisters."

"I don't particularly care *what* people think." I did care—about a milligram's worth.

I avoided Rikki as long as I could. Sounds cruel, I know, but she drained me after the party. Her behavior had wandered into new territory that I had no map for. She left long, apologetic messages on my answering machine. She said that I couldn't desert her now because she needed me more than ever. That all the doctors' wives had voted not to include her on the Foundation Board of Directors for the health clinic. "No one cares about me now, except you and Mommy," she said. "And Matt, that selfish bastard. He wants me to get rid of all my dogs. Even Mr. Thai. Matt's probably why God is punishing my womb. And he had the nerve to storm out of the house. I don't know where he went, but he should've stayed there."

I didn't return her calls. I just listened as she talked until the machine disconnected her. Maybe she'll just go away if she keeps getting the machine, I thought. But she didn't and continued to call at least six times a day. I gave in late one night. Eric groaned, turned over, and put the pillow over his head. Rikki sounded close to tears. My heart couldn't stand it.

"Oh, you're there," she said, calm. She knew that I was there all the time—I heard it in her voice.

"Where else would I be at"—I looked at the clock—"two o'clock in the morning?"

"I called you yesterday at two in the morning," she sniped. "You didn't pick up then."

"What is it, Arika?" It was late. So late that I hadn't known where I was when the phone rang.

"I can't sleep. And Matt isn't speaking to me."

"Make a soufflé or something," I groaned.

"A soufflé? That's a good idea." She carried the phone downstairs to the kitchen. Soon, the pots clanged and the pilot on the stove clicked.

"Rikki, I was sleeping."

"You don't have to talk. Just keep me company."

Despite distance, time, and a telephone, Rikki rambled on about her dogs, their fleas, about her fourth-graders, and the proper way to separate egg yolk from egg white.

I fell asleep several times during our conversation. She didn't notice because her mouth moved until five that morning. "You gotta eat dinner with us tonight," she said. "Because in a way, you helped me cook."

I brought a bouquet of sunflowers with me that night. I had invited Eric to come along, but he declined. He packed his overnight bag and returned to his apartment downtown. I promised to call him later. He told me not to bother.

Matt, in glower mode, sat at the table. Rikki clapped her hands once I sat. "Now that we're all here, let's eat."

Rikki had become an astounding cook. The soufflé

melted in my mouth. The same for the rack of lamb, scalloped potatoes, London broil, asparagus, macaroni and cheese, lima beans, and baked Alaska. I knew that I shouldn't have eaten this much food, but . . .

Matt eventually chilled out as we ate. We talked about gun control, the right to bear arms, and violent video games. Rikki tried to join us, but she brought up irrelevant points or rambled on and on until she gave up. Matt ignored her, which I'm sure frustrated her. She began to shovel food into her mouth.

Out of the blue, she threw her fork onto the table. "Can you two shut the hell up?" she shouted. She looked up from her plate. Crescents the color of avocado hugged the bottoms of her eyes. Grease shone on her chin.

"Sorry," I said.

Matt sat back in his chair with a look that I never knew he could make.

"You have grease . . ." I reached to wipe her face with a napkin, but she knocked away my hand.

"Have you realized," Rikki said, "that in the past two days I've only slept three hours? I made this wonderful meal and all you two can talk about are the bullshit Bill of Rights and Nintendo!"

"Arika," I said. "The food's wonderful, but we're both full. And you know, since I've been seeing my nutritionist, I have to stay within my calorie range."

"No one asked you to cook this crap," Matt snapped. "And no one told you to stay awake all night and day to do it, either!"

Tears filled her eyes. "All I ask from you, *lovebug,* is that you *eat!*" She grabbed the dish of macaroni and heaped two giant spoonfuls onto Matt's plate. She tossed the rest, straight from the bowl, onto my plate. Matt shoved his plate to the floor. All of its contents spilled onto the carpet. Rikki gasped and picked up her crystal wineglass and hurled it across the table toward Matt's head. He ducked, but the glass hit the back of his neck. I shrieked and hopped up from the table. Matt shouted, "Get the hell out of my house!"

Rikki ran from the dining room. Mr. Thai followed her. Matt held a napkin on the cut to his neck. "I can't believe this."

Shaken, I said, "I have to go and get her."

I grabbed my jacket from the foyer. "Wait, Stacy," Matt said. "I'll go with you."

Matt and I followed Rikki and Mr. Thai as they stormed up the sidewalk. We exchanged solemn looks when Rikki started to talk to the dog. "Did you like dinner tonight? You did? I'd do anything for you, my pumpkin pie. Forget that old Matt. He doesn't understand us. What do you want to eat tomorrow?" She placed his mouth next to her ear. "Oh, really? I'll buy that when I go to the grocery store."

"Damn it, Rikki, will you quit talking to the dog like he's a human?" Matt said.

Rikki knelt and hugged Mr. Thai around his neck. "Mind you own business, Matthew. Keep out of our conversation."

"Conversations happen between *people*, Arika, not a dog and a woman who can't see that she's talking to a dog."

"So what are you saying, Matthew? You've been dancing around it for days. Why don't you just come out and say it? Or are you the cowardly son of a bitch I always knew you were?"

Speechless, I stood behind my brother-in-law. This was

going to happen in public. A confrontation, a battle. The line would finally be drawn in the sand.

A few of the neighbors converged at their windows to witness the confrontation between the handsome doctor and the pretty wife who had the problem they couldn't exactly put their finger on. "Maybe we should go back," I suggested.

"There's this . . . place," Matt said. "In Rhode Island. They're participating in some groundbreaking work with this . . . nerve and . . . it's for people with . . . it's pretty impressive. And, well, it can help you with . . . well, with what's going on. And no one has to know." He looked back at me and said, "Sorry, Stacy, I didn't get to tell you."

I didn't respond. I wasn't pleased knowing that he wanted to put my sister away in some asylum—swanky asylum or not. Matt had probably visited a psychiatric facility during medical school, but that's different from visiting your grandmother who lived in one. Even though doctors didn't shackle people the way they did in the eighteenth century, or beat and isolate them, many of them worked for programs that still paralyzed you with drugs, shocked you with electricity, and poked you with needles, all in the name of science.

Rikki frowned, then nuzzled her dog's coat. "Does the dinner party have something to do with this?"

Matt nodded. "And all the cooking. And the dogs. The shopping. Then there's school."

Rikki stood and placed her hands on her hips. "What about school? I'm a damn good teacher! I've won awards! Teacher of the Year! Ask anyone!"

"Yes," Matt said. "You are a good teacher when you go to work. Dr. Frank called me this afternoon, Arika. She said you've been out fifty-six days this year."

"I have sick days." Rikki looked at me for help, but I looked at Mr. Thai. "I haven't been feeling well. Is that some kind of crime now?"

"No." Matt stepped toward her. "I know you've been . . . under the weather for some time, now. And Dr. Frank is concerned about that, too." Matt paused, then said, "It's just that . . . one of your parents complained to her. The parent saw you one afternoon at the mall when you had called in sick."

Rikki grunted. "So? I probably needed something. What business is it of hers? Nosy bitch."

Matt said, "Some of your students have told their parents that there are times when you sit at your desk and cry." When Rikki didn't reply, he continued. "Your behavior scares some of the kids, sweetheart. And your teacher's assistant, too."

Rikki sighed, stared at the heavens for a bit, then shook her head as though she had grown tired of the conversation. "I had just finished *Charlotte's Web*. It's a sad story, okay? I've read it six hundred seventy-three times, but it still affects me. And I can't help that."

The three of us stood there for a moment, all eyes on the ground. I finally lifted mine and considered my surroundings. This was really a nice neighborhood: houses that rambled on and on, green lawns as big as 7-Elevens, luxury automobiles parked in each landscaped and cobblestoned driveway. No helicopters. No sirens.

"Is there something else?" Rikki asked. "Other complaints or grievances?"

"Why didn't you tell me you've been missing that much work?" Matt asked. "I should know that, Arika."

"It slipped my mind." She chuckled. "I guess it's out of order."

Matt and I exchanged nervous glances.

"It's okay," she said. "You can laugh. It's called a joke."

"We just want the best for you," I said. "We know how much you love the kids and teaching and everything, so we don't want the principal firing you for something you can't control."

"So now I've lost control?" She looked at me. "So you want me to go to this place, too? This psychiatric Betty Ford clinic? It sounds pretty interesting."

Matt sighed with relief. He hadn't thought she would react this calmly. Especially since she had just lashed out with violence at the dinner table. As for me, though, I trembled so much I developed a migraine headache. I wanted to run home and never look back.

"They'll get you back on track," Matt said.

"But I take my medicine," Rikki said with a shrug. She reached into her sweatshirt pocket, pulled out a pill vial, and rattled it. "See? Prozac, lithium, uppers, downers, siders, backwarders . . ."

"Not regularly, though," he said, "which is a problem."

"Don't preach to me," she snapped. "I've been living like this every day of my life, okay? I take the pills when I need to, okay? I don't like being dependent on pills, okay? They make me dizzy. They make me thirsty and I can't deal with that every day, okay? I'm not some fucking guinea pig!"

"Then we should find an alternative method," Matt said. "Something with fewer side effects."

I felt uncomfortable standing there, listening to this. Even though my sister's illness was no mystery to me, this conversation still needed one fewer pair of ears.

"Is that fine with you?" Matt asked Rikki. "We'll do this together."

She sighed and threw up her hands. Then a low growl came from her throat. She turned to me. Or shall I say *on me.* "Hey. You can't even look me in the eyes." She pulled Mr. Thai into her arms and stood. "What do you think, little sister?"

"I agree with Matt. I'm sure the . . . place . . . will help us arrive at some sort of solution."

"Is this about the dinner party?" she asked again.

"Your problem isn't new to me, Rikki," I said, "so don't try to bullshit me into thinking that. I've seen you at your worst, and I don't want to see you that way again."

"Kiss my ass, Anastasia. You, too, Matthew." She dropped the dog to the pavement. He yelped in pain and ran over to Matt. "Everybody treats me like a fucking poodle who bit *once.* You wanna put me away now? Gas the pretty, rabid dog?"

"That's not it, sweet pea," Matt said, trying to stay calm. He stepped to her with his arms outstretched. Blood from his cut continued to drip onto his shirt collar. Mr. Thai, smart dog, hid behind me.

"Yeah, it is," she said, and slapped away his hands. "And you know what? I'm on to you two."

Confused, Matt and I looked at each other. Across the street, the living-room and porch lights flicked on. A woman in a sky-blue robe looked out to where we stood. Her husband, in matching pajamas, joined her. She held a telephone in her hand. I was sure the police would arrive soon.

"This bitch right here," she said, pointing to me, "she's always been jealous of me. And wanting what I have.

Remember when you stole Jacques what's-his-face from me back in high school? Huh, Miss Goody-Goody? And now I see it. You want my husband, too, don't you?" She pointed to Matt. "And you," she said, glaring at him, "you like banging her more than you like banging me? Huh? You like *whores* now?"

"Rikki, calm down," Matt whispered, now aware that this scene would get worse before it got better. "We don't have to go to Rhode Island. There's this therapist, Chris Nesbitt, right here in Los Angeles. He comes highly recommended by a psychiatrist that I know at work. This guy is very discreet."

Rikki didn't listen. "And now you two wanna lock me up, put me in the fucking crazy house so you can go at it like a bunch of rabbits?" she snarled.

I finally moved toward her. "Rikki, Matt and I aren't sleeping together. C'mon."

"Shut up, you fat, backstabbing bitch! I know you are! And you're telling me all these stories about my behavior and I don't remember them 'cause they never happened, 'cause you're making them up!" She stepped toward us. She wavered, however, as if her feet wanted to go toe-to-toe, to duke it out till death, but her mind wanted to stay put, to stay safe, to stay *there.*

"I'm not losing my mind! I'm not losing my mind! I'm not losing my mind!" she screamed again and again. Every light on the block came on. She sank to the ground in mumbles and screams. We all heard her deny that she was not losing her mind.

She ran to the house and got in before we arrived. She locked us out and refused to let Matt in, despite his pleas. She placed chairs and couches in front of the doors. She armed the house's alarm system.

Matt and Mr. Thai spent the night in my living room. Matt sought to commit her to a local mental facility before he left for work the next morning. He called the psychiatric ward at Cedars. He demanded that I listen in on the other cordless phone. We held on the line for several minutes as "Raindrops Keep Fallin' on My Head" looped around a recorded voice alerting us to the volume of calls. Matt grew more agitated as each minute danced into the past. When a human male voice asked him how he could help, Matt pounced on him.

"I need to admit my wife," Matt blurted. "She's lost her frickin' mind!"

"Okay, sir. You're gonna have to calm down and breathe."

"Yes. I apologize. I'm Dr. Matthew Dresden, a doctor at Cedars. My wife is bipolar. We had a huge fight last night and I'd like to bring her in for evaluation."

"Okay, sir. Due to Section 5150 of California's Commitment Law, I'm going to have to ask you a few questions before you bring her in."

"Will this take long?"

"Do you fear that your wife is a danger to herself?"

"Suicidal? Yes. No. I can't tell. She was mostly angry at me last night."

"So would you say that she's a danger to others? You included?"

Matt scratched his head. "She threw a glass at me, but is she a serious threat? No. But—"

"Is she gravely disabled?"

"What the hell does that mean?"

"Is there evidence of malnourishment? Is she unable to provide for her own food, clothing, or shelter?"

"No. She eats. She shops a lot. She locked me out of my house! That's why I'm calling!"

"I see. From what you've told me, neither you nor the state can force her to come in."

"So you're telling me that you can't do anything unless she does something drastic?" Matt shouted. The man didn't respond. "It'll be too late!"

"Is there anything else I can do for you, Dr. Dresden?"

Matt had nothing else. That was his last solution.

He was upset that I wasn't upset as much as he was. I agreed: yes, she needed help, but she had rights. From what I knew, my sister was still an American.

"I'm only trying to help her," Matt said. "I guess it's a *Moore* thing to ignore important shit like this." He spat out my last name just as Zenobia would have.

"Fuck you, Matthew." I stomped to my bedroom and slammed the door behind me. But maybe Matt was right. Maybe it was a *Moore* thing.

Later that day, Matt and Mr. Thai returned to their home. All of the locks had been changed. As he waited for the locksmith, Matt checked his voice mail from his cell phone. Rikki had left several rambling, incoherent messages. The locksmith came. Rikki wasn't there. Matt packed a few things and moved out of his house. He left her a note on the refrigerator: he wanted a divorce.

14

THE THERAPIST

AS HE'D said, Matt had already talked to psychopathologist Dr. Christopher Nesbitt before he'd broached the subject with Rikki. Matt told me that the doctor wasn't alarmed.

"He said that Rikki's just rebelling," Matt said. "That in marriage, people with manic depression grow irritable. Restless, even. Rikki just wants a little excitement in her life right now. She's rebelling against everything she loves about me: my kindness, patience, and stability."

Eric looked at me. "Maybe I should talk to this doctor about you, too."

I gave him the finger and said to Matt, "So he doesn't think Rikki's . . . ill?"

"And that it's your fault for being so damn patient and understanding?" Eric said. He chuckled and finished his Diet Coke. The waitress immediately flitted over and filled his and

Matt's glasses. She didn't leave first without a wink. Obviously, she didn't think I was married to either of these men.

Matt said, "Of course he thinks she's . . . no, it's not my fault. He thinks she has bipolar disorder."

"Manic depression," I said. "I knew that already. The doctor said that back when we were teenagers."

Eric crunched on his ice as he thought. "I don't know. Too many doctors blame everything that's wrong with the world on manic depression. If you're irritable, you have manic depression. If you cry, you have manic depression. If you're happy one moment, then sad the next, they want to shove a truckload of lithium down your throat." He shook his head. "It's a rush to diagnosis, if you ask me."

"But we're not asking you," I said. I turned to Matt. "So?"

"So Rikki's gotta go in and talk with him. He can only know what he's dealing with then. After that, we plan a course of action, which will probably mean more drugs."

I sighed. I turned around in my seat. The waitress hadn't filled my glass the entire time I'd sat there. Yet Eric and Matt were almost drowning in their sodas. No tip for her.

"So can he cure her?" Eric asked.

Matt shrugged. "It can't get any worse."

Rikki continued to call Matt at the hospital days after their public showdown. She still left rambling and angry messages on his work voice mail. He accidentally picked up his extension when his nurse told him he had a call. Of course it was Rikki. He told her that he was in the middle of an examination and asked her to call back. She insisted on staying on the line until he returned. He didn't argue. He returned to the phone minutes later.

Rikki told him that she would do anything to save their

marriage. Even if that meant seeing a psychiatrist. She said that she loved him. She asked for another chance. So she entered Dr. Nesbitt's Beverly Hills office at four-thirty sharp on March 16.

Rikki and I had dinner two hours later. She glowed. She spoke calmly and with much deliberation. She told me that she and Dr. Nesbitt had chatted about the weather and about freeway traffic, and the opera season at the Music Center. After her third cup of coffee, she told him that she really didn't know why she was there because she was actually feeling better.

"Better than what I've ever felt actually," she said. "I think I just needed to blow off some steam to get to the place where I am right now. Dr. Nesbitt said that this was a possibility, but he wanted to be sure. So he asked me a few questions. He told me that everything I told him was confidential."

"Should you tell me?" I asked, and eyed the waiter, who resembled Antonio Banderas.

"Of course." Rikki smiled and savored the spinach-and-artichoke dip we had already ordered. "Dr. Nesbitt's a psychopathologist."

"A what?"

"That's the scientific study of . . . I don't know. I kind of stopped listening. This man is *fine.*"

"Really?" I asked, wondering just *how* fine.

Rikki nodded. "He brought up that night when I cooked. When we had that huge fight. He asked if that happened to me much. The insomnia, I mean."

"You've always had trouble sleeping."

"Then he asked me how many hours I had gotten in the past three months." She dipped another chip in the thick cream. "About twenty-one hours a week. Three hours a night. But that's not all the time."

Then he asked her about those other times, about her energy levels, her concentration, spending habits, hallucinations, and overinvolvement at work.

"He asked if there was anyone else in my family who may have had some kind of mental illness," Rikki whispered.

I gulped and almost choked on my appetizer. "What does that have to do with anything?"

"Well, for some people, bipolar disorder is genetic. If he knows that there's a possible link, then my diagnosis will be more accurate." She shrugged. "So I told him that Nana had been locked up in some nuthouse near Santa Barbara. I don't know what for, though, since no one talks about it."

"So what did he say after that?" I asked, on the edge of my seat.

"What's happening is that my brain's electrical mood-regulating system isn't working right. There's this imbalance in my neurotransmitters. He said that I suffer from mixed-state rapid cycling."

"Rapid what?"

"It's when depression and mania happen at the same time more than four times a year." Tears filled her eyes. She dabbed at them with her napkin, then fiddled with a tortilla chip. "Basically, I'm a monster."

I frowned. "He didn't say that, did he?"

She smiled. "No. He's so sweet. He promised that he would walk me through this, especially since I'll have to pop pills. And I'll have weekly sessions with him, too."

I reached for her hand and squeezed it. "How do you feel about that?"

"I told him that I've tried the medication thing already. And that it doesn't work." She sighed. "It's stress, Stacy. I'm sterile, you know? And I've got forty-eight kids in my class, which is totally fucked-up. And Matt. He's away all the time, so I'm lonely. I'm lonely, that's all."

She rambled on for another five minutes on why she didn't need therapy. Once she calmed down, she said, "Dr. Nesbitt wants to check my thyroid status, and he wants to follow my moods, then analyze them against everything else that's going on in my life. It's called mood charting."

"Sounds New Age. Is he gonna use crystals next?"

She shook her head. "He promised it wouldn't be too intrusive. He's gonna track my medication use, my sleeping habits, my period . . ."

"And what if you don't want to do it?"

"He told me that in the end, it's up to me. And Matt."

So she took ten photocopied charts and made an appointment to see the therapist the next week. He wrote her a prescription for Depakote, a form of valproic acid, the treatment of choice for mixed-state rapid cycling. He would possibly augment her treatment with lithium for its antidepressant effects, but would monitor her for a few months before making that decision.

Rikki took out a leaflet from her purse and read, "Side effects include weight gain, nausea, bruising, hair loss, tremor . . . Basically, I'll feel as though I'm on your everyday lithium." She chuckled and shoved the paper back into her purse. "He even suggested that I carry a medical ID card or wear a bracelet to let the world know that I'm on this stuff. Sure. Thanks, Doc. I feel wonderful already."

"Sorry." I felt so bad that I paid for dinner.

She and I had lunch after her fifth session. She showed me her charts from the past weeks. She seemed proud. I was impressed, too, at my sister's diligence.

"Guess you don't need your other journal now," I said.

"You know who Dr. Nesbitt looks like?" Rikki gushed. "George Clooney."

Yeah. Okay. Yum. "Rikki . . ."

She pulled a picture of Dr. Nesbitt from her wallet.

"Where did you get this?" I asked. Cheese and bread, he *did* look like the actor, but . . .

"Off his Web site. Isn't he beautiful?"

"Yeah . . . Does Matt know that you have a picture of your therapist in your wallet?"

She cackled and examined the picture. "Matt? He's fucking around on me, so who cares if he knows. That's why he doesn't want to have a baby with me."

"Don't say that. You know Matt isn't like that."

"Oh, he isn't?" She reached into her wallet again and pulled out a piece of paper. She threw it in my direction. "Explain this."

"It's a receipt. So?"

"To Rex's." Rex's was one of the most romantic spots in town. "He sure as hell didn't take *me* there. Who did he have dinner with? You?"

"No. You know that. And you don't know that this means that he's sleeping around on you. And that certainly doesn't justify you—"

"Sleeping with my therapist?" She sipped her iced tea and put the receipt back in her wallet. "I could blame it on the madness."

"Yeah, but you're quite sane at the moment."

She shrugged. "Splitting hairs."

"Aren't you supposed to be there to get better? Not to screw your doctor, who's actually sworn not to mix it up with his clients? George Clooney or not, that's just ethics."

"Do you know what it feels like? To lie on a couch, telling this handsome, intelligent, and powerful man all of your secrets? And you can tell that he finds you attractive. You even catch him staring at your legs and your butt. And he's listening to you. He understands you. And there's concern in his big brown eyes and soft lips."

I shivered. I had no clue . . . How did she know his lips were soft?

"You'd be a hypocrite," I said. "If Matt's a jerk for having an affair, then you'd be an even bigger jerk for having one in retaliation. And you made *me* promise not to act like Daddy."

"Matt's beginning to act just like Daddy," she snapped. "Staying out all night. Meetings, appointments. He even lies and says that he's at his momma's house. And why'd he move out so quickly?"

"Leave Dr. Nesbitt alone, Arika."

She laughed and slipped a sliver of green pepper in her mouth. "Maybe I will, maybe I won't."

This conversation freaked me out, for obvious reasons. I wondered about this Christopher Nesbitt. Was he a quack who had gotten his degree from some sweatshop medical school down in Central America? Did he even know how to spell *psychopathology?* I found his Web site. He had a bachelor's degree from UCLA, and a Ph.D. and M.D. from Yale. So what? He was smart. Did he become a eunuch when it involved his beautiful female patients?

Feeling like Colombo, I stopped by his office, unannounced, a few days after my lunch with Rikki. Initially, his receptionist refused to get him. "He's in conference," she said. So I transformed into the Loud and Angry Black Woman. I did the whole neck-rolling, hands-on-hips thing and scared the poor creature. She called up to his office right away.

Dr. Nesbitt greeted me outside his office. He *did* look like George Clooney. Heavens. He held out his hand: soft, no cuticles or calluses.

"Pleasure to meet you, Stacy," he said. "I've heard so much about you."

"Thanks for seeing me. Don't worry. I won't take up too much of your time. Seeing that you're in *conference* and all." He had a gorgeous office. Italian leather furniture, fresh flowers, and lithographs, including a limited Ed Ruscha. Several framed pictures sat on his desk and credenza of him in front of world landmarks with this beautiful brunette. There was a picture with him and Madonna, too.

"What can I help you with?" he asked.

I gave him a brief history of Rikki's illness in childhood all the way up to recent events. I also shared my concern that my sister was attracted to him.

He laughed. "I take my oath very seriously. I'd never do anything to compromise my professional relationship with a client. And that includes your sister."

"So, is she getting better?"

He gave me the "can't say anything" smile.

"Did she tell you about our grandmother?"

"I know about your grandmother."

"Rikki told me that it's genetic."

He nodded. "Could be, yes."

My heart sank. I wanted him to say that she had misunderstood because now I felt guilty. I should've been the one with this illness. I'm stronger than Rikki. But then again, Rikki *was* me, but with manic depression. I would suffer just as she did.

There was a knock on the door. "Yes?" Dr. Nesbitt called.

His secretary poked her head into the office. "Your three o'clock appointment's here."

Our conversation ended with a promise that he'd keep our talk confidential. He walked me to the waiting area. "Again, it was a pleasure meeting you," he said. He shook my hand, then squeezed my elbow.

Whatever anxiety I had about Dr. Chris Nesbitt started to evaporate once I noticed how well his approach to treatment worked. Rikki soared with her new drug. She did late spring-cleaning and even had a painter throw up new coats of paint on the inside and outside of her house. She got rid of all the dogs, except for Mr. Thai. She returned to church and even played piano for special music.

"You look fabulous," Mommy said after one service. She did.

"I feel great," Rikki said. She and Matt treated us to lunch afterward. They laughed and kissed, just like in the old days. "We're going to Paris for Christmas," she said. "It's been a while since we've had a break."

"That's good to hear," I said. I was now free to think about things other than alleged adultery in my sister's marriage. My marriage, for instance.

Eric and I had separated completely by now. He sold the condo, which meant I had to move into a dinky one-bedroom apartment on the Westside where you couldn't walk the streets at night or turn on two faucets at the same time. It was a crappy place, which I still couldn't have afforded without financial help from Eric. He had moved to another swanky, high-rise apartment in downtown Los Angeles, complete with concierges and a brand-new dishwasher. We still spoke, though. And we still slept together. But he also mentioned the D-word after one of our trysts. I cried in the bathroom that night. He had left my apartment by the time I returned to the bedroom.

I've never had a lover as skilled as Eric, and I don't just mean sex. He listened to me whine and served as a tester for my puzzles. I held him when he came home upset and near tears because of a dying patient. He encouraged me when I wanted to give up on everything in life, and I encouraged him. We would play video games for hours and lie on the futon watching bad martial-arts films. He didn't mind if I watched *Close Encounters of the Third Kind* fifty times. He'd sit and watch it with me every single time because he watched *Star Trek* movies just as much. We could be nerds together. I trusted him and he trusted me, even now.

I wondered if my weight had something to do with his mention of divorce. I never asked him outright if he found me less attractive. Don't think I'd want to know the answer. But that was fine. He was just one less person I had to think about.

Be sober, be vigilant; because your adversary the devil, as a roaring lion, walketh about, seeking whom he may devour. —I Peter 5:8 Be sober, be vigilant; because your adversary the devil, as a roaring lion, walketh about, seeking whom he may devour. —I Peter 5:8 Be sober, be vigilant; because your adversary the devil, as a roaring lion, walketh about, seeking whom he may devour. —I Peter 5:8 Be sober, be vigilant; because your adversary the devil, as a roaring lion, walketh about, seeking whom he may devour.
—I Peter 5:8 Be sober, be vigilant; because your adversary the devil, as a roaring lion, walketh about, seeking whom he may devour. —I Peter 5:8 Be sober, be vigilant; because your adversary the devil, as a roaring lion walketh about, seeking whom he may devour. —I Peter 5:8 Be sober, be vigilant, because your adversary the devil, as a

15

He's Gone

RIKKI'S RECOVERY convinced several people who saw her over those months that her life had mended. She didn't mind taking her new medication, and she never missed therapy with Dr. Nesbitt. She baked Toll House cookies for him, sent him fresh tiger lilies once she found out those were his favorites, and got her hair done every week before her appointment. Whenever she mentioned "Dr. Nesbitt," she giggled and blushed as if he were Denzel Washington. I didn't know how to handle this. I was just glad that my sister had found the direction that no one else could provide. But, at the same time, she was falling in love with her doctor.

Mommy still loathed the idea that Rikki saw a therapist, but enjoyed the fringe benefits of a balanced daughter. Although they were still separated, Rikki and Matt returned

to church and sat with Mommy and me on our pew.
Mommy sat, beaming, as each of her daughters flanked her
again. "Just like old times," she repeated to herself. "Just like
old times." Then she'd take both Rikki's and my hands and
squeeze them. She'd kiss us both on the cheek. Matt got a
bear hug and a pat on the back. "You're a good man, son," she
told him. "You will be rewarded."

My sister even volunteered to tell the children's story and
work on the food-for-the-hungry program. Sister Vernell
Lamont, the head deaconess, told her that she'd contact Rikki
as soon as possible for her to begin.

Rikki called Sister Lamont after a month passed with no
word on when she'd be able to start. The woman never called
her back, so we went to church to catch her at prayer meeting. Sister Lamont's face darkened once she saw my sister
and me waiting to talk to her. "You were supposed to get back
to me," Rikki said with a smile.

Sister Lamont grunted and shoved her Bible in her purse.
"Yes, well . . ."

"Is there a problem?" Rikki asked, still smiling.

"Well, to be honest, there *are* some members of the congregation who have concerns."

"About?"

"Well, are you still having your . . . problems?"

Rikki frowned. "Which problems are those? Marital
problems? Financial problems? Menstrual problems? Which
problems?"

Sister Lamont sighed. "*Well-being* problems."

"Well-*being*," Rikki repeated, and nodded her head. She
knew that Sister Lamont really wanted to say *mental* but considered herself too polite. "I'm fine. I'm ready to serve."

"Does she need to bring in a doctor's note? Rorschach tests?" I asked.

"That won't be necessary." Then Sister Lamont launched into a speech about the serious matter of telling stories to children during the eleven o'clock hour, as well as handling food for the public. The church couldn't let any old body be involved. And with the myriad problems Rikki had had in the past, well, the church couldn't take any chances.

Rikki's blood pressure rose as she listened. A thin coat of sweat lay across her forehead. Tears glistened in her eyes, but didn't fall. She swallowed and took a deep breath.

"Are you telling us that her help is not needed?" I asked, my fingernails wanting to scratch out this woman's eyes.

"No," the head deaconess said. "We hope that you will still support us with financial gifts."

"Ohhhh. You want my money." Rikki reached into her purse for her checkbook. She scribbled out a check for $700 and left without saying another word.

"I've never been so humiliated in all my life," she said as we drove to the hospital to have a late dinner with Matt. Rikki pulled into the parking lot. At the same time, Matt was leaving the parking lot. He didn't see us. A beautiful blonde sat in the passenger seat of his Benz. "What the fuck is going on?" Rikki said. She peeled out of the lot to follow her husband's car.

"Maybe he's dropping her off," I said. "He knows we're coming for dinner, doesn't he?"

Rikki shook her head. "I wanted to surprise him."

Oh, God, I thought to myself, please let the car pull to the curb in front of a bus stop. Let the blonde get out and wave good-bye. Please let this be *anything* other than what it seems. But his car never stopped.

Meanwhile, Rikki switched lanes to keep up with her husband on the freeway and to remain hidden at the same time. "That *bastard!* I knew it!"

"You don't know anything," I said, unconvinced. "Where the hell are we going?" We were driving over the Sepulveda Pass toward the Valley. "Maybe Matt moved to San Fernando and she's his neighbor who works at the hospital."

"That bastard *hates* the Valley," Rikki spat. "It's that bitch, Jen . . ."

"His *nurse* Jen?"

"*She* lives in the Valley."

Sure enough, Matt got off the freeway and eventually pulled his car into a duplex's driveway. He and the blonde hopped out of the car, laughing. She was a tiny, slender thing who needed to do something about those brown roots growing in her hair. Rikki zoomed into the driveway and skidded to a halt. I held on to the door to keep from flying out the window. She hopped out of the car before it stopped moving. Matt and Nurse Jen froze like deer in the middle of the road. Their jaws dropped from shock.

"And what the hell's going on here?" Rikki shouted.

"Rikki . . . ," Matt said. "What . . . what are you doing here?"

"What the fuck are *you* doing here?" Rikki stormed toward the couple. Her fists were clenched so tight it looked as though her knuckles would pop out of their sockets.

"Matt," Blondie said. "What's going on?"

"Rikki, just calm down," Matt said with his hands up. "This isn't what—"

Rikki slapped Blondie. Blondie clutched her cheek and crouched over. I hopped out of the car and rushed toward my sister. She and Matt began shoving each other and shouting obscenities. Jen was crying. I found myself wrestling my way in between my sister and my brother-in-law, hoping that the fight would end before the cops came.

Finally, Matt pushed Rikki hard enough to gain some distance. "Stacy, you better get her 'cause I'm one minute from—"

"Do it, you son of a bitch! I dare you! Hit me!" Rikki shouted.

"Rikki, let's go." I grabbed her wrist and pulled her toward the car.

Matt placed a hand on Jen's shoulder. I'm sure he asked her if she was okay. I don't know because I hopped behind the Volvo's steering wheel and careened toward the freeway, back to Los Angeles, with my hysterical sister.

So Rikki slipped again. She avoided the world. That included Mommy and me. She wouldn't eat. She didn't comb her hair. She canceled her therapy session for the week. She didn't go to work. And as a result, on the Tuesday before Thanksgiving, the principal at 59th Street School left a message on her answering machine, sent a fax, and couriered a letter. The message was clear: do not return to school after Thanksgiving. She was fired.

A sheriff's deputy arrived at Rikki's one Monday morning, two weeks before Christmas. He handed her a package. Inside, Rikki found a restraining order and a petition to file for divorce. On December 19, the day before her fourth anniversary, Rikki called me. Good news, she said. She and Matt planned to retreat to the cabin in hopes of reconciliation. She told me he had agreed only after she said she'd subject herself to inpatient psychiatric treatment, and that was only if he promised to hold off on divorce proceedings. I wished her luck, assured her that I loved her, and told her to call me once she returned to Los Angeles.

I tried to concentrate on me again. My agent suggested that I create fifteen more puzzles for her to submit to newspapers and magazines around the country. To facilitate this, she told me to buy new crossword puzzle software that would make this chore easier. I bought the program and installed it later that night. The software corrupted the hard drive on my already-ancient computer. Serendipity smiled on me—Eric called. I complained about my brain-dead 486. He offered to loan me his laptop.

"You wouldn't mind?" I asked.

"No. Of course not. I'll bring it over right now."

Right now? No problem.

I ran and hopped in the shower as soon as I hung up the phone. Afterward, I slathered on lotion, light perfume, a little eyeliner, lip gloss, then pulled a thin, white T-shirt over my head. You know, my usual bedtime attire.

Eric arrived twenty minutes later and immediately began to hook up his computer, then install the software. I watched him work from the doorway.

When he finished, he smiled and said, "What are *you* all gussied up for?"

I shrugged. "There's no gussying here."

He nodded. "Guess what I have in my bag?"

"What?"

"The anniversary edition of *Close Encounters*. Wanna watch it?"

"Now?"

"Yeah, unless I'm interrupting something."

"No. Well, work, but who cares."

He nodded. "Still seeing what's-his-face?"

Who? There wasn't a what's-his-face in the picture and hadn't been since I'd married Eric. What had he heard? And from whom? Maybe Rikki told Matt something . . . "Nope," I said. "Are you still seeing what's-her-face?"

"Nope."

"Well, there you go."

We studied each other for a moment. Then he smiled. I sighed. Then we . . . you know. That man gives great house calls.

But damn that phone. The answering machine clicked on.

"Stacy?" It was Arika. Her voice trembled. And since we were miles apart from each other, I thought it was natural for her voice to sound distorted. Maybe she was winded from hiking a few miles in the woods or Jet Skiing on the lake across the road. Or having great sex with her husband. I made several assumptions on the night Rikki called me from the cabin in Marin. But I never asked myself, "Why was she calling me when she should've been working on her marriage?"

"Stacy, don't," Eric said as I reached for the telephone.

"I won't talk long. Promise."

He rolled away from me and found his boxers discarded in the doorway. "Fuck this," he muttered.

I placed the receiver over my ear and said, "What's up?"

"Nothing. It's pretty cold up here."

"Uh-huh." I mouthed, "Don't go," to Eric.

He shook his head and threw up his hands. "I'm sick of this, Stace."

"Matt's gone," Rikki said.

"At least you tried." I wanted her off the line. I wanted Eric in my bed. I wanted to be touched and nibbled and stroked. I beckoned him over. He considered my command and beckoned me back. Something in my stomach pulled each time his finger moved. I stayed in bed.

"No," Rikki said, "you don't understand. Matt's *gone.* As in *disappeared.*"

"He'll be back. Probably took a walk to clear his head. He always does that when you piss him off."

Eric said, "Hang up."

I motioned, *One minute.*

"Who's there?" Rikki snapped.

"Eric. He says 'hey.' " Yeah, right. By this time, Eric couldn't stand Rikki.

"Don't you understand?" Rikki shouted over the phone. "My husband's not here! And I don't know where he went!"

"Cheese and bread, Arika, calm down, okay?"

Eric pulled on his jeans.

"When was the last time you saw him?" I asked.

"Two nights ago. On our anniversary. After dinner."

I heard a pill vial rattle, then land on the floor—a sound as dangerous as a rattlesnake's tail for my sister. "Okay, don't freak out. And take it easy on the pills."

"I don't know what to do."

"Why'd he leave?"

The front door of my apartment slammed. My man had just disappeared into the night, too, but you didn't see *me* freaking out.

"Hell, Stacy, I don't know."

"Okay, what happened *before* he disappeared?" I tucked my cold feet back under the goose-down comforter.

She inhaled, then slowly exhaled. "It's been so romantic up here. You know, we hadn't had a night like the night before he disappeared in a long time. We talked, took walks, held hands. He was so sweet.

"I cooked coq au vin and those baby potatoes that night. He loved my coq au vin. I made this Roquefort salad dressing from scratch, too. I even baked bread in that machine you gave me, you know, after you and Eric separated. And I opened that bottle of '74 merlot we got from Provence two years ago."

Rikki arranged the table in front of the living room's fireplace. Since it was the holidays, she created a centerpiece out of candles and white poinsettias. Matt showered after his three-mile jog on a nearby trail. She wore a champagne-colored peignoir with her hair in a tumble of long, loose curls. He chose blue UCLA sweatpants and a matching sweater.

"I feel overdressed," she said when she emerged from the bathroom. She tugged at her flimsy lingerie, which had been purchased at one of the finest boutiques in Beverly Hills.

Matthew grunted. "Everything smells good. Did you let the wine breathe?"

Rikki nodded.

They sat at the candlelit table as the fire roared and the Isley Brothers crooned. They clutched hands and blessed their meal. Matt asked God to repair their marriage. After they both said, "Amen," he squeezed her hands, she kissed his, and they ate.

"He enjoyed dinner," she said. "He even had seconds."

After dessert—crème brûlée—Rikki and Matt took the near-empty bottle of wine to their bedroom. They kissed and fondled until both fell out of their clothes. "Matt lay back on the bed," she said. "I got silk scarves from the dresser, then tied him to the bedposts. Not too tight, though. He never liked me to tie him too tight."

"Should you be telling me this?" I asked. And why would I want to hear about her sex life when mine had abruptly ended minutes ago?

"Believe me, he was in heaven," she purred.

Rikki and Matt had *lots* of sex that night, with and without scarves. They drank the rest of the wine, and their lovemaking turned rough and loud. "So much so that I thought the neighbors would come over and complain."

But we didn't have neighbors up in Marin; at least not in the traditional way. It was incredibly secluded. No peeping eyes and no other ears to hear.

Rikki slept heavily after their fourth round: too much wine, food, pills, and sex.

"A typhoon could've blown in from Malaysia and I would've stayed knocked out," she said. "When I *did* wake up, the room was dark and so cold. I was sore, and my skin felt damp and sticky. The fire in the bedroom fireplace had died, so I turned toward Matt to get warm. But he wasn't there. His spot in the bed was cold. Like a corpse had lain there. I called him, but he didn't answer."

Rikki rose from the bed and pulled on her peignoir. She called Matt again. She checked each room in the cabin. The bitter chill forced her to turn on the central heat. She sat at the breakfast table and waited for him to return. Then she stood at the bay window in the living room. She clearly saw the trail that led into the woods. She waited until six that next evening to panic.

"But he never came home," she said. "He's gone."

I knew that she hadn't told me everything. I heard it in her voice.

16

THE HUNT BEGINS

ACCORDING TO police transcripts, the police department's automatic service directed Rikki to the operator when she first called to report Matt missing on December 22. A woman on the other end of the line said, "Marin Police. How may I direct your call?"

RIKKI: Yes, my husband's missing.
OPERATOR: Would you like to file a missing person's report?
RIKKI: Yes. I guess I would.
OPERATOR: Is your husband over eighteen?
RIKKI: Yes.
OPERATOR: Does he suffer from Alzheimer's or any other mental incapacities?
RIKKI: No, but he's been gone for two days.

Operator: Are you sure he's missing? He didn't just
    leave?
Rikki: He's *missing*. I don't see what difference that
    makes.

The operator told Rikki that thousands and thousands of
people around the country are reported missing to the police.
Some are children, some are adults, some turn up alive, and
others turn up dead. Some adults don't want to be found,
which means that they weren't actually victims.

Rikki: Yes, I understand that. So my chances for get-
    ting cops involved are . . . ?
Operator: Well, it's our duty to immediately assist
    any person who's reporting a missing person. But
    you should also think of hiring your own private
    investigator. May I have your address and phone
    number, please?

The operator told her that officers would be out some-
time that week to complete an official report. "Marin's a
small town," the operator said. "We care. Oh. You should
probably check with the morgue or the hospital. Sounds
awful but . . ."

Rikki called me on Christmas Eve afternoon. She
sounded drunk and I told her so. She said not to worry, that
she had popped Depakote, then Eskalith just in case the valproic acid didn't work. She had taken a shower to make the
dizziness go away. It hadn't, so she had finished a bottle of red
wine. "I'm much better now."

I closed my eyes and rubbed my temples. "Do you need

me to come up there?" Had she just overdosed? Was I taking this all too lightly? Should I call an ambulance? *Cheese and bread.*

"No," she said. "Not yet. I just filed a missing person's report. It's just a matter of time now."

Rikki told me that once she hung up the phone with the operator, she took a deep breath. She headed straight to the bathroom and stepped into the shower for the second time that day. After twenty minutes under the water, she stepped out, toweled off, and then marched naked outside to the Volvo. She found her fabric-covered journal on the seat next to her Bible. "You should've seen me," she said, laughing. "Buck naked in a Volvo. But I got cold and went back in." She found a marker in the desk drawer.

She flipped through the Old Testament's delicate, worn pages and searched for texts that she hadn't marked. I'm sure by that time, every passage except lineage and health laws screamed in yellow, orange, green, and purple. She fumbled to the New Testament and pored over the Gospels. "I tried to find any new words spoken by Christ. Or by Paul. Or John. But I couldn't find anything," she said.

Frustrated, she dropped to her knees and tore sheet after sheet from her twelve-year-old Bible. The pages floated until they covered her thighs like ashes from a volcano. She reached for a book of matches and lit one. She blew out the flame and threw the matches behind the credenza.

Rikki ran to her bedroom and threw open the closet door. She found her pill case on the top shelf. She dumped three pills into her palm and swallowed them dry. She pulled on a pair of gray sweatpants and a T-shirt with the word *Princess* across the middle. Then she returned to the living room. "I just wanted a promise that everything would be fine. That *I* would be fine, you know?" She needed a promise that she hadn't read or heard or considered or memorized. But the Bible lay dry, spent, and torn: it couldn't help her now.

She pushed her journal to the floor into the heap. "I walked back and forth until I realized that I had to tell Matt's mother *something*. It was Christmas Eve and she'd expect to get a call from him." She finally snatched the phone from the cradle and dialed. "Mother Dresden," Rikki said. "How are you?"

Zenobia said fine, then asked her what she wanted.

"Well," Rikki said. "Ummm . . . I'm not sure if . . . well . . . Matt's . . . he's been . . . I haven't seen . . . have you seen him lately?"

"What?" Zenobia shrieked. "No, I haven't seen him! What are you—"

"He came up to the cabin with me, here in Marin, but he left. I haven't . . . it's been a few days."

Zenobia wailed into the receiver. "What have you—" Her boyfriend, Louis, grabbed the phone from her hands. Rikki heard Zenobia tell him that Matt was missing. Louis told Rikki that they were on their way up.

Later that night, I sat at my mother's breakfast table snapping green beans in two for Christmas dinner. I had planned to tell Mommy that I had lost ten pounds that week. That I had sold four puzzles to the *New York Times*. And that Eric and I were talking again. Life always seemed to shape up when Rikki was more than seventy-five miles away from me. But the phone rang. Mommy picked it up. Her expression told me that it was my sister.

I froze when Mommy clutched her heart and whispered,

"Oh, sweet Jesus." Her skin paled to an ashy cinnamon. "Oh, sweet Jesus." She leaned against the counter for support. I stared at the scar on her chin, the one she got after fainting the morning Rikki slit her wrists.

"What's going on?" I whispered. "Mommy?"

"We'll be right there. Don't worry. We're on our way." Mommy hung up. "Matt's disappeared." She wouldn't look at me.

"What? When?" I wondered if I sounded surprised.

"We gotta go up there. His mother's on her way." Mommy wandered down the hallway, touching the walls to ensure that she wouldn't fall. She disappeared into her bedroom.

I called Rikki once Mommy was out of sight. Rikki picked up on the first ring. "Did you call the police again?" I asked.

"They don't care."

"Did you try calling Matt down here? Maybe he came back home. I can drive by and see—"

"No. He's not there," she slurred. "Remember, you don't know anything. We ain't talked about *any* of this, 'kay?"

"Yeah. But I don't see why that's important." I looked behind me to see if I was still alone. "Are you okay? You sound a little . . . Where's the dog?"

"His maid has him. Man, Zenobia freaked out. You should've heard that old bat." A note of glee sounded in Rikki's voice.

"Can you blame her? Her only child is missing in the woods somewhere. Aren't you supposed to be freaking out, too?"

"Whose side are you on?"

I took a deep breath. "Your side."

"Good. Now hurry up. I'll need someone to protect me from the hunters." She laughed—the Witchie-Poo/Scarlett O'Hara Cackle—then hung up.

Around two that Christmas morning, Mommy and I loaded the trunk of my Ford Taurus with enough luggage for a year. Mrs. Drake from next door agreed to stay at Mommy's, in case Matt called. We hopped in the car: eight hours *alone,* with my mother. It would be dark as we drove, so the scenery wouldn't distract her. She couldn't read her *Woman's Day* magazine, either. What had I done to deserve this?

Mommy started in as soon as I put the key in the ignition.

"Why did you let her go up there alone?"

"Why didn't you force her to stay down here for the holidays?"

"Have she and Matt been arguing lately?"

"What did Zenobia say when Rikki called her?"

"Did you know any of this was going on?"

"Where do you think Matt is?"

I shrugged away most of these questions. I wanted to be flippant and say, "I'm not paid to be Rikki's shadow nor am I Dionne Warwick and have friends who can predict the future." That would only make Mommy talk more. Shrugs only blocked her efforts.

We stopped at Denny's to eat. Mommy continued to barrage me over her pot roast and Dr Pepper with questions I couldn't possibly answer:

"Are they divorcing?"

"What did she tell you?"

"Was Matt sleeping with that nurse?"

"What are you keeping from me?"

"Is she still seeing that therapist?"

And if I *did* know, I would *never* tell her.

When I had to fill my tank at the gas station, she asked through the passenger-side window:

"Have you told anybody yet?"

"What do you think I should tell the pastor?"

"Can you come up with something good but believable?"

"Don't say anything until you tell me what you're going to say, okay?"

This last one was actually an order, not a request. My mother rarely *asks* me to do anything, even though she liberally sprinkles question marks on the end of her sentences.

As we got back on the freeway, I had a decision to make. Do I take a chance and drive eighty miles per hour on a highway that's radar-enforced by overzealous cops in Ford Mustangs in order to end this trip? Or do I abide by the law and slop up the state as my mother yaks herself hoarse? As we continued our drive up Highway 5, fortune smiled on me. Mommy fell asleep three hours into the drive. I didn't play music or a book on tape, in fear that she'd wake up.

On the afternoon of December 24, up in Marin, two cops, Arrigiano and Flowers, had arrived to assist Rikki as she completed a missing person's report. They politely refused Rikki's Christmas cookies and eggnog. Rikki thanked them for coming out, especially since it was Christmas Eve. They saw how she bumped into tables and tripped over her feet as she led them to the living room. She polished off two glasses of eggnog before they sat on the couch. Then they noticed Rikki's shaking hands as she filled in the report. They watched her pause at the section that authorized the release of dental and skeletal X rays.

They took notes as they asked Rikki routine questions:

FLOWERS: How long has your husband been missing?

RIKKI: Since Thursday night.

FLOWERS: That's ninety-six hours.

RIKKI: Yes. That's right.

FLOWERS: Why did you wait that long to file a report?

RIKKI: I watch a lot of TV. And the cops on TV always
    tell the loved ones that they have to wait at least
    two days before they can declare someone missing.
    It's procedure, right? And, at first, I didn't think he
    was missing.

ARRIGIANO: You thought he would come back?

RIKKI: Yes. Of course.

ARRIGIANO: Is that your car out there?

RIKKI: The Volvo?

ARRIGIANO: Yes.

RIKKI: It's a lease.

ARRIGIANO: Did he drive up from Los Angeles?

RIKKI: No. He flew in from the airport. Caught a cab
    here.

FLOWERS: Any other vehicles?

RIKKI: We have one of those three-wheel, all-terrain
    things.

FLOWERS: Is that out there?

RIKKI: It should be.

ARRIGIANO: I didn't see it.

RIKKI: I'm not aware if it's missing or not.

ARRIGIANO: Could your husband have taken it when
    he left?

RIKKI: Possibly. I don't know.

FLOWERS: They're pretty loud.

RIKKI: Yes.

FLOWERS: You would've heard him driving it.

RIKKI: Then I guess he didn't take it.

ARRIGIANO: Why didn't he drive up with you?

RIKKI: He couldn't leave until later in the day. He's a doctor, you know. He has patients.

FLOWERS: You didn't want to wait?

RIKKI: I needed to get out of Los Angeles. It was driving me crazy. You've been there, haven't you?

"Mrs. Dresden, we can't make any promises to find your husband," said Officer Flowers, a lean man with a face covered in pockmarks. "Over four thousand people disappeared under unknown circumstances this year in California. We suggest that you put out a couple of flyers, keep a log, and document everything that you do. Meanwhile, we'll submit your husband's name to the FBI's National Crime Information Center and the attorney general's office in Sacramento, just in case."

"People get lost up here all the time," Officer Arrigiano said. "Especially people from Southern California."

"Don't worry, ma'am," Officer Flowers said. "Your husband's probably on his way to the Pacific Ocean. But we'll find him."

On their way out, the officers took a cursory look around the cabin. Officer Flowers noticed the brilliant sheen on the hardwood floor in the dining room. The officers noticed several towels piled high on the washing machine in the utility room. Officer Flowers made a mental note and would bring it up to his partner later. Officer Arrigiano smelled something sharp and rank in the area. He would bring that up to his partner later. They didn't look in the bedroom or the bathroom. Rikki walked them to their squad car.

"It'll work out," Officer Flowers said again.

"From your mouth to God's ear," she said. "Thank you, officers. You try and have a happy holiday, okay?"

Rikki waited until the car disappeared down the road. She went back into the cabin and took another shower.

17

SO MANY QUESTIONS

MOMMY AND I parked next to Rikki's Volvo on the steep driveway that disappeared behind the house. I prayed that life had resolved itself during our trip north. That right then, Matt was sitting on the bed, unshaven and exhausted, with a blanket draped over his shoulders. He would be holding a hot mug of tea as he told his wife and mother about his harrowing days lost in the forest. Rikki would be buzzing between her husband and the kitchen, preparing a celebration feast. Zenobia would be there, second-guessing the blanket, the beverage, and the menu. Life would be swell again.

The cabin was cedar and A-framed, tucked in a patch of redwoods that protected it against the sun's bossy glare. Its bay windows were divided into eight panes that glistened from the recent rain. Inside, there were four tiny bedrooms that had originally been two, and a huge stone fireplace that was rarely lit. Sunbeams broke in through random skylights. A redwood deck surrounded the front and the sides of the house. An old-fashioned swing creaked near the front door. Across the gravel road were the forest-green waters of the tiny lake. Live oak trees guarded it from strangers.

I saw my first shooting star on that porch. My first firefly and deer, too. I lost a tooth here; the tooth fairy found me anyway and left a dollar. It was magical in the woods, at the cabin. I hated when vacation ended and we had to return to our boring house in the city with its regular old flies, smog-filled night skies, and the occasional backyard possum. That was so long ago.

Mommy and I plodded into the house. I entered Rikki's bedroom, which held the sweetish odor of vomit, the sharpness of chlorine bleach, and the artificial aroma of lilac air freshener. I remembered that smell from the days when I lived with my sister at Cal.

The sight of Rikki shocked and frightened me. She sat up in her bed when she saw me. Her face was bloodless and covered mostly in shadows. Her eyes were sunken and hollow. Her lips were swollen and outlined with white grit. Her hands sat on top of the blanket. Her finger joints were swollen. Her palms, too. The room sweltered even though it rained off and on that day. The dry air attacked my joints, too. It looked as though my sister was severely dehydrated, in addition to something else.

"She's having fainting spells," Zenobia said once Mommy and I entered. The old woman who hated my sister now spoon-fed her hot grits. She pressed a cold hand towel against Rikki's forehead and gently nudged her back to the pillows.

I opened a window and pulled back the curtain. I took my bottle of water from my pack and placed it on Rikki's dinner tray.

"I'm so glad you could make it," Rikki said from bed. "Merry Christmas." Despite her appearance, her voice was strong and her tone intentionally saccharine. She held out her hands for me to take.

I took her hands and sat next to her. "You need to drink some water, Rikki." I opened the water and held it out for her. She pushed the bottle away.

"Poor Arika," Zenobia said. "She was a total mess when we got here. All pale and hungry. She's such a trouper."

Huh? Wait. What have you done to Zenobia Dresden, you space alien?

I smoothed back Rikki's tangled hair. Her skin didn't feel clammy. Her grasp was not weak. The hope chest at the foot of the bed drowned beneath several bath towels that had been folded and stacked neatly into twin towers.

I took the compress from her forehead to rewet it. "Any word from the police?" I asked from the bathroom. No one responded. As I ran the hand towel under the water, my eyes skated around my surroundings. Matt wasn't in the bathroom: No whiskers from a recent shave were in the sink. No underwear had been tossed to the floor. The toilet seat was clean and dry. No second toothbrush, no aftershave . . . no Matt. I ran the towel under the water once more, then twisted it until the water dripped into the drain.

I returned to the bedroom, wondering what would happen if I mentioned my observation. "Any word from the police?" I asked again.

Rikki said, "They just had me fill out some stupid report!"

She turned her head away. Zenobia plucked the towel from my hand. Mommy, racing Zenobia, pushed me, and beat the widow to Rikki's side.

"I have it under control now," Mommy told Zenobia, snatching the wet cloth from her hand.

Zenobia snatched it back and said, "No, Olivia. You just got here. I'm sure it was a long drive. You need your rest."

"Stacy drove," Mommy said. "And Arika needs her family now."

"Well, I *am* her mother-in-law," Zenobia sniffed.

"And?" Mommy said with a hand on her hip. "You've never considered her family before. As a matter of fact, this is the first time that you've treated her with a little dignity."

Louis left the room. He hadn't said anything since Mommy and I arrived. The old women continued to cluck about Rikki's proper care. I watched my sister's reaction. A small smile stayed at the corners of her mouth. Two women, one who treated her like a porcelain doll, and one who treated her like a promiscuous leper, were haggling over who could care for her better.

Like the bathroom, something was off in the bedroom, too. I couldn't say what. The room was just . . . wrong. I felt as if I stood on a set for a play: too sterile and deliberate for real life. And those towels. Rikki caught me staring, so I shifted my eyes to the feud. Had they forgotten why we were up here? This wasn't about cold compresses and grits.

"Well, are we going to hire a private investigator?" I asked.

"I don't know *what* to do," Zenobia said. She reached to place a fifth pillow behind Rikki's back. A fine spray of dried, reddish brown fluid was on the pillowcase. We all froze. Zenobia's face crumpled. A choked gasp escaped from her throat. She dropped the pillow and staggered away from my sister. Then she screamed.

Louis rushed in from the living room with a cheese sandwich in his hand. His face was ashen and heavy with exhaustion. "What's going on now?"

"It's blood!" Zenobia shouted. "There's blood on the pillow!" She picked up the pillow to show him. "She's done something to my baby!"

"What?" Mommy said. "You're crazy!"

"I can't believe you're accusing me of hurting my husband!" Rikki shouted.

"Everyone just calm down," I said.

Louis studied the pillow. "This could be anything. Hot chocolate or something."

"It *is* hot chocolate," Rikki snapped. "It's cold up here!"

"Are you calling me a liar?" Zenobia asked her. "Are you saying that I don't know hot chocolate from my son's blood?"

"Zenobia, you need your rest," Louis said. "Where are your blood pressure pills?"

"I *know* she had something to do with it!" Zenobia shouted. "She's never liked me, and she didn't love Matt. She's a lunatic who had somebody kill him!"

"Get her out of my house!" Mommy shouted.

"You *killed* him!" Zenobia shouted even louder.

I wanted to laugh; not because of her ridiculous accusation, but because of the way she pointed at Rikki. Just like a character on a *Perry Mason* episode.

Zenobia then rushed to the dresser and rifled through the drawers. Then she threw open the closet door. She slammed hangers from one side to the other.

"What in the hell are you looking for?" Mommy asked.

I glanced at Rikki, who sat up in bed wide-eyed. The compress fell to her lap. Both of us knew what Zenobia wanted to see.

"Where are his things?" Zenobia demanded. "Where are my son's clothes?" She stormed toward Rikki. "Answer me, before I beat it out of you!"

Rikki cried out. Zenobia closed her eyes and covered her ears. Rikki kept screaming as Louis grabbed Zenobia and pulled her toward the door. "Come on, darling," he said. "Some cops are outside, wanting to talk to us. Let Rikki get her rest."

"Are you sorry he's gone?" Zenobia shouted with her fists clenched.

Rikki continued to scream even after the bedroom door slammed. "She's gone, Rikki," I shouted. I repeated myself three more times. Mommy wouldn't go near Rikki until she finally settled down. As we moved closer, Rikki sighed and turned toward the window. She pulled the covers over her head and shouted, "Leave me alone!"

"Rikki, honey," Mommy said.

"Leave me alone!"

Mommy and I obeyed. We left the bedroom and joined Louis and Zenobia in the living room.

"Your son's Matthew Dresden?" Officer Flowers asked Zenobia.

"Yes. Do they have to be here?" Zenobia shot a look over to Mommy and me.

The cops ignored her question. "Did you want to add anything to the missing person's report Arika completed?" Officer Arrigiano asked.

"He's not *missing!*" Zenobia shouted.

He asked her if she knew of any criminal intent toward Matthew, a notion that was not rooted in the hatred of her daughter-in-law.

"But she killed him!" Zenobia shouted. "Or had him killed! My son was well-off. He has a life insurance policy worth five million dollars. He has a trust that will mature on his thirty-seventh birthday. That's worth four hundred thirty-seven thousand dollars! We own property and stock!"

At that point, Louis grabbed his girlfriend's shoulders. "She really needs her rest," he explained.

"Of course," Officer Flowers said.

Officer Arrigiano shouted after them that a few off-duty cops would be out to help organize a search, that it was the least the city could do. Louis told them that they were staying at the Intercontinental in San Francisco. Even with a missing son, Zenobia still needed a fluffy white robe and mints on her pillow. Officer Arrigiano watched the pair march to their car.

"Can you believe that woman?" my mother said back in the hallway outside of Rikki's bedroom. She began to pace. "What a bitch! Rikki broke her neck trying to please people every day of her life, including Matt. Including *her.* And now Zenobia thinks she's some ax murderer!"

"Mommy, calm down," I said. "You know Zenobia will never—"

"Rikki's never hurt anything around her." Mommy paused and rubbed her temples. "That's not true. I take that back. She accidentally killed Hopper, but that's all."

"How? Daddy wouldn't say."

"She was just a baby when we got that rabbit. She'd pick

him up by his ears and drop him. Pick him up, drop him. He died, but it was our fault for getting a four-year-old a damn rabbit for Easter. And she cried twice a day for a month after Hopper died. Oh, it was awful." Mommy shook her head as she remembered. "A woman who gets herself that worked up over a rabbit can't kill her husband. That just doesn't make sense."

Then Mommy nodded. She had convinced herself that Rikki was harmless. Good job. "I'm going to my room to take a nap. Watch over your sister."

"As always."

After Mommy disappeared into her room, I opened the door to Rikki's. "Rikki?" I sat on the bed beside her and pulled away the comforter. The breeze from the window had chilled the air. The smell still lingered.

Rikki turned to me. Her eyes glistened, not from tears, but from drugs. She took my hand, kissed it, and smiled. "And how are you, little sister? Haven't seen you in a while."

"I'm doing okay. Considering . . ."

"How was the drive up?"

"Okay."

"How's the diet?"

"Okay."

"How is Eric?" she asked.

"Fine."

"And the crossword biz?"

I shrugged.

We sat there in silence.

"What, Stacy? It's obvious you have something to say. Just spit it out. Damn."

I walked to the window and looked out at the encroaching wall of swaying greens and browns. Some of the trees had been stripped—it was winter, after all. The branches from the bare big-leaf maple lightly scraped against the window. No birds chirped. No chipmunks frolicked. The bats and owls would feed once the sun set. Early fog ascended from the ground like heat. The forest looked haunted. The whiteness reminded me of John Carpenter's movie *The Thing*. Who knew what was out there? Who knew what was in here?

"Want me to confess? To plead to God for mercy? To throw myself at Zenobia's feet and beg for forgiveness? They'll find Matt. I know they will." Rikki pulled the comforter to her chin and turned away from me. "You know, it's so lonely here without him. It's darker. Colder.

"I got lost in the woods the other day. I didn't go farther than a stone's throw, really. As I walked, my legs moved like they were made of lead because of all the leaves and dirt. And I couldn't see the sun. Just redwoods. The fog. It was so cold." She sighed and looked at me.

"I didn't find him out there, Stacy. And when I realized that, I stopped walking. No use in going further. And when I looked around, nothing looked familiar. And I couldn't breathe. I got so scared I just started running. I found my way back. And I cried as soon as I saw the front porch. I was so glad to be back. I fell to my knees and just cried and cried. I thought I wanted to be with Matt, wherever he was out there. But when I came inside, where it was warm, I realized that I didn't want to be out there. That I was a liar. I took it back. I take it all back." She yawned, then closed her eyes. I watched her until she fell asleep.

Zenobia's accusations were wild, but then again, where *were* Matt's things? I tiptoed around the room and opened the closet. Not many of Rikki's or Matt's clothes hung from hangers. No men's clothes were stuffed in drawers. If you weren't paying close attention, you'd never notice that no one—especially two people—had enough clothing to wear for a week.

Twenty minutes had passed since Rikki fell asleep. Someone knocked on the bedroom door. I opened it. Dr. Nesbitt stood there. Sweat glistened on his face. He breathed as though he had run all the way from Los Angeles. He held his doctor's bag.

The shock on my face must have been obvious.

"Stacy." His whiskey-wet voice made my stomach flutter. "The front door was unlocked. So I just came—"

"Dr. Nesbitt. What are you doing here?"

He peeked around me to see Rikki in bed. "Is she okay?"

"She's asleep." I stepped in front of him to block his view.

"No, I'm awake." Rikki sat up in bed and held out both hands for Dr. Nesbitt. "Oh, Christopher. Come in. Please."

Christopher?

Dr. Nesbitt stepped around me and found Rikki's grasp. "Are you okay?" He pulled out his stethoscope and checked her pulse.

My throat burned. The blood in my veins curdled. My head almost shot off as I watched him sit next to her on the bed. I wanted to bite him, to clamp my jaw around his neck, then thrash him about until he no longer moved.

"How are you feeling?" he asked, touching her forehead.

"She was resting," I said, and shut the door a bit too hard. I stood over them. Grrr.

"I'm doing better." Rikki batted her eyelashes. "Now that *you're* here."

"Well, do you do this for all of your patients?" I asked. "I

mean, it's a hell of a house call. Three hundred and something miles away."

"Well, Rikki . . . ," he said, glancing at my sister. "Look . . ."

"I don't mean to be nosy," I said. "But it's just—"

"I called him, Stacy, to be with me. For support," Rikki
said. "And he rushed right up. Isn't he sweet?"

"Yeah. What a doctor," I said. "Who told you how to . . .
Did you know the way to get up here? I even get turned
around a bit and I partly own the place."

Dr. Nesbitt shrugged. "I've got Cherokee in me." Both he
and Rikki giggled. "And I have a *Thomas Guide.* Any word
about Matthew?"

Rikki shook her head and frowned. "I'm just hoping to at
least *know.* For closure."

"It's a bit early to talk about closure, don't you think?" Dr.
Nesbitt was right. Matt had only been missing since Thursday night. "Everything will work out," he said. "You have to
believe that. And don't do anything rash, okay? Promise me."

"Anything for you."

"Arika, you really should get more rest," I said. I reached
around Dr. Nesbitt and started to tuck the comforter beneath
her legs. He had to move aside.

"She takes care of me," Rikki explained to him. "Good ol'
Stacy."

Dr. Nesbitt nodded. "You're lucky to have her."

Good ol' Stacy *indeed.*

"Chris," she said. "My back hurts. Got anything in that
magic black bag of yours?"

"Why does your back hurt?" I asked.

"I really don't think you should take anything else," he
said, examining her eyes with a penlight.

She jerked away. "A fucking Tylenol's all I want," she snapped.

I rushed to the closet to find Rikki's pill case. She was probably the only person in the world who kept her medicine in the closet. I found it and froze. Close to ten empty vials were in her bag: lithium. All prescribed by Dr. Nesbitt. The label on the oldest vial went back to September. Only one vial—Depakote—remained partially full.

Dr. Nesbitt shouted, "Stacy, do you mind leaving? I should thoroughly examine her."

I jumped and shoved the case to the back of the closet. I closed the door, my heart pounding, my mind racing. I turned to consider the doctor and my sister on the bed. Again, I realized that something wasn't right with this scene: Dr. Nesbitt and Rikki's relationship, his presence here, and the way she called him by his first name. And I'm her *sister*. Why did he want me to leave? Why did her back hurt? Why did she call him? Why were those pill vials empty? Where were the pills from those vials now? What *had* she been doing those two days before she called me? What was she doing those days before she talked to the police? And where in the hell were Matt's clothes?

18

Just the Facts, Ma'am

SOUTHWEST Airlines told Officer Arrigiano that Matthew Dresden had bought a round-trip ticket from Los Angeles to San Francisco for December 20. Matthew hadn't made a reservation—he just showed up at the counter. He didn't check in luggage. He didn't use his return ticket, scheduled for the next day, back to Los Angeles. He hadn't made another reservation with them, either. No other airline confirmed that Matthew Dresden was a recent passenger.

The weather cooperated with us the morning of our first search, even though the cloud deck dropped lower and became fuller as each minute passed. It would rain, but not now. For this, we were grateful. Who wanted to search for the body of a loved one, dead or alive, when the sky was gray and the forest floors soggy? On the other hand, it would seem inappropriate if brilliant sunlight in a cloudless sky shone down on us as we beat back bushes in search of a body.

There were nine of us, including Mommy, Zenobia, Louis, and me. As promised, a few police officers had volunteered to help us look. Kinko's donated two hundred flyers and a staple gun. Matt's description was included on the goldenrod-colored sheets. It said that his wife had last seen him the night of December 20. That he was a Los Angeles–area pediatrician. That a $25,000 reward was being offered for information leading to his safe return. Rikki had selected a picture of Matt that she kept in her wallet. It was one of those silly $5 photo-booth pictures, where you made faces for the camera.

"Didn't you have a better picture of your husband?" Zenobia asked. "He looks like a fool."

"Didn't you?" Rikki snapped back. "He was your only child. And if I knew beforehand that he would disappear on me, I would've had him sit for Ansel fucking Adams, okay?"

"Folks, let's just calm down," Officer Flowers said.

Zenobia, smarting from Rikki's remark, tugged her red sun hat over her head. She zipped up her scarlet-and-orange jogging suit and tucked her crimson-and-white lace-edged handkerchief in her pocket. She selected a long, thick branch from the ground. I thought she was going to beat my sister with it; instead, she used it as a cane for the long walk in the woods.

My mother, just as tacky in her shiny purple jogging suit, found a similar walking branch lying nearby. She wore purple-and-white Reeboks with matching purple socks and a baseball cap. Her T-shirt said, "WWJD: What Would Jesus Do?"—she thought that was pretty clever. The bill of her cap was studded in rhinestones. My mother: always the belle of the ball.

I carried insect repellent in my knapsack, as well as protein bars and water. What would Jesus do today, out here in the woods? I know He wouldn't need a stinking walking stick.

Our group circled Officer Flowers once he spread out a map of the search area on his Chevrolet's hood. I glanced at Rikki, who stood back with Dr. Nesbitt. She didn't seem very interested in the search perimeter or what we could find during our time out. She just stared at her feet and threw wary glances at the woods.

Officer Flowers finished the briefing, folded his map, and started toward the mouth of the dark green and gold forest. We followed him and the other officers into the scrub and towering redwoods. Dr. Nesbitt started to move with us, but Rikki grabbed his arm.

"Rikki, aren't you coming?" I asked, walking backward.

"I can't." She rubbed her arms and winced as she considered the tall trees a hundred yards away from where she stood. "The woods scare me. Chris, please. Stay with me."

Dr. Nesbitt nodded. "Whatever makes you feel safe." Then he placed a protective arm around her shoulders. He had stayed at a motel off the highway the night before, even though Rikki had insisted that he stay with us.

"Oh, God!" she shouted. "What if they find him? What if he's dead?" She grabbed the doctor around his neck and sobbed into his chest.

"She'll be fine," he assured me. "Don't worry."

"I know she's in good hands," I said, and turned away. I entered the forest alone. Despite what I thought, I wanted to believe that Dr. Nesbitt didn't love my sister like *that*. But why was he up here? Moral support? Bah . . . maybe. Rikki tells me everything. Wouldn't she have bragged by now that she had nailed her sexy doctor?

I looked back at the house one more time, but they no longer stood on the porch.

Our party walked on and across those trails for three hours. The insect repellent failed, and as I searched in the bushes, bugs snacked on every part of my body. We spanned across the forest, side by side. We called Matt's name. Zenobia called the loudest. "Matt, darling!" she cried. "If you're out there, say something! Anything! It's Mother!"

"Maybe we should've prayed before we started searching," Mommy said.

Zenobia stopped walking. "Please, Olivia . . ." She grabbed my hand and Mommy's hand. Louis joined our small circle. The cops just watched and waited. We bowed our heads.

Mommy began without her usual theatrics. "Dear Lord, we know You are aware of this situation, so please, sweet Jesus, guide our footsteps. Be with Matthew, wherever he may be. Bless the officers that look for him. Bless his mother, Lord, who wants to see him again. Be with Arika. Give her strength and patience. In the end, your will is done, so we rejoice right now because You have answered our prayers. In Your name, we pray, amen."

We all said, "Amen."

Zenobia hugged my mother. "Thank you, Olivia," she said. Then she cried for another three minutes with her arms wrapped tightly around Mommy's neck.

The sun pushed the clouds lower. The wind struck our

faces. The air turned angry and frigid. More clouds in the distance rushed toward us. We needed to return to the cabin, but we kept on. We followed a horse trail northward. The path stopped and started, uncertain if it wanted to lose us or lead us. We weaved our way through forest and ferns. We didn't hurry or stop moving, even when patches of wildflowers or mushrooms made us catch our breath and wonder at their beauty. As we trekked deeper into the woods, the moss-covered trees leaned toward each other, sometimes blocking out the thin light. It was as if they were conspiring to, literally, keep us in the dark.

We left the redwoods and entered a Douglas fir forest. The fragrance reminded me of the Christmas that I didn't have that year. Darkness slipped over us again, like gauze that blocked light from the eyes. It was beautiful here. And scary and wild and miraculous.

It was God's will for us not to find Matthew that day. We walked back dusty, sad, and unable to figure out why He had made this difficult situation more unbearable. No one spoke— not even the cops. We all knew what it meant if we couldn't find Matt. Even if he had committed suicide, he couldn't have buried himself, right?

On our way back to the cabin, we passed the lake. A small boat glided across the water. Two uniformed officers drove the vessel toward the shore.

"What are they doing out there?" Louis asked. "Dragging the lake?"

Zenobia screamed, "Oh, sweet Jesus! Did he drown?" She fell to the ground in sobs. Louis threw his arms around her and rocked her until her cries softened.

Alarmed, Officer Arrigiano looked out to the water. "Oh,

gosh, no! We just bought that boat a few days ago. It's like a department Christmas present. They're training!"

I knew Matt's body wasn't in the lake, anyway. I didn't think that this would comfort Zenobia any if I said it aloud. It was just a hunch.

The small search party made its way into the cabin. I tarried behind. I wandered over to Rikki's Volvo. Dust covered the windows. Unlucky bugs stuck to the grille. A few of these insects looked really fresh, as though their fate with a Swedish import had just occurred. I peeked into the car. I didn't know what I wanted to see. And I couldn't see it. I squeezed the door handle. It was unlocked. I opened the door. A map, the kind you get at a gas station, sat on the front seat. It was folded the wrong way, perhaps in haste. A wheelchair was in the back. It was collapsible—easy enough to store in a Volvo station wagon's fold-down seats. The backseat's fabric looked darker in some places. I touched it. My fingertips came away moist. I sniffed. It was sour and acidic, just like the smell in the house.

A set of keys lay on the floor. The key ring had a metal fob with a snake wrapped around a staff. There was a Mercedes-Benz key, too. Without thinking, I scooped the keys from the floor and stuck them in my knapsack.

"Are you coming in?" Mommy asked from somewhere behind me. "Rikki cooked supper."

I jumped, hit the automatic door lock, and stepped away from the car. I tried to close the door without much ceremony. Mommy stood on the porch. "Is Dr. Nesbitt still here?" I asked. I stepped farther away from the car.

Mommy, with her head slightly tilted and her eyes narrowed, looked at me, and then at the Volvo. "No. He's gone.

I don't see why he came up, anyway. Intruding, that's all he was doing."

I sighed. "Mom, you didn't make him leave, did you?"

My mother frowned and crossed her arms. "Rikki needs her family, not some witch doctor."

"Don't worry, Stace. I didn't need him anymore." Rikki appeared next to Mommy. "And he *does* have other patients to care for."

I looked back at the lake. The officers had loaded the boat on a trailer hitched to their cruiser. On their trailer bed was a very wet, very damaged three-wheel ATV covered in algae, sludge, and a piece of white material. There wasn't a body. The water hadn't surrendered what it didn't own.

"How in the hell did *that* get in there?" I asked. I turned to the porch, but I was now alone.

Officers Flowers and Arrigiano had been invited to stay for dinner. Louis and Zenobia stayed, too. Just one big happy family. Over peach cobbler, the cops took advantage of this time to probe deeper into the mysterious disappearance of Matthew Dresden.

"We found an ATV in the lake," Officer Flowers said to Rikki. "Yours, maybe."

Rikki said, "Yes, I saw that."

"Have any idea how it got to the bottom of the lake?" Officer Flowers asked.

"Those things are quite heavy," she said. "I don't think they can stay afloat too long."

Officer Arrigiano nodded. "I think what Detective Flowers is asking . . . well . . . did it drive itself into the lake?"

"I didn't hear anything." Rikki clutched her neck. "Are you implying that my husband committed suicide?" She rose from her seat. "That he drove in and drowned himself to death?" she shouted.

Officer Arrigiano held out his hands. "Please calm down, Mrs. Dresden. Have a seat, just relax. We just find the circumstances of your husband's disappearance somewhat curious. That his ATV was found at the bottom of a lake. That you didn't hear him take it. You said he went for a walk, not a drive."

Mommy went and placed her arms around Rikki's shoulders. "They were *very* happy." Then Rikki hid her face in Mommy's neck and cried.

"Please don't cry, Mrs. Dresden," Officer Flowers said.

Mommy shouted, "Her husband was an honorable man! He saved lives! He was a pediatrician!"

Officer Flowers said, "No one is questioning his integrity."

"Why aren't you looking for him?" Mommy asked. "Why are you sitting here?"

"Will you calm down, Mother?" I asked.

"We don't search once the sun sets," Officer Flowers explained.

"Rikki insisted that we stay and eat," Officer Arrigiano added.

Rikki wiped tears from her eyes and said, "Can you excuse me? It's been a long day. I'm not feeling well." Then she and Mommy left the dining room.

"Did Dr. Dresden have a drug problem?" Officer Arrigiano asked Louis, Zenobia, and me. "Could he be involved—"

"Of course not!" Zenobia said. "Matt was an honorable man! He valued life. He was a doctor!"

"Was he schizophrenic?"

Zenobia sighed. "Matt saved lives. He'd never take his own! His *wife* has told you that, countless times."

Officer Flowers turned to me. "Did she and Matt argue before he disappeared?"

I faked a smile. "They were in love. Their marriage, like every marriage, had its rough patches. They came up to reconnect. That's all."

"No! They had separated," Zenobia said. "Matt wanted a divorce!"

The officers sighed. Emotions clearly dictated tonight's Q&A. So, I walked them to their car. Officer Arrigiano was a tall, beefy guy who looked as if he had played rugby in college. But his skin suggested that he never went outside—ever. "So what do you think of all this?" he asked me. "Do you think your brother-in-law is the type who'd just walk away and wouldn't tell another living soul where he is?"

"No. But I've only known him for ten years." As if *that* weren't long enough.

"Think he ran off with a girlfriend? Or a boyfriend?" Officer Arrigiano asked.

I shrugged my shoulders. "I don't believe he was seeing anyone else. Not anyone he'd want to leave town for."

"And your sister," Officer Flowers said.

"What about her?"

"Is she okay? I guess I mean to ask, Is she under a doctor's care?"

I folded my arms. "Yes, she is."

"That was her therapist who came up?" Officer Flowers asked.

"Yeah."

Officer Arrigiano grunted. "Manic depression?"

I turned to him. "How did you know?"

He smiled. "Before I put in for a transfer, I was a cop for the LAPD. Saw manic-depressed nut jobs all the time."

I smirked. "The cops or the criminals?"

His smile disappeared. "Both. And neither are good to be around when they haven't been medicated."

On the second morning's search, Rikki insisted that everyone have a full stomach before leaving the cabin. She decided that she would prepare oatmeal, pancakes, and turkey bacon. She wanted me to squeeze fresh orange juice, but we didn't have oranges. Regardless, she rummaged through the refrigerator in search of citrus. She had forgiven Flowers and Arrigiano.

"Did Matthew have any identifying marks?" Officer Arrigiano asked as he inhaled the aroma of bacon. "Tattoos? Scars? Anything like that?"

Rikki had given up on the juice and had started on the meal. "No," she said as she stirred the pancake batter.

"Yes!" Zenobia said. She glared at her daughter-in-law. "She *threw* a bowl at him—"

"It wasn't a bowl," Rikki said, beating the batter. The thump-thump of the spoon against the bowl sounded so . . . violent. "It was a wineglass."

"And it almost cut his head off!" Zenobia shouted.

"You're lying." Rikki dropped the spoon and crossed her arms. Pancake batter splattered across her face and the top of the counter. "It just cut his neck."

I smelled burnt bacon.

"He needed three or four stitches." Zenobia touched the back of her neck. "He has a scar there. On the back of his neck. It looks like a slice of watermelon." She glared at Rikki again. "What did you do to him this time?"

Rikki rolled her eyes, tossed the bowl of pancake batter in the sink, and sat on the couch with me. Zenobia stomped to the bathroom. We didn't have breakfast that day.

New Year's Day came and went without celebration. For another week, we searched the woods. Each search became shorter than the last. Broken bottles of beer, used condoms, and a State of Georgia license plate were the most interesting items we found. The police decided to drag the lake officially after the ATV was found, but discovered nothing under the water's surface. "Missing Person" flyers with Matt's picture were tacked all over the neighboring town and rustled uselessly in the wind.

Our church sent a fruit basket and a card to the cabin. "Thinking of You," it said. Pastor Phillips's secretary signed it on behalf of the congregation. They promised to keep their eyes open for Matthew just in case he returned to Los Angeles. When asked by cops, some of the townies here in Marin remembered the handsome doctor. A nice guy, they recalled with a sad shake of the head. No one had a clue where he'd gone or when they'd seen him last. Some also mentioned his pretty wife, who had recently come to town. She had visited the grocer and a medical supply store.

One afternoon, Officer Flowers held out a piece of material for Rikki to examine. "What's this? We saw it near the garbage can outside. In plain view."

"It's a scarf," Rikki said.

"Yours?" Officer Arrigiano asked.

"Yes."

"And this nightgown?" Officer Flowers held out a dirty, white piece of silk.

Rikki nodded. "Yes. Where did you get that?"

Officer Flowers said, "What are these stains? Right here and right here?"

Rikki shrugged. "I don't know."

"Is this blood, ma'am?" Officer Flowers asked.

Rikki shrugged again. "I don't know why it would be."

The cop sniffed the scarf. "It smells strange. And what's this other stain here? It doesn't look like blood, maybe—"

Rikki looked away. "My sinuses are clogged, so I can't really smell."

Officer Flowers grunted. "It smells like, well, vomit. That's what I think. I could be wrong."

Rikki frowned. "Yes. You could be wrong."

"We found this nightgown tangled around the ATV," Officer Arrigiano said.

"What? What was it doing there?"

Officer Flowers smiled. "You don't know?"

"No."

"Was Matt planning to stay up here long?" Officer Arrigiano asked.

"We don't see many of his personal belongings in the bedroom or the bathroom," Officer Flowers added. "And we found this." He held up a plastic bag. A Tag Heuer watch was inside. "We found it in some leaves on the shore of the lake."

I recognized that watch. Rikki had bought it for Matt on their third anniversary.

Rikki stood up and walked toward Mommy, who also stood. "Should I contact my lawyer?" Rikki asked. "I mean, this line of questioning has become ridiculous."

"Rikki, they just want—" I started to say.

She went on. "You continue to harass me, asking me how this got there, how that got there! Meanwhile, my husband is out in the wilderness somewhere, needing to be found, yet you continue to engage me in some Colombo/Agatha Christie–wanna-be interrogation. I ask again, Officers, am I a suspect? Should I speak with my attorney? If not, I ask that you please leave. I'm entertaining guests. I actually smell my pie burning."

And with that, she and Mommy rushed to the kitchen to rescue her pie.

19

THE LAST TIME

IT WAS inevitable. We concluded our "missing person" search for Matthew after two weeks of no solid leads. "There are close to eight hundred and fifty thousand people missing in the country," Officer Arrigiano pointed out.

And Matt was now one of them.

"We want to find him almost as much as you do," Officer Flowers said. "Who doesn't like happy endings? Some cases are never closed, which can be a bad and a good thing." He looked down and rubbed his neck. "But I gotta be honest. Any cop will tell you, if you ain't found him in two months, then . . ."

"So what happens now?" I asked. "Does the FBI get involved?"

Officer Arrigiano shook his head. "They only assist with providing data. But Matt's missing person's file will remain open until he's located. If he's still missing after thirty days from the date Rikki filed the report, then she's gotta take the release form to get the skeletal and dental X rays. We'll use that to compare against the Unidentified Persons File. For unidentified bodies."

Zenobia lost control and collapsed hearing that. She was forced to realize that Matt just wasn't *there*. That he was gone. That he went from being a "Matt" to being just a body. "But we'll keep looking," Louis said in an attempt to calm her down. "I promise you."

Officer Arrigiano gave us the business card of a Los Angeles–area private investigator. "He's good. Especially if you got a little money."

Zenobia could not be placated with promises and a private eye. She kept crying and pulling at her hair and clothes. She eventually had to be sedated by a paramedic. Loaded on Valium, she clutched her remaining flyers to her bosom as though they were the last connection to her son. Louis loaded her back into their car. He asked Mommy to ride with them in case Zenobia lost control again.

"Everything's gonna work out," Mommy said to Rikki and me. "We're all gonna be surprised when Matt turns up." She kissed me, then Rikki, then joined Zenobia and Louis in their car.

From the front porch of the cabin, Rikki and I watched our mother and Matt's family disappear down the road. "Are you coming back home?" I asked my sister.

"Not yet. I still have some things to do."

"Want me to stay with you? I will . . ."

"No. I'd like to have a little quiet."

"Why *was* the ATV in the lake?" I asked.

She shrugged.

"Why was your gown wrapped around it?"

She shrugged again.

"Are you sleeping with Dr. Nesbitt?"

She sighed. "Stacy, you ask so many questions."

"Because there are many questions to ask."

"What do you think? You'd sleep with him, wouldn't you?"

"Rikki . . ."

"Christopher Nesbitt is a lying, double-dealing son of a bitch. He's not as smart as Matt thought he was. He's just another *man* who has ruined my life."

Her hair was bunched around her head in coarse tangles. The smell that wafted in the breeze suggested that she hadn't showered in days. Her eyes stuck in her head like dull pieces of coal. I could not see my reflection there. I couldn't see her there, either.

My eyes stung with tears. "Arika, please. What happened? Please tell me."

She shrugged and offered a weak smile. "You should go now, Anastasia."

"Please."

"Go. For once in your life, listen to me. Do as I say."

Tears slowly slid down my cheeks. I nodded, then threw my arms around her. No matter what, she was still my big sister. "I love you," I said. "You know that, right?"

"Of course I know that. Only love puts up with someone like me after all this time." She smiled. "But I'm determined not to live my life in chains. You can understand that, can't you?"

I nodded. I wanted to tell her that we all had chains. That

she wasn't the only prisoner in the world. She wasn't alone, no matter how screwed up this life was. But I just nodded.

She wiped my tears with the back of her hand. "I won't take long." She looked up at the sky. Lavender and gray clouds pushed toward the earth. The warm, heavy smell of ozone tinged the air. Rumbles a few miles away cut through the forest's silence. "A storm's coming," she said. She took a deep breath and smiled.

I kissed her on the cheek and rushed to my car before that . . . *thing* burst from the place that I always kept locked.

"Rikki," I shouted. "There's a wheelchair in your car. Why?"

She stared at the sky. She scratched her head and shrugged. "He was heavy." Her eyes met mine. She stepped forward, but remained on the porch.

I don't remember how I got into the car, but I do recall how I trembled, how my fingers fumbled around as they tried to guide my car key into the ignition. I found the slot, turned, and jumped when the engine roared to life. I pressed too hard against the gas and screeched a few yards away from the cabin. I slammed on the brakes and gripped the steering wheel. I took a couple of deep breaths, said a quick prayer, and eased my car away from the cabin.

Rikki, in her robe, remained on the porch. As I drove away, she waved good-bye. She blew me a kiss and waved again. I watched her hand move across space before large drops of water covered my car's rear window. In my final glimpse, I saw my sister as she stood in the rain with her arms stretched, her face to the sky, and her robe open.

20

No Words

ON THE drive home, my mind started and stopped. I was confused about *everything* in my life. I had to drive 315 miles to Los Angeles: it was a long time to spend alone. The vast nothingness off the highway provided my mind with some escape. Creek beds cut in, out, and through the landscape. Bleached rocks and sand had darkened from the cool, quick rushes of freshwater. The hillsides were gold and green from the rain. Brush and trees and wild grass covered the land's face. And where there wasn't color, there was a darker brown, even black, from the ravages of a farmer's controlled burn.

Almond trees, oak trees, old trees, dotted the hillsides. Many of them stood high or at impossible, miraculous angles. Angles that wouldn't have been possible if their roots hadn't been buried deep, deep into the ground. Cows—mottled, chestnut, and black-and-whites—lounged in the high grass. Calves tottered behind their mamas. Daddy looked on, uninterested in his family. The cows moved toward ponds or gathered at high fences to watch the cars and trucks fly past. Power lines and windmills fit here, in this fusion of wild and man-made.

The speedometer on my car never passed sixty-five miles per hour. Motels off the exits of Highway 5 beckoned me to get a room. To never go back. To join the tumbleweeds and never take root again. More than once, I considered pulling off the road. I didn't, though.

I thought about taking another highway, seeing where that led, maybe staying there once I arrived. No one would know me. They wouldn't expect much from me. I would have no obligations. I stayed the course, though, and headed for Los Angeles.

Fast-food signs beckoned the modern nomad—me—to stop awhile. To have a break today. To have it my way. I had no appetite, despite their promise of satisfying my every dietary need.

Then the scenery repeated itself and my mind became bored with what it saw. Once again, I was forced to think— about Rikki, Mommy, God, Life, Death, Love, Eric, Truth, Not-Truth, and Half-Truth.

It had stopped raining by the time I passed Pyramid Lake. It sat below the highway, tucked between two hills. In the middle of the water was a tiny island. Granite walls surrounded and contained the lake itself. On the stone, bands of light to dark to black marked the water levels over the past thousand years. Trails of white froth bubbled behind a tiny human on a tiny Jet Ski. Someone was having fun.

I remembered that for a time, a short time, it used to be

my family. Coolers full of cold chicken, potato salad, and red soda water. Frisbees and blankets. Mosquitoes and plastic thongs left on the sandy banks. Falling asleep in the backseat of the car on the ride home. Tired from hopping in and out of the water. Sticky and damp from the heat and spilled soda pop. Itchy from bites and scrapes and dry, ashy skin. Daddy would carry Rikki and me into the house, into our room, when we were still small enough to carry. And we'd thank him and Mommy for taking us away before we fell asleep and dreamed about more picnics and rubber rafts.

But I left the lake behind and continued to inch my way toward the big city. A family in a Suburban passed me—all smiles, hoots, and sunscreen. That used to be my family. No. I'd like to think that it was.

When no one was around, I had gone back to Rikki's closet and swiped those empty vials of lithium with my sister's name and fingerprints all over them. What about Matt's keys? What if the police discovered them in my bag? Could I be arrested? Maybe I shouldn't have left Rikki. What if she needed me . . . ? I thought about throwing the vials and the keys out of my car window. Let the golden hillsides of California claim them and make them a part of the wild. No one lived out here. No one would piece it together. I didn't, though.

What I had done, up in Marin—was it a crime? Did I steal evidence? Was it really "evidence"? Did I actually think Rikki did something evil with those pills? Despite what she said, did I really believe she did the unthinkable to Matt? This last thought disturbed me the most—thinking the worst about someone I loved. Rikki had stopped short of telling me everything, but she had told me enough. Matt was dead.

Once I understood and acknowledged this, the car's speedometer dropped to forty-five.

I knew that I had reached Los Angeles County once I passed Magic Mountain. A stretch of road still lay before me. Again, I thought about Matthew's keys, which were still in my purse. I no longer thought that he sat on his couch, enjoying a rerun of *Cheers* and eating a Fat Burger. He wasn't outside washing his Benz or watering the grass. I didn't wonder about him as much as I wondered about what I would find if I stopped at the house he had rented after he and Rikki had separated.

I exited the freeway once I saw the Hollywood Bowl. I slowly drove up those tight, winding roads, sometimes pulling over to let a car driving in the opposite direction pass first. The sun had set hours ago. Only a few streetlights brightened my path. I found Matthew's house. His car was still parked in the driveway. A light burned in the room toward the back. Maybe . . .

I reached the porch. Newspapers piled high. Mail stuck from the slot. Most had drifted to the ground. I pulled Matt's keys from my purse, then placed what looked like a house key into the lock. I thought about an alarm three seconds after I'd opened the door. I didn't hear any screech or beep. I closed the door behind me and wandered to the living room.

There wasn't much furniture here, just a small couch. A folding chair sat before a card table in the middle of a cavernous dining room. A milk crate held a twenty-six-inch television and a Sony PlayStation. All the walls, except for the one with a calendar from a dry cleaner, were bare. It was too big a house to be so empty; but Matt had lived in big houses all of his life. He didn't need "stuff" to make him comfortable. The heat clicked on. I walked around and found the thermostat. I pushed the button off.

A newsmagazine sat open on the couch. A soda can perched on the coffee table alongside the remote control. A pile of stuffed manila folders gathered on the floor. I wandered to the kitchen and opened the refrigerator door. A few items remained on the shelves: one half-empty bottle of Evian, a withered mango that had a splotch of fungus on the skin, and a box of Frosted Flakes.

I found the bathroom that Matt had used the most. His toothbrush hung in the holder. The razor and shaving cream hadn't moved in weeks. A used bathtowel had been tossed to the floor. His bedroom was messy and manly. His suitcases were still in the closet. His clothes looked undisturbed. I didn't find a bra or a thong or a tube of lipstick; none of those negligible leftovers that a woman abandons to secretly mark her territory. One side of his bed had been slept in. He used only two pillows. His wedding picture sat on the nightstand behind the answering machine.

The answering machine . . . A "12" blipped in the display: twelve messages. My finger pressed the button. The tape spun backward, stopped, then spun forward. The recorded time stamp said, "Thursday, December twentieth." My sister's voice, urgent and pleading, filled the room:

"You don't believe me, do you? I will fucking do it—I'll slit my fucking neck if you don't come up here. If you don't want me, no one else can have me. I will not live without you. I swear, I will do it, Matthew. I have nothing to lose. Pick up the phone . . . pick up . . ." I heard feedback—Matt had grabbed the receiver from the cradle.

I fell to my knees as the other messages played on. I was

too scared to cry. I just hugged myself. "Oh, God," I said. "Oh, God." Over and over again, always close to tears, but dancing away from the precipice every time. I eventually dragged myself from the floor and stumbled to my car.

I reached my apartment. Eric's Corvette was in the driveway. I parked next to him. He got out of the car. He looked rumpled and tired in his scrubs and tennis shoes. Circles darkened the spaces below his bloodshot eyes: he hadn't slept for days. "Hey," he said. He ran his finger along the ridge of my nose. It rested on my bottom lip.

I tried to say "Hey" back, to come up with something sarcastic. I couldn't. I just stood there.

"Your mother called. I had left a message, wondering . . . well, Matt . . . He's still not . . ." He looked away. He squinted to contain his tears. His eyebrows met and crumpled into a single line. His lips quivered. A tear escaped and ran down his cheek.

He opened his mouth to speak again, but no words came. He raised his arms and placed both of his hands on my shoulders. My eyes stung and my heart thumped. My breath caught as he touched me. He pulled me into his arms and kissed me with a tenderness that I had never before experienced in life.

"I love you, Anastasia," he whispered. "And I'm sorry. For everything. I still want to be a part of your life. This may be the wrong time . . . I know I'm selfish . . . I wouldn't blame you if . . . But I just . . ." He kissed me on the forehead. "I just love you . . . I love you so much."

And I cried.

My mail had piled up: subscription notices, gas bill, car note, credit card offers, grocery store circulars, and a check

236 ~ RACHEL HOWZELL HALL

from a puzzle sale. Everyone wanted something from me. I had nothing to give. There weren't many messages on my answering machine. I didn't have many friends now.

Eric and I lay on the couch beneath the quilt Nana had made for Mommy fifty years before. He stroked my hair as I lay beside him. The room glowed with the light of a single raspberry-scented candle.

We hadn't talked much since we'd come in from the driveway. But then, I didn't have much to say. I needed to remain silent for once and figure out what *I* wanted from life, what I *needed* from life. Sharing the quiet with him was enough for now.

The phone rang.

Eric sat up and reached for it. I gently pulled him back onto the couch. "No phones," I whispered, and kissed his cheek.

"Okay." He rubbed my arm as the phone continued to be intrusive, harsh, and disrespectful of the peace we had created. Finally, the answering machine picked up. The tape rolled to ready itself for the recording. It was Mommy.

"Anastasia, pick up . . . Stacy . . . I guess you haven't gotten back yet. I just called to . . . well, okay . . . what do you think? She seemed fine to me. A little out of sorts, but with Matt gone and all, I'm sure she's not sleeping that well, you know? Are you gonna call her when you get in? Maybe you should, don't you think? Maybe you should stay with her for a while, when she comes home, until this whole mess blows over. Yes, I think that would be good. Until she's back on her feet, okay? Zenobia's still acting crazy. Oh, and Eric called. I think there's some love there. Call me as soon as you get in. Bye."

There was a click, a beep, and the room fell into silence.

21

SO IT WAS

I SPENT the rest of the week in the dark—literally. I had closed all the blinds in my apartment, didn't answer the phone—the answering machine had been unplugged since it could no longer take any more messages. I didn't erase calls, nor did I return them. No television. No newspaper. I reread parts of *Anna Karenina* at times, then napped when I couldn't read. I didn't eat much. Lost seven pounds. Eric kept me company, but we didn't speak much. No. *I* didn't speak.

When my mind cleared, when it could once again house more from the world, I trudged to the mailroom. My mailbox was stuffed and offered the usual: grocery store circulars, magazines, and utility bills. Only one piece of mail unnerved me.

I knew it was Rikki's suicide letter even before I tore my letter opener across the flap; even though she hadn't written

a return address on the upper left-hand corner of the envelope, or on the back. Return address. But then you can't
reach the dead, can you? No little yellow sticker with a new
address for *that* group of people.

I retreated to the solace of my apartment's balcony to read
the letter. Rikki's words seemed ordinary, almost rote. You
know, milk, cheese, toilet paper, pick up suit from cleaner.
But she used her personal stationery—Howard Linen with
her name imprinted in silver on the letterhead. She used her
Montblanc fountain pen—jet-black ink. I guess she considered this a special occasion.

Dear Stacy,

*You know what this means. I can't apologize, and you
can't save me from it like you've done before. All of your hard
work and intervention (is that the word?) and now look
what I've done. Can't do it anymore. Life is hard, especially
inside my head, not that the world will last long anyway
with the Apocalypse and all. I will be damned; so don't look
for me in the resurrection of the righteous dead.*

*How many commandments have I broken? Thou shall
not kill. Thou shall not covet your neighbor's (or sister's)
stuff—you have it all and I wanted it. Thou shall not bear
false witness (lie, right?). Thou shall not commit adultery.*

*I lusted for Christopher in my heart—a sin as bad as
fleshly pleasure. He probably lusted in his, too. Yes, he turned
me down again and again, but I could tell. A woman knows.
He was going to give up being a doctor so he could be with
me. He's too late, though.*

*I am off the subject. Thou shall not kill. Matt didn't
come to Marin to reconcile. I threatened to kill myself. That*

scared him. He hated me 'cause I was okay. He wanted to divorce still, after all that I did to get him up here. He wanted to leave. I begged him to stay for dinner. Perhaps he should have left. I would not turn the other cheek—another sin. He did not deserve my forgiveness, so after it was over, I tied him to the ATV and tried to drive it into the lake. He came undone and fell on the bank. The thing kept going. It ripped off my gown. It was kinda funny, if you think about it. But then I paid for it when he started to drip after I came back with the wheelchair. What a mess.

Matt will understand, though, and he'll probably tell you he does when you see him on that Day, that is if he confessed to God about his affair, since he never confessed to me. A wife knows, though. But he no longer lives in misery, or in guilt. He won't have to mourn my absence. I won't have to mourn his.

Please look after Mr. Thai. He's still with his maid, who's fine for a short time, but not as a full-time mother. I know you have allergies and everything, but he's so high-strung and difficult. If anyone else takes him—like Mommy—they'll gas him. And I don't know if dogs go to heaven. Hopefully they do so it will be one less thing for me to think about. You can find the maid's address and phone number in my organizer by the phone in Matt's home office.

I love you, Anastasia, and I have reconciled the fact that we will never see each other again, despite our love.

> *Love always and forever,*
> *Arika*

I scanned the single page five times. I followed the original creases in the paper to refold it, then slipped it into the envelope. I sat with the letter for over an hour. No tears this time—I had already cried the day's allotment of pain away.

You know how it feels to know something is going to happen, but you don't want it to happen, so you make yourself think that it can't happen, even though you know there's a strong possibility that it will eventually? Yeah. That was me. And I had no idea what to do about that feeling or how to classify it. Had I failed my sister? Could I have done better? I didn't know this, either, and there wasn't any comfort in this.

Mommy kept calling me, especially after the Marin Police Department had called her the day before. A third of the messages on my machine were from her:

"When are you going back up to Marin to get Rikki?"

"Should we bury Rikki next to Matt?"

"Who's gonna pay for the funeral, the casket, oh, and the dinner?"

"Will Rikki's life insurance cover . . . this? You think you can help out some since we spent all of your father's insurance money on Rikki and Matt's wedding?"

"Think Eric will help? Can you ask him?"

"You there, Stacy? It's Mommy. Call me, okay?"

Sister DeHaviland, Mommy's friend, called twice. To check up on me, she said. Right. Mommy had already warned me that rumors were flying around about Matt and Rikki, and to just keep my mouth shut for the time being. No problem.

Pretty soon, though, the media began to camp out near the front of my apartment building. I grew tired of the popping flashbulbs, of being pushed and shoved, of being shouted at, so I stayed at Eric's place. The double-paned windows blocked out all sound. The building's security kept the mobs at bay.

Pastor Phillips called me, too. "And I'll say it again. 'It is better to dwell in the wilderness, than with a contentious and angry woman.' King Solomon sure knew what he was talking about."

I said, "Sure, Pastor," thanked him for his call, and disconnected the telephone. He had talked to every television station and newspaper in town about my sister. That's fine. I would just find a new church home.

It's sad to say that I never knew what I wanted when it came to Rikki. No. I *did* know, but those kinds of thoughts reddened my cheeks and quickened my breath while I waited for that bolt of lightning to strike me down for having not-so-pure thoughts. For so many years, I had wished her out of my life. The religious fanaticism, the drug abuse, the mental illness: she was tortured and she made life so unbearable for all of us who were around her. I know: it wasn't right that I wanted her to succeed in ending her life. But it wasn't that I wanted her to succeed, it's just that I wanted my phone to ring and to have ordinary conversations. I wanted my mother to see *me,* not as my sister's keeper, but as a woman with my own problems, with my own successes. And I wanted a life with Eric.

I wanted, for once, to be free of shame and guilt.

But then, Rikki was gone. And I still felt guilty, ashamed, and selfish.

I don't know if my sister was sane or insane when she decided to poison Matthew. Does it really matter? Rikki and Matt aren't alive now to explain their marriage or their motives. And no scenario—poisoned food by a calculating murderer or by a scorned wife with a mental illness—offers any comfort or solution. Some will say that my sister deserved worse than death. Some will choose Matt's family over my family. I'm sure the Dresdens will win, although this is no contest.

People whispered that my father, a teacher at school, or someone at church had sexually abused Rikki. Hmph. I wish that I *could* explain things away by saying that some pervert did unspeakable things to her. Maybe more people would've shown Rikki mercy. But I can't say that since it's not true. It's difficult to accept that invisible, indescribable things can haunt a person. Things that you don't know exist until they sneak out at a dinner party or sleep for days in a darkened room.

I'm prepared to be quietly offended, though, since I can't debate this with every person every day. Still, what do they know? About anything? Rikki's beauty, her secrets, her desire to be close to God, who seemed, at times, too far away from her. Or how, in those quiet times, she could fly as smoothly as a dragonfly across the water. They didn't know.

Ozone tinged the air. I looked up and saw rain clouds stalk across the sky. They squished down so low, I could almost touch them. Rain began to slip upon the streets below. I stood up and moved to the edge of the balcony. I closed my eyes and opened my mouth. A few drops fell upon my tongue.

God's tears.

Yes. It was beautiful.

Epilogue

MISSING MAN'S BODY FOUND;
WIFE FOUND DEAD
Crime: Love and Madness Ends in Murder-Suicide,
Part 2 of 2

Herbert Gustafson is a native of Ely, Minnesota. Herbert, a manager of a local computer repair shop, decided to treat his family—his wife, Kimberly, and their sons, Timothy, 12, and Edgar, 7—to a winter in California. His older sister, Marge, lives in San Simeon, California, a beautiful coastal town located between San Francisco and Los Angeles. She hadn't seen her family in over a year and invited them to stay with her.

The Gustafsons arrived in San Simeon on January 20. Marge drove them to the beach for their first glimpse of the Pacific Ocean. Then they toured the mansion built by eccentric billionaire William Randolph Hearst. A day before her family planned to return to Minnesota, Marge capped off their visit with an old-fashioned picnic at Lake Nacimiento, 130 miles south of Marin, California. Timmy and Eddie darted to the water as soon as Marge's Plymouth Voyager pulled to a stop in the parking lot. But ten minutes later, Timmy shrieked. The adults ran to the lake's shore and were horrified to see Timmy's right leg wrapped in strings of algae, twisted beer can rings, and the torn sweater worn by a bloated corpse.

The body was that of a black man. His skin had started to yellow in color, to loosen and burst open to expose muscles and fat. Some of his fingernails had come off, as well as patches of hair on his head.

Kimberly fainted.

Park Ranger John Ramirez called 911. "Minutes later, police, fire trucks and the paramedics were everywhere," Ramirez said. "Usually it's pretty quiet here." Police officers pushed back curious civilians as they cordoned off the area with yellow crime-scene tape. More patrol officers arrived on the scene and began to take names and addresses of witnesses.

Detectives from San Simeon arrived close to 3:30 that afternoon. They photographed the area from all angles and took close-up shots of the body. "It was somewhat difficult to gather evidence in such a wild environment," said Detective Arnold McMillan. "The area was overrun with footprints and trailer tracks. Blood could easily have washed away into the water. But we pulled on rubber gloves and grabbed specimen envelopes just in case."

Walsh Chilton, the county coroner, arrived. He made note of the temperature, humidity, and the weather. It would help him establish the time of death. He pronounced the man dead and watched as the body was slipped into a heavy plastic bag.

Chilton's minivan whisked the corpse to the morgue for the autopsy. There, the body was identified as "John Doe," assigned a number, and toe-tagged. Chilton took more pictures of the man fully clothed. In his report, he wrote that the victim wore mud-caked sweatpants and a crew-neck sweater that had started to unravel. There were no gunshot burns in the man's clothing. There was a dry-cleaner's tag in the sweater. Chilton set that aside to compare the serial numbers against his running database of dry cleaners up and down the state.

John Doe's clothes were cut away. Even though he was in his late 20's–early 30's, identification was still impossible. The man had decomposed significantly due to his exposure to water, insects, and fish. He weighed approximately 170 pounds, 190 before his death. He had brown eyes. Dark red specks, caused by pressure in the head, stained the eyeballs. Chilton searched the body for needle tracks to indicate drug abuse, but found none. The man had a healthy build with no lesions or tattoos. His skin was flawless except for the crescent-shaped scar on the back of his neck.

Chilton ran swabs underneath the remaining fingernails. There was skin there that didn't belong to the victim, as well as fragments of silk or a similar material. He examined the hands. There were scars circling the man's wrists, as though he had been tied with rope. He took fingerprints and made a mold of the man's mouth.

The coroner started with the internal examination of the body. Since there was no visible sign for cause of death, the

246 ~ Rachel Howzell Hall

coroner knew that the answer lay in the organs. He took a blood sample from the heart to determine the victim's blood type. He gathered samples of the stomach's contents for toxicology. After he removed the bladder, he removed the urine and sent samples of that for toxicology as well.

Finally, he examined the head and brain. Even though the eyes told of some trauma in the head, Chilton couldn't find a fracture or a puncture. John Doe didn't die from a hard hit to the skull. There were no marks on the neck to signify strangling. Choking was the only remaining explanation for those crimson specks in the eyes.

Toxicology test findings came back. John Doe's last meal was chicken, potatoes, and a green salad. There was a high lithium concentration in the urine—about 22 tablets of that drug. Chilton determined that the salty meal had probably disguised the saltiness of the medication. There was also high bile content in his stomach and esophagus. He had choked on his vomit as a result of lithium toxicity. He was already dead before he was disposed of in the lake.

The fingerprints were quickly compared to those in the National Crime Information Center's Missing Persons database. The prints were those of Matthew Dresden, a resident of Los Angeles, California. He had been missing since December 20.

It was the opinion of the coroner that Matthew Dresden, a 33-year-old male, choked to death on his own vomit due to fatal doses of lithium. He ingested the chemical orally, which caused stomachache, nausea, muscle spasms, vomiting, seizures, and death. Those ligature marks on his wrists suggest restraint and struggle. And since suicide victims can't dispose of their own bodies, the manner of death was homicide.

After early unsuccessful attempts to contact Dresden's wife, Arika Dresden, 30, the victim's mother, Zenobia Dresden, 60, was alerted that the coroner had completed the autopsy. She signed the death certificate, and a mortuary sent a hearse to the hospital to bring Dr. Dresden's body back to Los Angeles.

The motives for the murder? Money. Sex. Madness.

When asked if there was an accomplice to the murder, head detective Casey Simpson said, "There was only one additional suspect but he was cleared this afternoon."

That suspect was Los Angeles–based psychopathologist Christopher Nesbitt, who was brought in for questioning, but released once his whereabouts at the time of the murder were confirmed. Nesbitt, 40, was leading a symposium for 150 psychopathologists at UCLA at the time. When reached for comment, Dr. Nesbitt said, "She [Arika] needed more help than what I could offer. Once she and her husband separated, she threatened suicide regularly. I never knew when to believe her, but because of her history, I didn't take any chances, especially when she called me from Marin in December." Dresden had contacted Nesbitt as efforts to locate her still-missing husband had gotten under way.

Two teams of police officers and detectives were dispatched once Chilton finished his work. One team retreated north with an arrest warrant for Arika Dresden. The other team was assigned to gather evidence at the homes owned and rented by the couple.

The cops reached the cabin in Marin. After no one answered, they kicked in the door. The police called out to alert Mrs. Dresden that they had a warrant for her arrest. She was not in the house. They found, instead, an empty bottle of vodka, an empty vial of Depakote, a form of valproic acid (a medicine used to reduce the frequency and severity of some forms of manic depression), and an open kitchen door that led to the dark forest.

"For many manic-depressives, the bottom falls out," says acclaimed author and psychiatrist Dr. E. W. Anderson. "Their thinking becomes frenzied. Nothing makes sense. Memory is often compromised. Manias and depressions have violent sides. This patient [Arika Dresden] also seems to have been abusing alcohol, which would have aggravated those symptoms."

A former fourth-grade teacher at 59th Street Elementary School, Dresden was loved by many. "But she cried all the time," fourth-grader Craig Fremont said. "Especially when she read us *Charlotte's Web*."

"I thought she was too involved with the students," said Gina Jackson, a concerned parent. "I found it strange that she baked cookies for them every Friday. *Homemade* cookies. What sane working woman bakes Toll House cookies for forty-eight fourth-graders?"

The family of Arika Dresden has repeatedly declined to offer comments or a formal statement.

"I know Matt deserved a lot better, but I always supported his choice," said the victim's mother. "I was always so patient with Arika. Despite everything."

"She [Arika] always cried in church," said Vernell Lamont, head deaconess of Bethany Seventh-Day Adventist Church and close family friend of the Dresdens'. "Every song the choir sang, she'd stand up and cry. Every appeal the pastor made, to be rebaptized or rededicated, she always went up front. Sometimes crying, sometimes weeping. And I always thought to myself, 'Ain't nobody that sorry unless they're sinning big time.' "

"I miss Matthew, Dr. Dresden," said Jennifer Norse, RN, who recently married and is three months pregnant. "The entire staff misses him; but I miss him the most. We were really close."

READING GROUP GUIDE

A QUIET STORM

DISCUSSION POINTS

1. Religion is a persistent theme throughout *A Quiet Storm* and Seventh-Day Adventism is the cultural backdrop for the book. Is religion, as it is seen in the Moore family, a burden or a blessing? What do the biblical excerpts from Rikki's journal mean in the context of the unfolding story? In reference to the characters' developments?

2. In chapter 5, look at Jacques's shocked reaction to the disparity in how the sisters are treated. Similarly, look at the paragraph in chapter 6 that begins "I told Mommy about my conversation . . . ," especially the paragraph's last four lines. Explore the concept of "favorite" or "spoiled" children and why you think Rikki gets such special treatment from her mother and father. Why is Stacy considered last, if she is considered at all? Explain whether or not you think Stacy's mother cares for her less than she does for Rikki, and why.

3. How does Rikki's family react (in chapters 5 and 6) to her attempt to kill herself? What did Rikki want when she tried to kill herself? What message is she sending to her family? Discuss the Moore family's reaction to the event, including Pastor Phillips's "exorcism." What was your reaction?

4. *A Quiet Storm* explores family and personal guilt. Look at the paragraph in chapter 7 beginning, "In my heart . . ." after Rikki describes her dreams to Stacy, and at Rikki's statement "I'm not worthy of God's grace. And I'll get mine. Watch. I'll get mine." How do you think Rikki came to feel so guilty?

5. To what extent did Stacy and Rikki's father's affair, and his hiding his heart disease from them, affect their lives and their view of men? What are the differences between Stacy and Rikki's reactions to these startling revelations?

6. Why does the Moore family (including Stacy) insist on denying that Rikki is ill? Does their denial play a role in causing Rikki's illness? Why do they persist in keeping her illness secret? What other secrets does the family have? What about their persistence in maintaining family secrets? Have you known families who have this dynamic?

7. Why does Stacy allow her relationship with Eric to deteriorate in favor of trying to help her sister? What do you think made her sacrifice her happiness and well-being so constantly to save Rikki?

8. Discuss your take on the role of heredity in manic depression and other mental illnesses. Look at the paragraph in chapter 14 beginning: "My heart sank . . ." Talk about whether or not you think Rikki inherited Nana's emotional disturbance and if Stacy had the potential to follow the same path.

9. Examine the paragraph in chapter 19 that begins: "I kissed her on the cheek . . ." When Stacy left Rikki for the last time, did she know her sister was going to kill herself? How did you come to your conclusion? Did Stacy want her sister to kill herself? Would it have been possible for Stacy to live her own life if Rikki didn't kill herself? Examine personal responsibility and discuss where you think the responsibility for a loved one ends.

10. Does Stacy believe that she can change her sister and actually save her from her internal demons? When, if ever, does Stacy see that Rikki is beyond her help?

11. *A Quiet Storm* is a story of two sisters and a particular family dynamic. How much of a difference does it make that the characters are African-American? How do the book's themes transcend race and culture? How might members of other cultures or ethnic groups deal with Rikki's manic depression differently from the Moore family?

12. Examine how the author uses the themes of storms and earthquakes and natural beauty throughout *A Quiet Storm*. How do these nature themes amplify and parallel the emotional and social fluctuations of the characters? How do these themes help the evolution of the story?

13. Examine Rikki's capacity to love others. Did she ever display any real signs of love for Stacy or Matt? What actions or words does she use to express this love?

14. From chapter 15 on, Hall introduces a kind of murder mystery subplot into *A Quiet Storm,* complete with detectives, clues, and a Q&A. Explore how the introduction of this additional plot device advances the earlier, essential themes of the book. How do you think the epilogue serves to resolve the story or the characters' relationships?

15. With her beauty, superior intelligence, and creativity, Rikki is a magnetic figure. Discuss your impressions of the phenomena of "charisma" and "celebrity." Examine to what extent people are attracted to those kinds of people and what they hope to gain by associating with them.

A Note from the Author

All families have secrets. Unfortunately, mental illness is one of those secrets. Too often, we prefer not to think of it as a problem. Instead, we laugh at it when it manifests itself in that strange uncle you avoid during Thanksgiving. Or we think we can pray it away, without seeing a professional about it.

I wrote *A Quiet Storm* out of my frustration with families who refuse to deal with this silent killer, and with the sanctimonious who simply label it as sin. Manic depression is a disease that crosses gender, racial, and class lines. It does not develop from a person's lack of willpower, his or her economic status, or bad circumstances.

We can choose to ignore mental illness, to belittle it, or to be ashamed. But we should know: it *will* destroy. You only need to consider the number of people who are imprisoned, homeless, and institutionalized because of this illness to know that this is true.

As a Christian, I believe that God heals; but I also believe that He works through psychologists and psychiatrists just as He works through neurosurgeons, obstetricians, and allergists. How can we expect God to heal us when we are too ashamed to even admit that we're sick? Can't we meet Him halfway? *A Quiet Storm* shows what happens when a family won't.